THE LAST LONGSHOREMAN

A Chilling Tale of Crime and Corruption on the Boston Waterfront

MARC ZAPPULLA

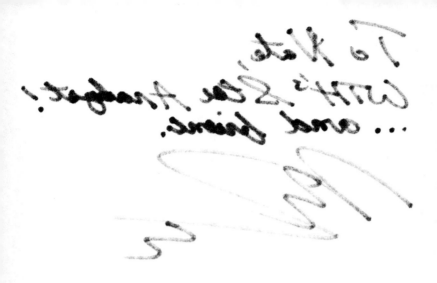

This is a work of fiction. As in all fiction, literary insights and perceptions are based on experiences. Therefore, all names, characters, places, and incidents are a product of the author's imagination or are used fictitiously. Any resemblance to actual persons, living or deceased; events; or locales is entirely coincidental.

Published in the United States by True Emperor Publishing

© 2016 Marc Zappulla
All rights reserved.

ISBN: 1535367539
ISBN 13: 9781535367530
Library of Congress Control Number: 2016914245
CreateSpace Independent Publishing Platform
North Charleston, South Carolina

Cover art and design © 2016 Mike Petrillo

Acknowledgments

First and foremost, I'd like to extend much love and gratitude to my mom and dad; without your encouragement, love, and support, I may not have been able to see this book through. I love you both very much.

Thank you, Google, Wikipedia, and to the entire staff—living and deceased—involved with the production of the 1954 Academy Award winning film *On the Waterfront*. To the International Longshoremen's Association (I.L.A.)—the greatest union in the world—thank you for existing. A big thank-you to my friend Mike Petrillo for outstanding work in designing the cover as well as the inspiring words you offered every step of the way. Thank you also to the rest of my family and close friends for your continued loyalty and support, as I wouldn't be here without you; I love you all dearly. Lastly, a special thank-you to Amazon, Amazon Kindle, and CreateSpace for your professionalism, insight, and logistical work in getting this book off the ground.

I saw a lot of bad things on the Boston waterfront. Things I ain't never seen before, and hope to God I never have to see again.

—Former longshoreman

Prologue

My mother, may her soul rest in peace, always told me God had a plan for everyone. In truth it was her only way of letting me know that my evil ways would inevitably catch up to me and that there was a special place in the world for kids like me, the "rotten" ones, and I should brace myself for the horrors that lay ahead.

But I mocked each and every one of her religious and spiritual omens, so she opted for another approach—a good beating with a belt, a wooden spoon, or the heel of her rigid, scuffed-up Italian clog. And after the lumps went down and the bruises faded, again she would say, "God has a special place in this world for you, Tony."

And so God put me on the waterfront.

CHAPTER 1

WELCOME TO THE DOCKS

It was like nothing I had ever seen, not even in my worst nightmares. And it happened just a few feet from where I was standing.

Butchie was an ill-tempered madman, clearly overwhelmed by an intense rage when he gripped that blade underhand and readied himself to do his worst. Then, in lightning-quick fashion, he stabbed the pudgier fella repeatedly while he had him pinned against the ship's railing, with his wide-set shoulders nearly bending the cold, rusted steel.

He plunged the blade so many times into the guy's doughy midsection and upper chest that he fell like a house of cards, and when he hit the deck, he shifted and quivered uncontrollably.

It was disgusting.

The blood—it ran across like a bucket of paint had been kicked over, and worse, it flowed in my direction.

I was fucked.

The poor bastard's convulsions slowed, and after a few residual jerks and kicks, he lay there cold and dead.

It happened just after 5:00 p.m., moments after my shift on the waterfront ended. I was a longshoreman. The dead guy was a longshoreman, too, but I didn't know him; I didn't even know his name, but I had spent much of the day with him in the hole of the ship—which is more commonly known as the cargo hold—where the goods were stored.

I felt bad for the guy, I really did, but I wasn't going to interfere. I wasn't stupid. It was bad enough I had to see his brutal end; if I had come another inch closer, I would have ended up alongside him, and that would have been a bad thing.

It was toward the end January of 1958 on the waterfront in Boston when I saw the incident. Most of the guys unloading cargo that day had cleared out. I was alone on the portside of a ship doing nothing but having a smoke and admiring the view of the cold and quiet harbor before heading home. That's when I heard an argument of sorts taking place not far from where I was standing. It was to my left, near the bow. When the voices got louder, I decided to call it quits.

I savored one more drag, flicked the cigarette overboard, and decided to "whistle past the graveyard," as they say.

Big mistake.

I began to walk along as inconspicuously as I could toward the bow, hugging the edge to allow myself enough room to scoot by. My hook—the principle tool of any longshoreman—was dug into my back left shoulder with the handle bouncing gently on my chest. It was a convenient way to carry it when I wasn't using it. As I got closer, I noticed the yelling had quieted down, so I picked up my pace. But when I turned the corner, that's when I saw Butchie Shea, another longshoreman. He was seething and holding the handle of that good-size blade to the guy's chin while he had him levered against the side of the ship with nowhere to run. This guy was shaking like he'd just passed a fistful of razor blades through his colon.

Butchie, now seemingly content, bent down and wiped the blade clean on his victim's black pea coat. That's when I turned ever so gently to leave in hopes of finding another way off the ship, but as I changed direction, I heard him call out to me.

"Hey!"

So I twirled back around to acknowledge him.

He stood up, and using the point of that blade for emphasis, he said, "You didn't see nothin'."

He was just so calm, so collected; I got the feeling he knew I'd been there watching the whole time and didn't give a shit, and that concerned me. I, on the other hand, was flushed, and my body was warm; even in the stiff, cold wind I could feel my pulse thudding from my head to the soles of my feet. I thought my heart was going to explode out of my chest. But despite all of that and the jarring nature of what I had witnessed, I remained still, acting like someone who was wholly unaffected by the gruesome show, and I had to, at least long enough to shake my head and say, "I didn't see anything."

"Good," said Butchie, "now give me a hand over here, would ya?" He bent down, readying himself to grab hold of the fat guy's cold, dead wrists.

"What?" I said, naturally bewildered.

"I said give me a fuckin' hand! Look at the size of this son of a bitch," he went on. "I can't do this alone."

"I gotta do this, really?" I asked.

He stood up slowly, postured himself, and said, "You either help me now, or someone else will, kid. But that's no good, not for you, because then I'll have two bodies to get rid of, if you catch my meaning."

"I do," I said.

"And I don't have that kind of time," he said, "so get the fuck over here and help me!"

I was between a rock and a hard place with no way out, and I knew that. I was no stool pigeon, but sometimes people find themselves at the wrong place at the wrong time and end up taking a dirt nap anyway. I prayed this was not one of those times.

I was leery of Butchie because he was crazier than a shithouse rat. He was cold, and he was callous—a man of few words, but with a history of wicked endeavors that spoke volumes for him. He simply was not a longshoreman you'd want to get in a beef with over anything.

And he wasn't a big guy, maybe five foot six, if he was lucky, with a stocky build and a rugged-but-youthful look to him. Only a few years my senior, in fact.

I was just eighteen at the time.

But what he lacked in stature and maturity, he made up for in cold-bloodedness. For all intents and purposes, he was demented.

So I stood over the body, though I wouldn't look downward for fear of locking on its open, dead eyes.

"Where are we putting him?" I asked.

He straightened up again and looked overboard. But with the railing around four feet in height, even I knew we'd have a tough time heaving the fat bastard's deadweight over the side. Through the railing—well, that was out too, as it would have been like trying to stuff a pillow through a mousehole.

"How about down the hole?" I suggested.

"Down the hole?" he said curiously.

I said, "We'll stuff him between a couple of pallets and leave him there. By the time anyone finds him, we'll be long gone."

Still, he pondered for a moment. "I think I like that idea, kid," he said.

Perfect, I thought. *Anything to get this train moving.*

I bent down and grabbed his boots, and immediately the weight of the fella had me nearly convinced he was glued to the deck. He had to be over three hundred pounds at least, if I had to guess.

Butchie said, "I told ya."

Then he grabbed the man's arms and started pulling him, with me hanging on the other end and stepping through the trail of blood being left behind. Butchie stopped when we came upon a door that led to the hole He turned the knob as cautiously as he could and gently opened it. He took a peek inside.

I was getting impatient, looking sharply in all directions, fearing someone was out there lurking and ready to blow the whistle on us. But there was no one on the ship, and everyone on the pier was heading home, so it was just the two of us…or three, depending on one's point of view.

"We're clear," said Butchie, much to my relief.

But instead of taking the wrists once again, angling him straight, and dragging him down the stairs, he let go of the guy, walked behind him, took his left leg, and then ordered me to grab his right one. Together we lifted him up like he was a two-wheeler and pushed, moving him forward until his face bounced off the top step and onto the second, and then we thrust him forward one more time and watched him tumble down the stairs to the bottom.

In the hole we took his limbs one last time: Butchie had his arms, and I had his legs. We tugged and dragged, then paused, then tugged again. It was a friggin' workout. We aligned him perfectly to go straight in between two pallets piled high with cases of whiskey. Butchie then went in between them, grabbed his arms again, and pulled him with everything he had. It was a tight squeeze for sure, but he didn't care; he was determined. So he pulled again, straining every particle in his body.

Quite honestly, I thought the guy was going to burst. With every jerk backward, his arms were forced above his head like a corkscrew until Butchie gave one final lunge backward and let him go.

"We're done," he said, huffing and puffing.

He leaned back against a pallet and took a pack of smokes out of his pocket, turned, and offered me one.

"No, thanks," I said.

He was in no rush, it seemed; in fact, he acted like a guy waiting for his car to be fixed at the mechanic's. So casual. So carefree, but just a little out of breath.

I had nothing to say except, "I'm just gonna go."

"Go ahead," he said, "and remember what I said."

"Of course."

I took a few steps toward the stairs before he stopped me. "Hey, kid," he called to me. I turned around, and as I did, he used the body like it was a plank and walked right over the guy. Then he reached inside his jacket pocket. My blood pressure rose like a bastard. I thought for sure he was going to pull out a gun and do away with his only loose end—me. But I was wrong. It was a bottle of booze, twelve-year-old Glenlivet, that he took out and tried to hand to me. "Here, you earned it."

But I balked and waved my arms—respectfully, of course.

"Relax, kid," he said. "Here, take it."

Still I hesitated.

"Take it," he said with a more commanding tone, and then he grinned. "Don't worry; I won't tell nobody."

I got a kick out of that statement. "Thanks," I told him and took the booze.

"You didn't know this guy, did ya?" Butchie asked.

"No, I didn't," I said. "Today was actually my first day on the waterfront."

"No shit, huh? Welcome."

"Thanks," I said. "I guess."

"I knew you looked unfamiliar," Butchie went on. "And don't worry about this bum, because nobody gets whacked on the waterfront for nothin'. Know what I mean?"

"I do."

That's when I got the feeling I was going to come out of there OK and in one piece.

"What's your name, kid?"

"Tony Costa," I told him.

"A guinea, huh?" Butchie said.

"That's right," I said proudly.

"Butchie," he said.

"I know who you are."

"Go on now. I wouldn't want you to catch a cold out here or somethin'."

"Yeah," I said. "Thanks for the booze."

"Hey, don't mention it."

As bad as I wanted to get the hell out of there, I couldn't help myself; I needed to know, so I came right out and asked him, "Hey, uh, what would you have done if I wasn't here to help you?"

"I always think of something, kid."

With that, I turned my back and headed off, all the while clinging to the suspicion that I was not yet free and clear, to the point that I felt a sharp, pinhole pain in my back where the blade or bullet might penetrate me.

But there was none.

Finally, I reached the gangway and made it off the ship safely and then headed straight to my car.

It was a long walk back through the yard and to the lot where my 1955 Ford Thunderbird was parked. I glanced back at the boat every ten steps or so, but with each turn of the head, it seemed less and less believable that something so horrible had actually taken place back there.

But it had.

So when I approached the main gate, I felt an incredible sense of relief. I walked through it and waved to the guard, Freddy, and he waved back.

All I wanted at that point was to get home, close my eyes, and chalk it up as a bad "first day at the office." But in processing what happened, I became nauseous, and so I sought out a secluded area where the edge of the lot met the harbor. I stood on the gravelly surface, bent over, and heaved twice, violently, into the water. I gave it a minute and stood there until the cool air soothed me and brought me back to a comfortable state.

It was a curious thing. I had seen much growing up on the streets of East Boston—guys getting their heads knocked in with bats and pipes, a stabbing here and there. I had even seen a guy run over by a car twice and live, but nothing like what I saw that day on the pier.

Sadly, it would not be the last time I witnessed a brutal, senseless murder.

I was a boy among men, learning my way on the harsh terrain of the Boston waterfront as a longshoreman. I was young and brash and tough, but you wouldn't have known it, not then. I kept to myself when I first landed on the docks, and with good reason.

The late fifties were a tumultuous time down on the pier, with local gangsters and Mafia crime families all vying for a piece of every shipment and union dollar that came in, and if you acted up or got in their way somehow—well, you ended up like that poor fellow who had his guts spilled all over the ship.

I finally got home to my modest one-bedroom place across the bay in East Boston; I had chosen the location to be closer to the docks. It was a simple place with a bed, a bathroom, and a stove—not much else. It was enough for me at the time, certainly.

I remember turning the key to the front door, still wondering if Butchie had sent someone, and that someone was lurking behind a car, fixing to eliminate me once and for all. But there was no one but a vagabond, a colored guy named Willie, who was in plain view, sitting with his back against the side of my building and eyeballing the Scotch in my hand like it was the last drop of alcohol left on earth. I looked him off, but he was harmless anyway.

So I walked in and quickly closed the door behind me. I placed the bottle on the kitchen table, took my pea coat off, and flung it carelessly somewhere.

Then the phone rang. I hesitated to grab it, as I was feeling kind of jumpy, but the rotary-dial device was right next to me on the counter, so I took the call.

"Hello?"

It was my father.

"How was your first day of work?" he asked.

"It was, uh, pretty uneventful…it was good," I said. "I kept busy."

"Sometimes that's not a bad thing, ya know?"

"Yeah."

"It's a different world, ain't it?" said my father.

"It sure is, Pop," I said. "It sure is."

"Meet anyone from the neighborhood?" he asked.

"No, not today," I said. "Maybe tomorrow, who knows?"

"Well, listen, hang in there. I just wanted to give you a quick call to see how it went, but I'll get in touch with you in a week or so, OK?"

"You got it, Pop," I said, "and tell Ma I said hello."

"I will, Tony."

"Thanks."

I hung up.

The next call came from the Scotch, and I answered it. I twisted the cap off, grabbed a short, tumbler glass, poured myself a healthy dose, and gulped it down like a sailor on shore leave. Then I drank another before I put the bottle down and headed to the bedroom. I tossed my scally cap on the floor and then fell backward onto my twin-size bed.

What a day. I had processed enough, and the jitters and paranoia I was feeling just moments earlier had finally washed away, thanks in part to the brief exchange with my father and the downing of some Scotch. Regardless, I had finally found the peace and quiet that had escaped me on the ship.

After a moment or two of deep reflection, I dozed off, emotionally exhausted. My last waking images were of that bludgeoning on the ship, the stuff nightmares are made of.

CHAPTER 2

BUTCHIE THE KILLER

The following morning, the carved-up, bloated, and squished corpse of Butchie's victim was discovered by a couple of crew members on the ship—two guys trolling the hole, probably looking for some product to take home themselves. Whatever the case, they alerted the captain, and he in turn called the authorities.

Within an hour of the find, the state and local authorities descended on the pier like the Germans over Poland. They questioned everyone from the guys working security at the gate to the captain on the ship. But they got nothing. And when my turn came around, I didn't flinch.

A cold and agitated state cop stopped me as I was on a break—or a "lap," as we called it. In his thick Boston accent, he asked, "Anything you can tell me about the body we found on the ship, kid?"

"No."

"Have you seen anything out of the ordinary lately, witnessed any argument or altercation…anything at all?" he asked.

I shook my head. "No."

If I learned anything growing up in Eastie, it was this: you never volunteer information. A simple yes or no will do, because the last thing I wanted on that day was to self-induce a cloud of suspicion hanging over my head by getting into a lengthy conversation with one of these detectives. So a dense look, a gentle headshake, followed by a one-word answer—that's how it's done.

"Thank you for your time," said the cop, and then he walked off and evaporated into the yard.

They weren't stupid, those detectives—they knew someone on the pier had something to do with the murder—but gathering any evidence that could potentially lead to a viable suspect was tough going because we were all "D and D," or deaf and dumb. We never saw anything, and if we did, we pretended like we didn't. It was a code followed religiously—and not just in Boston but in every port up and down the East Coast and every terminal on the West Coast too.

When the dust settled that afternoon, I met up with a guy named Mickey Con in one of the coffee rooms we had down on the docks.

Mickey was fairly new, with a tenure of about eight months of sporadic employment on the docks. He was tall and wiry, with a shaggy do protruding from his flat cap and an unrelenting, bare gaze that, quite honestly, freaked out a lot of guys on the pier. And the guy never shut the hell up. Mickey could talk the balls off a brass monkey if he had the opportunity. He had no sense. He was a sex fiend, a gambler, a smoker, and a drinker—and quite erratic—but he was a good guy in my opinion, just a little nuts.

According to him, as a young fella he once bought a car off a used-car dealer on the South Shore, but after just a couple of days of driving the thing, he somehow convinced himself that he got a raw deal on the sale. So the crazy bastard went back down to the dealership and drove the car right through the showroom window.

He did some time for that.

Not too long after he got out, he picked up some Chinese food from a place in the South End of Boston and had an argument with a guy behind the counter, so he went home, had his dinner, and then went back and drove another car through the front of the joint and did it with a smile, I was told.

Thankfully, no one got hurt in either case.

He did more time for that, which included a stint in the psych ward.

How did he end up on the waterfront?

His brother Sam had a union card passed down from his father before him. That was the only way to get a job on the docks back then: you had to have a relative who had previously been a union member or one who was currently working on the waterfront. If a person wasn't qualified by family, a connection through a union official or organized crime was always a surefire way of landing the union card.

Unfortunately, Sam was killed in Korea just as Mickey was let out of the nuthouse, so he took his card and started working immediately.

Mickey and I grabbed a coffee, sat, and spoke at length about the spectacle of that day, which was the cops swarming all of us, trying to excavate our brains and get to the bottom of what had happened.

Not surprisingly, Mickey started poking and prodding. "I heard it was one of the fellas that did that guy in," he said.

"Is that right?" I said.

"That's what I heard," said Mickey as he brought his hot cup of joe up to his lips and slurped a sip. "Just sayin'."

"People say funny things sometimes," I told him.

"Yeah," said Mickey. "You hear anything?"

"No."

I wondered at that point if Mickey knew something of the truth and was testing me. After all, I'd just met the guy. But I relaxed rather quickly and came to the conclusion he wasn't bright enough to even think that up. But I figured, why take a chance? So I told him I'd see him tomorrow and cut the conversation short.

Two days after the murder, I showed up to the pier and "faced" for a job in the hiring hall. That's when a good number of guys literally face the stevedore and wave their arms in the air to get his attention in hopes of getting picked for a job. Hence the term.

The stevedore pointed to me right away to work on a ship unloading again. It struck me as odd, as I had the feeling he'd sought me out in the crowd. In any case, I was happy to be working that day.

There were roughly the same number of guys on the ship that morning, minus one, of course. But also present was that crazy son of a bitch Butchie.

We spent all day on the ship, working. For Butchie, it was just another shift. For me, well, it was pretty messed up. I wasn't ready to interact with him so soon, but I lent nothing to the effect of a guy looking to avoid contact. I was cool, calm, and collected, just a kid who didn't know any better. Had I shown signs of anything less, Butchie would have taken notice.

As the day progressed, the conversations were minimal—"Pass me this" or "Hand me that"—and that was fine with me. It wasn't until the end of the day, when the monotony was busted wide open, that Butchie said, "You do good work."

I replied, "So do you," boldly referring to the way he murdered that guy a couple of days ago.

He looked sharply at me and at my grin, and he gave a slanted grin back. He was impressed, I figured, at the fact I could make light of the incident.

"Walk with me," he said.

He took a few steps, and I followed him to a quiet spot near the port side of the ship. He stopped and said, "Listen… thanks."

"For what?"

"I think you know."

"Nah, forget about it," I said.

"I can't do that," he said. "So I'm going to make sure you're taken care of around here…Starting tomorrow you'll get the good jobs from the stevedore, with me, on the pier counting the pallets or directing traffic in the warehouse when they're loaded inside, instead of lugging this shit off the ship. And no one is gonna get in your way—no one."

"That sounds like a great thing, so it's much appreciated," I said. "But won't the other guys get a little…you know, a little upset, seeing how I just started working here?"

"No."

"OK, I guess," I said. "Thank you."

"Don't mention it," he said.

"So…what brings you on the ship today then?"

"You," he said.

"Me?"

"That's right," said Butchie. "I needed to know what kind of guy you are; wanted to make sure you'd keep your mouth shut, and, uh, I think you will."

"So now what?" I asked him.

"Now I'll introduce you to Jimmy G, the union president. He's a solid guy and a good person to know around here."

"Known him long?" I asked.

"Jimmy has been here just a couple of years, give or take, so not too long," he said. "We'll see how long he lasts."

"How long?"

"These days," he said, "anyone who has any sort of control in the union might as well have a bull's-eye on his back. Everyone's looking for a piece of the pie out here, and if they're not careful, it's lights out."

"Then why would anyone want the job?"

"Greed," he said. "The temptation to make a lot of dough seems to outweigh the risk for a lot of these guys."

"Crazy..."

"It's war out there, kid, between the ones who want control over the docks. But as long as you don't get caught in the crossfire, you'll be all right."

"Understood," I said.

"What are you doing later, after work?" he asked.

"Nothing really," I told him.

"Let's get a beer."

"Yeah, that sounds like a good idea, as a matter of fact," I said.

We met up at a place in South Boston called the Brothers' Pier. It was owned by a couple of former longshoremen, brothers, of course, named Rick and John O'Callaghan. They opened early, at 6:00 a.m. on most days, to allow the longshoremen a few drinks before they reported down to the waterfront for work. And believe me, there were some guys who couldn't make it through the day without having a few before, during, and after work.

So Butchie and I had a few beers, and then a few more, and spoke almost entirely about our upbringings, turning the evening into a prolonged bonding session.

He began, "I was young when my parents came over from Ireland, just two years old. We settled in South Boston, not too far from this place, in fact. It was right at the tail end of the Depression, and my father, who was a carpenter, naturally had a tough time finding work in them days. When I got old enough, I started contributing to the family the only way I knew how—by stealing whatever I could to help us out. Then my kid sister was born, which was nice, but it made things that much tougher to survive."

"I was born on January 3, 1940," I told Butchie. "My mother had me, and after the Japs hit us at Pearl Harbor, my dad joined the war. I was a bastard from the get-go. I told my parents to fuck off as soon as I could talk, so I got more beatings than I could count as a kid…"

"Makes two of us," Butchie said. "And happy belated."

"Thank you."

Maybe it was the beers giving me the courage, but I had to ask him, "Was that the first time you ever…"

"What?"

"You know," I said.

"What, killed a guy?"

I answered, "Yeah."

He pitched a squinty, uninterrupted look. "No."

I let it go—at least, it was my intention to.

"You want to know about me, so I'll tell you," said Butchie.

"No. No," I said. "I don't want to know your personal shit."

"It's too late," he said. "Let's see, I was thirteen when I stabbed my eighth-grade teacher with a scissors for telling me I was no good."

"No shit?" I asked.

"He was right, but still, you don't say that to a kid."

"No, you don't," I said.

"I didn't kill him," said Butchie, "if that's what you're thinking."

Shaking my head, I said, "No, I wasn't."

"But after I tried making a paper snowflake out of the guy, the cops came calling," he went on. "The assault landed me eighteen months in a reform school over in Dorchester. At my sentencing, the judge addressed me and said, in not so many words, that I was by far the worst kid ever to come through his courtroom. So I stood up and yelled, 'Hey, Judge, go fuck yourself!'"

"Get out, really?"

He nodded and took a sip of his beer. "He'd seen me before in that courtroom, so…"

"I see."

"Anyway, after serving the eighteen, plus six more for telling that cocksucker to fuck off, I was released," he said. "At that point, though, for me, there was no shot at rehabilitation.

It was just a couple of weeks before my sixteenth birthday when I was told that a kid from my high school was heckling my baby sister—who was twelve at the time—each day as she walked home from school…It drove me mad, so I decided to shut him up."

I actually started to sober up as I listened to his stories. I was wide-eyed, intently hanging on every last word.

"I caught up with him walking on a quiet street in Southie, not two blocks from my own house," he went on. "It was around five o'clock or so when I approached him. His name was Paul. He was a good-size kid, bigger than I was, and older too. I couldn't have given a shit less, though. I walked right up to him and asked if he had a problem with my sister. Before the kid could answer, I coldcocked him. He hit the sidewalk, and I jumped on him and stabbed him repeatedly. I can't tell you how many times, but when I finally stopped, the kid was a bloody mess and barely breathing. So I got up and took off."

It was eerie, because by his tone, it seemed as though he was describing what it was like to kill your first deer, but it was in fact a human being.

"Anyone see it?" I asked him.

"I'll get to that," Butchie said. "So when the kid never came home for dinner that day, his parents sounded the alarm. The search party ended when the family got a call that the kid was in critical condition over at the Mass General. As it turned out, a little girl peeked through a window, saw the whole thing, and told her father, who then positively ID'd me. When the cops picked me up at home, I remember my mother whacking the back side of my head as they escorted me past her just before the front door."

I said, "The kid died, I take it?"

After a swig of beer, he shook his head. "The son of a bitch lived, Lucky for me, right?"

"No doubt."

"I'll tell ya, though, I vowed after that day that if I ever used a blade on someone again, I'd finish the job and then some…Well, you saw what I mean."

"I certainly did," I said.

"Anyway, I did more time for that, a couple of years up in Billerica, but word got around, ya know? And so I was approached by several hoods around town looking for favors, either to collect money, bust someone up, or worse. They asked me, and 'they' included that knucklehead down there on Broadway, the one who owns the dry cleaning business," he said. "You know who I'm talking about."

"I do," I said.

"Then a guy who was in the rackets named JR asked me if I was interested in working on the waterfront. I had nothing else going on, so I said, 'Yeah, sure, why not?'" He went on. "The other stuff, though, I do it for the money. That guy the other day, the one on the ship…he was a degenerate gambler who ran up a tab to around twenty-five to JR."

"Twenty-five hundred?" I asked.

"Twenty-five thousand," he said. "The shithead was ready to skip town, so I was called in, naturally, because I could get to him so easily on the pier. I had the stevedore put me on the ship with him, and that was that."

"That's a helluva story," I said.

"It would have been even better if I got to his brother, James, too," he said. "He was a cocksucker who we knew was going to make trouble after we took his fat fuck brother out, but he's gone…got twenty to life on murder two or something, so he's out of the way."

"Good timing," I said.

"For him. Anyway, the money is pretty good and all," he said, "but I'll tell you what, though—if I could make a fuckin' score off one of these ships one day, something big, that'd be the end of it for me. I'd buy a boat, sail to Florida, and never come back."

"That'd be nice," I said.

"One day, I tell ya," said Butchie, "it'll happen. And I'll need people I can count on—if you catch my drift."

"You can count on me."

"Good," he said.

"I'll cheers to that."

"To the biggest goddamn score the waterfront ever seen," Butchie said.

We clanked beer bottles and took a swig, and then Butchie said, "So, what's *your* story?"

CHAPTER 3
SCHOOL IS OUT

I attended Saint Mary's of East Boston.

The place sucked. The halls smelled of one thousand pits on a scorching summer afternoon, and so did the nuns. It was old and decrepit and deeply begged for a new roof, walls, and all else in between.

I was stuck there at the behest of my parents, who foolishly believed the "ladies of the cloth" could offer me some guidance, discipline, and respectfulness, but they were dead wrong.

It was 1949. I was nine years old and sitting in class, boorishly tapping my pencil's eraser on my desk one day, with my left arm pillared against my left cheek, keeping my melon from crashing on the desk. I was chomping at the bit, waiting for the bell to ring, but this old, wrinkly hag, Sister Isabella, was going on and on and on about an assignment, for which I had no clue. I wasn't listening. My biggest concern that day was tying the perfect knot on my tie; it was a cheap black cotton piece of crap throttling my neck.

Then, *rinnnnnnng!*

I sprang from my desk and crashed into the bottleneck formation of students who had rushed the door.

It was recess, and it was Friday, and that meant we had forty-five minutes to screw around versus the typical thirty minutes of freedom we were afforded Monday through Thursday.

A mass of kids had spread out in the schoolyard like a giant web, as the cliques formed in their respective corners of the yard.

There was no agenda, just the opportunity to take a breather from the ear sore developing from the spiritual lectures and other tedious academic endeavors.

I sought Mike, Lorenzo, and Chris, my three closest buddies. As on most afternoons, we were being scoped out vigorously by Sister Mary McLaughlin, who often took on the role of watchdog during recess. We saw her speaking rather intently with a student, Sarah, but her peripherals told us something else. She eyeballed us, as when trouble ensued, my friends and I were never far behind. Nonetheless, I took it as a sign of aggression and disrespect from the whiskery old nun.

I was so hopped up from being outside with my buddies and away from the blackboard and from knowing we were on the heels of the weekend. I was brimming with excitement.

I wanted to run or scream or hit something. So I picked up a golf-ball-sized rock and said to my friends, "Watch this."

And so I wound up slowly, like Dizzy Dean with no runners on base, and then hurled a fastball, hitting the nun right in the ass! I spun around like a top so as to not be detected.

She screamed, "Jesus Chri—!" while all the kids erupted in laughter.

I maintained my composure. I was so cool and went on as if nothing had happened, but it meant little. Before I had a chance to enjoy the moment with my friends, Sister Frances, who had been watching from a distance, stampeded over and grabbed my wrist as tight as a duck's ass in water and escorted me back in the building and into a vacant classroom.

There, she ordered me to bend over, while in the meantime, she plucked a yardstick from the closet. I knew it well—so well that on some days, I could measure small objects from the imprints it made on my ass. She placed her left hand on my back for pressure, pushed me forward over the teacher's desk, and then proceeded to deliver ten whacks to my ass with an unholy purpose. It hurt like hell; I didn't cry, though. I wouldn't. I winced like a bastard, gritted my teeth, and bore the pain, but I never cried, even though for some reason that beating was worse than any other in the past.

Remember, that was 1949. Nuns back then were big and bulky and had no qualms about setting a kid straight with brute force by the hand or any other object fit to perform the task.

I can still feel the threadlike scars left behind by some of the lashes I collected from many of those beatings. At least, I think they are from them.

The school was sure to call, I figured, and I had assumed I'd catch another beating, but this time at the hands of my mother, Antoinette.

It was a bad day that was about to get worse.

It was around four o'clock when I carefully opened the front door to my house and crept up the thick brown-carpeted staircase one level to the second floor, sliding my left arm on the railing, peeking left and right and even behind me in case I needed to thwart off a sneak attack.

So futile.

My mother appeared at the top of the stairs with her arms folded over her flowery muumuu with a disgusted, stone-cold posture and crabby expression.

She was a big woman, imposing, and had no misgivings about beating someone like a hired mule if she needed to.

Behind her and to her left, hiding behind the wall and poking one eye out to see the beating, was my kid brother, Tommy, who was the "good one," as my mother always put it. He was a couple of years younger than I was, and the little bastard never did anything out of the way. The closest he ever came to a licking was when the two of us went in my mother's purse and stole ten dollars to buy some fireworks to light off on the beach in Winthrop, the next town over from us. But when Ma found out, I could see the fear in my brother's eyes, so I took the rap for the kid.

When I reached the top of the stairs, I saw my brother bolt in the other direction.

Anything but the ass. Anything but the ass, I thought.

She gripped the back of my neck like her hand was the Jaws of Life and guided me down the hallway, nearly lifting me off the floor, and then chucked me against the foot of the bed, where her weapon of choice lay—the belt. My schoolbooks were still tied and wrapped around my shoulder when she began slapping me with her open hand across my left cheek; she bunched my shirt up in her left fist, holding me so I couldn't fall. Five or six good whacks, and then she yelled, "Turn around!"

I did.

She then grabbed the belt and swung a half dozen times or so across my back. There was a pause, a cease-fire, so she could catch her breath. She then delivered a few more lashes, tossed the belt on the bed, and left the room.

I thanked the Lord it was over.

What a shit day that was. Truth be told, I had plenty just like it, but as fate would have it, the nuns would soon realize they had messed with the wrong kid and for the last time.

Later that evening I was summoned to dinner at around five thirty. I took up my usual spot, sandwiched between my parents, with Ma on the left and Dad on the right; Tommy sat directly across from me.

My dad, Joe, was lean and mean. He worked in the navy yard in town, boxed at a local gym, and tended bar for a little extra dough in his spare time in the West End of Boston. As tough as he was, he left most of the disciplinary duties to my mother. Dad had a good heart; he was a very caring guy and a great provider for the family. But he had a short fuse, and with his skills as a boxer and his fearless nature, it was always best to leave punishments up to Ma.

I was slow to hit the cushion on the seat at the dinner table. My ass was still throbbing from round one, and my hesitation caught the attention of my mother.

"What's wrong with your ass? I didn't whack you there," she said.

"I know, Ma."

"Then what is it?" she asked.

"Sister Frances did."

"She did what?" she asked leaning toward me.

"Sister Francis whacked me in the ass a bunch of times for throwing the rock."

She exchanged a look with my father and then rose quickly and said, "Get up; let me see."

I stood up, and she pulled down the back of my knickers until she saw the fresh bruises and distinct, red track-like marks across both cheeks of my ass.

"Look at this," she said to my father.

So he peeked over, and by his expression, I could tell he was pissed. Ma pulled my pants back up and told me I could eat standing up.

She was seething, I could tell. Strangely enough, the notion offered a reprieve in a sense—she actually felt bad for me for an instant.

The very next Monday, I walked to school with my mother beside me. We waited patiently outside amid a sea of less-than-enthused students for a nun, preferably Sister Frances, to call us in with a cowbell. I remember my friends looking over and feeling bad for me, like I was in serious trouble.

The giant oak doors of Saint Mary's opened, and there was Sister Frances in the usual commanding pose she struck when she waved the bell back and forth.

"That's her, Ma," I said.

My mother let go of my hand and then cracked her knuckles. Still, she waited until all the kids went in. When that happened, she nonchalantly walked up to within a few inches of Sister Frances but said nothing.

It's important to note that even though nuns in that era were big and brutish, they were still revered by most people as sacred beings in the church and schools. My ma was no exception and believed we respect the nuns no matter what. I guess that day was different.

"Can I help you?" Sister Frances asked in a very smug tone; sadly, that's all it took for Ma.

What seemed like forever lasted about two seconds. That's when my mother clenched her fist and then darted after her like a hound chasing a hare. The nun spun quickly, though, and took off. I had no idea where my mother chased her to, so, being left alone for a good minute or two, I decided to go to class.

I walked in, and the kids were all dumbfounded because our teacher wasn't there. My eyes popped out of my head when I looked out the window and saw Sister Frances still being chased past the classroom outside and around the building. My classmates saw my expression, turned around, and observed the whole thing. On the next pass, though, my mother needed a break and stopped; she bent down to catch her breath but then retreated. She turned around and went home.

Moments later, Sister Frances returned to class and gathered herself as best she could. But boy, she looked like shit; her clothes were wrinkled, and she was sweating bullets. She shot me a look and then immediately ordered us to open our history textbooks to chapter 7, as if nothing had happened.

She was a big woman, that Sister Frances, but surprisingly quick on her feet, more so than my mother, who ran with a purpose.

In any event, that was the last time a nun at that school put a hand on me. In fact, I had a tough enough time getting them to make eye contact with me in class and at recess. Every time I raised my hand, they looked away. They never called on me again, so I finally gave up.

At eleven years old, I played baseball for the Little League Dodgers. Being part of a team was great; I really enjoyed it.

Now, on the field, even at that level of play, there was constant trash-talking, and most of the time, it was I who started the chatter. One particular game, a player on another team took a verbal thrashing from me after we were ahead by ten runs or something. It just so happened that this kid took to the mound that day when I was heckling him. When it was my turn at bat, I braced for the inevitable. He wound up and tossed a fastball right into my back, so I threw the bat at his head, but the lucky prick ducked and got out of the way of it. So I chased him out of the park and down a side street until I ran out of breath. The son of a bitch had some wheels on him. He ran fast and far, and he never looked back. He went right home.

When I got back, I could see my father sigh with disappointment. The good news was I only got suspended. I never received punishment for it at home either; I just got a lot of comments such as "What are you, an idiot or something? It's part of the game, for Christ's sake!" After all, I didn't hurt anyone—just scared the kid a bit.

I was young and stupid, and I simply did not get it. Quite honestly, it would be a long frigging time before I actually did…a very long time.

CHAPTER 4
UNCLE DOM

His ever-commanding presence, broad shoulders, and snarling expression caused most to avoid eye contact. The smart ones sidestepped his very being at all costs. On the street he was known as the Handyman because no matter what type of altercation he got in, he'd always grab something within his reach—a pipe, a branch, a rock, whatever else he could get his hands on—to swing the odds in his favor. He once beat a guy to unconsciousness in the back of a restaurant kitchen with a ladle that had been submerged in a fra diavolo sauce.

He was a friend to few, feared by many, and an enemy to a score of others, but to me, he was my father's brother and my uncle Dominic.

Uncle Dom was part of a Mafia crew out of the North End of Boston, and I thought it was the greatest thing.

I was just nine years old when he began asking me who I thought would win in any given sporting event, professional or college, and if I picked right, he'd always throw me a few bucks, depending on how much he collected.

He was very good to me—and I looked at him as a hero of sorts.

Among his many illegal activities, he was a bookmaker and took bets out of the Hill—a social club in Eastie that I became well acquainted with at the tender age of eleven.

The card games were loud and frightening. I remember the heated arguments at the table, the swearing, and on occasion, even a gun being drawn, either out of frustration or in an accusatory manner to challenge a cheater. And a few did get killed over card games back then—not at the Hill, but we did hear about it from time to time.

It was a social club with forty or so members. It was a great place for guys to unwind, have a few beers, and play some cards or billiards. The demographics ranged from cops, lawyers, and probation officers to gangsters, construction laborers, and longshoremen.

There were two floors. The lower level showcased a U-shaped, dust-filled bar clamped to the wall on the left as you walked in. The operation was manned by a sweet old guy named Gus. He was one of the original members and, oddly, found it abundantly satisfying to serve the guys, as he had little else to do outside the club. According to him, his kids and grandkids were no good, and since his wife had passed on quite some time ago, he found the club his escape from the outside world.

There were two poker tables, a cigarette machine, a jukebox, and one Cathedral radio that never worked nestled in the far left corner just below the ceiling. The bathroom was tiny and smelled like urine if we were lucky.

The top floor had a nine-foot pool table, a dozen or so warped sticks hanging on a rack, and a few padded steel chairs scattered about, with some stacked on top of one another. And there was the office. It was small but roomy enough to hold a modest-size desk with drawers and a chair to sit on. That's all it needed. The only work that was ever done there was balancing the books for the club and bookmaking.

Understandably, my parents never warmed up to me hanging out at the club with my uncle, but I never listened anyway.

When I turned twelve, I began spending more and more time there. Even when my uncle was on the phones taking action, I stood close and paid attention to every word. I studied the spreads, what the payouts were, and how to record them using a simple college-lined notebook.

I loved it. It was exciting to watch him work, and I became even more enthralled when he walked away from the office, thus giving me the opportunity to peek at the day's totals. I could cipher the info backward, frontward, and every which way till Sunday.

One day when I was upstairs playing pool, I heard him complaining of stomach pains. Without warning he leaped out of his chair yelling, "Watch the office!" as he ran downstairs to the bathroom. So I did. I watched an empty office and the open notebooks spread on the desk. I saw the usual: a lot of numbers, plusses and minuses, number and letter codes, dates, times, and locations. And then the phone rang.

I shot out of the office to see if my uncle was coming up, but apparently whatever he had eaten previously had worked him over pretty intensely.

So I went for it. I picked up the receiver cautiously, like I was afraid to set off a bomb, and then I said, "Hello?" in the deepest tone I could muster,

"Who's this?" the person on the other end asked.

"Tony?" I said, skittish.

To my surprise, the caller said, "You got the lines, Tony? This is B5."

So I rummaged through the notebook, frantically looking for this B5 character, but as it turned out, he was on the open page in front of me facing up; I was just too excited to see it.

I asked him, "What do you need, B5?"

"Just the NFL."

I saw the NFL spreads on the previous page and began to rattle them off. All of them, until he said, "OK, I'll call you back."

"OK," I said and hung up the phone.

I took a moment to gloat to myself but was interrupted when I turned around and saw my uncle standing over me with a very stern look on his face.

"Was that OK?" I asked.

"That was very good, as a matter of fact, kid," he said. "Now get the fuck up and let me finish."

"OK," I said and went back to the pool table.

When the last game kicked off that day, we took a ride to grab something to eat. That's when he spoke about me helping him out so I could earn a few bucks, but it wasn't to take calls; it was to collect money.

It seemed strange to me at the time—a kid my age collecting cash from bettors—but not all guys (or twelve-year-olds) who collected walked around with a baseball bat, spitting out threats if a guy didn't pay. That only happened when the bettor showed a lack of payments or the effort to make payments over a period of time. In my case, if someone didn't pay me, I took what he gave me and reported back to my uncle. He handled the rest.

For the most part, everything went smoothly. They were small jobs my uncle put me on, naturally, and local, so usually I'd just take my bike to get from place to place. Anything that needed attention outside of that, he called on others, who likely had the ability to use a car.

The closest place was a dental office just a block from my house. The customer was Dr. Benton, fiftyish, a bit overweight, with a double chin so big it dangled in front of him like a Jell-O mold. He was my dentist, in fact, so it was a bit awkward at first to learn he was a gambling degenerate, but I got used to collecting dough from him—and the cold looks he gave me even when I showed up just for a routine appointment.

Looking back, I'm not sure if the guy talked too much or just talked about things I didn't care about. But every time he had to pay, he'd give me a song and dance about his practice and how tough it was to run and tell me that my uncle should be a little patient (no pun intended) with him, and this and that. Still, though, the guy was never short. The doc always paid, and I always left with a lollipop.

But things got real on September 23, 1953, when my uncle sent me down to the C Street Tavern about a mile away from my house. I was thirteen at the time. He said the customer there was a waiter, a young guy who said he'd have his dough that day. He was already late, so my uncle let me know, "If he doesn't have it, give me a call from a pay phone."

So I hopped on my bike, and when I got to the place, I leaned it against the outside wall next to a steel bench fit for about three people.

I walked into the rectangular-shape business and felt the curious looks from a handful of customers sitting at the bar. I asked the barkeep, a real disheveled-looking character, where the guy was. He told me to wait a second—probably thought I was a nephew or little brother or something. I took a quick scan of the place and the people in it, but I didn't know anyone. I would soon, though.

The barkeep and the waiter appeared in a doorway leading to the kitchen at the end of the bar, which was situated on the right and ran parallel to a slew of random tables and booths. I could see the bartender point right at me, and then the waiter walked over to me. He was young, maybe college-aged, with a crew cut, and he was wearing an apron and an expression of utter disgust on his face.

He looked at me like I had three heads and asked, "Can I help you, kid?"

"I'm here to collect for Dom," I said.

He chuckled, but I stood unamused.

"You're kidding," he said.

"Not even a little."

"I don't have it, tell him. I was supposed to pick up the late shift yesterday, but it didn't pan out. Tell him next week."

I just stood there recalling in my head what my uncle had explicitly said to me. I contemplated what to say to this clown, but nothing came out. I'd never had to call my uncle before, so I figured I'd just ask him again.

"Do you have anything at all?"

"Hey, kid," he said with an aggressive tone, "I told you I don't have the dough, so jump on your tricycle and go home! I'll have it next week. This place ain't bringing any customers in like it should anyhow."

"Watch it," said the bartender, who was presumably the owner.

"OK," I replied.

I turned, walked outside, and panned the street both ways in search of a pay phone. I found one on the next block, on the same side of the street as the bar and to my left. So

I took a walk up there, picked up the phone, and dialed the club. Gus answered, and I asked for my uncle.

After a few moments, my uncle said, "Hello?"

"Hi, Uncle Dom."

"What's up, kid? I'm busy."

"I'm at the restaurant…or outside of it, and the guy doesn't have the money."

"What do you mean, he doesn't have the money?"

"He said he doesn't have any money at all; he'll have it next week."

Uncle Dom took a deep breath and sighed.

"Stay right there; I'm coming now," he said and then hung up the phone abruptly.

I walked back and waited just outside the bar for his arrival. In the meantime, the turd that owed the money came outside for a smoke. He looked at me, bewildered, and said, "Are you lost?"

"Just waiting for my friend," I said.

I didn't want to say I was waiting for my uncle in case the kid had an idea of taking off to avoid him.

After a few drags, he flicked the cigarette into the street and went back in. Just then my uncle pulled up and got out of the car. He passed me in a hurry and said, "Wait here."

Of course, I did, but I couldn't help but take a peek in to see what was about to transpire. And what I witnessed I will never forget.

Uncle Dom made a beeline for the guy—no words, just sheer determination and rage; when he got close, he grabbed a wine bottle that lay on the bar and smashed the kid across the head, busting the bottle and his melon wide open, spilling and splattering blood all over the place. When the guy hit the floor, my uncle took a broom away from the busboy, who was frozen in fear, and gave the waiter a few more whacks for good measure.

A couple of waitresses shrieked. The bartender did nothing, as did the few patrons sitting there.

I turned white. I had never seen anything like that in all my thirteen years. I thought about the beatings I took, but they were nothing compared to what this idiot experienced that day. It was the way the blood exploded out of his head and took flight, spraying the wall and ceiling. The kid lay on the floor and cried like a baby.

To some degree, I found it amusing that my uncle never said a word. He went in, beat the guy, and walked out.

He put my bike in his trunk, and we took off.

On the ride home, I was quiet. He knew I was a bit shaken, so he asked me if I was OK, and for the most part, I was. He dropped me off at home and said, "I'll see ya later."

It was as if nothing had happened. Like we had grabbed a burger down at the beach or something, and that was it. He showed no signs of being worked up or agitated and most certainly was not remorseful.

I was proud to call this guy my uncle.

CHAPTER 5

THE ATTEMPT TO MURDER

Back in the summer of 1955, I had no agenda. I was fifteen, bold and brash, and fearless as the day was long.

School was out, and with no desire to make good, honest cash, I made a choice: I continued to meddle in my uncle's business, and every now and then, he gave me a taste of some work and a bit of the money that followed.

I delivered packages to a produce store near Logan Airport, to a local thug named "Whistling" Willy Summers. I didn't have a driver's license—I was too young—but I got behind the wheel anyway. I was stopped numerous times by the local cops, but as soon as I let them know what I was doing and who I was doing it for, they let me go.

I delivered a lot of seafood as well to many of my uncle's friends in the neighborhood and to those who had loved ones serving time in prison. It was a nice gesture on his end and a sign of respect. My mother's brother, Uncle Sal, owned a fishing company up in Gloucester, Massachusetts, so the shit was easy to come by.

That was a good job for me. Uncle Dom paid well, and I always received a healthy tip—anywhere from ten dollars up to fifty dollars in some cases—from whoever I brought the food to, and that was a lot of dough back then.

I was hustling and making cash, and lots of it for a kid my age. So I decided to treat myself, and when I finally turned sixteen and got my driver's license, I went out and bought a nice car: a 1955 Ford Thunderbird, red, with a white convertible roof, off a lot in Somerville.

Unfortunately, my plush job came crashing down in a hurry when my uncle Dom was indicted on a slew of charges, including bookmaking, loan sharking, and extortion. But that wasn't the worst of it. He beat a guy to death, and over nothing really. He had an argument with a low-level gangster over an extortion payment. My uncle had a few drinks in him already when he caught up with the guy in a bar in the North End. He punished him severely and ended up putting him in a coma, and after a few days, the guy slipped away. So, adding a murder charge to everything else and considering all of his priors, the judge, who inevitably knew who Dom was and what he was a part of, hit my uncle with twenty years in Walpole State Prison.

It was a devastating blow to me. We were very close. I didn't trust anyone else in the business he was involved in, and without his guidance, I took a step back and terminated my involvement in any criminal activities…at least for a while.

Academically I got by, but it was a foregone conclusion that I would not continue my education beyond high school. I had some cash saved and managed to score a part-time job as a gas station attendant fixing cars.

The job sucked, and the boss was a prick, but I learned valuable skills as a mechanic, and it put some money in my pocket.

I had a girl, too, named Betty—a gorgeous, petite thing with long dark hair. I met her at the station one day when she came in for a brake job…that was a good day.

She didn't last long, though.

One evening I took her out to a local diner, and it was packed. From where we sat, though, I recognized a kid from my neighborhood named Angelo Cota. I never really liked him. He had a big mouth and lacked the balls to back it up.

I saw that Angelo was with a few of his friends. They were hanging around my car, sitting on it, even putting their brown paper bags on the hood, and that did not sit well with me.

I took a deep breath and told myself I wouldn't let anything get out of hand. But it never worked out that way, not for me.

I told Betty I'd be right back and very casually got out of my seat and headed for the exit. I went outside to confront them.

Angelo was no threat to me, but there were others I needed to be aware of, and I felt each one of them sizing me up—all five of his buddies.

Very politely I said, "What's up, Angelo?"

"Tony," he said very macho-like.

"Listen, you guys mind getting your bottles off my car?" I said. "It's a new ride…and I kinda like it the way it is, with no scratches and stuff."

They all exchanged a look as if I was speaking a foreign language, until the biggest of the group stepped forward, got to within an inch of my face, and said, "Make us."

Betty appeared out of nowhere and found a way to wedge herself between me and that punk, hoping she could defuse the situation, but as long as they were near the car, I was staying put.

It all happened so quickly. The straw that broke the camel's back was when the big guy, with his big mouth, simply offered a grin, as if to imply I needed my girl to fight my battle.

And so I snapped.

But first, I gently held Betty by the shoulders and moved her out of the way to my right. Then I launched myself at the guy. I threw a punch and connected and knocked him to the ground. Angelo and his buddies made halfhearted attempts at holding me off, but they couldn't. They knew I would have killed them. They did, however, distract me enough to slow my assault on his friend, and so the goon seized the opportunity and punched me—closed fist—right in the fuckin' balls.

Oh, it hurt. I fell sideways between my car and the one parked next to it, on my driver's side. I was utterly incapacitated. The big guy then kicked me over and over until I heard someone shout, "Come on; let's go!"

The next thing I knew, I was lying in a hospital bed. I vaguely remember my mother standing at my left side, shaking her head in a most disparaging fashion.

I spent the night at the hospital.

The following day I went home with one thing on my mind—revenge.

I had never seen the guy before, so I paid a visit to Angelo. I went right to his house. I rang the bell, and he promptly appeared.

In a guarded position, with his right hand gripping the inside handle, Angelo said, "What do you want?"

"Relax," I told him. "I don't have a beef with you, not yet anyway. I'm here because I want to know who your friend is. And I'm going to give you one shot to tell me who he is and where I can find him. If you don't want to tell me, that's fine; like I said, I'm not here to cause any trouble, not today. But just know, I will catch up with you again, and when I do, you will be sorry. It's up to you, because whatever you decide, I'll find him anyway, and I'll kill him. It's your call."

He thought about it. He knew I was dead serious. After a moment of silence, Angelo caved.

"His name is Carl, Carl Bradley," said Angelo. "You'll find him down near the pier, at the basketball court every

Sunday playing ball with a few of his buddies, but I don't know any of them."

"With his friends, huh?" I asked.

"Yeah."

"He'll be there?"

"He'll be there," he said.

"You did a good thing today, Angelo," I said. "You better not open your mouth and tell him I'm coming."

"I won't."

"Good," I replied.

I had turned to leave when he said, "You're not really going to kill him, though, are you?"

"No. Just going to scare him, that's all," I told him.

Just then I reacted to a wonderful smell emanating from Angelo's front hallway. "Is that a pot roast I smell cooking back there?" I asked.

Stuttering, Angelo said, "Yes…Yes, it is."

"I might have to come back for that one of these days," I said.

Angelo had no expression.

"Take it easy," I said.

I waited impatiently for Sunday to come. But before I marinated myself in the vision of me ripping Carl's face off, I decided to enlist a friend to help me out—not with the actual fight but to serve as a mere presence in the event someone decided to interfere. So I called my good friend Mario. He was a tough son of a gun. I'd known him my whole life. He was a loyal friend, reliable, and loved to get his hands dirty.

Sunday.
Mario and I showed up around 9:30 a.m. I saw Carl—he was one of six guys playing a pickup game at the court by the pier, just like Angelo said. The court wasn't fenced in, which made for easy access, or escape, depending on the situation.

So I wasted no time. I trotted up to him, paying no mind to the game, and just as he caught sight of me, I pounced on him like a lion on a gazelle. And once I got on top of him, I had no ambition to let up. I punched the living shit out of him, over and over until eventually he slipped into unconsciousness. I took a breather and looked around. The rest of the kids there were in awe, and afraid, judging by their pale expressions. Carl's face was bloodied; my hands were, too. Then I felt Mario tugging at my shirt, so I got up.

Carl's friends stood motionless, unable to digest what had happened. Finally, one dropped by his side and lightly tapped a cheek in the hopes of bringing him back.

Mario grabbed me by the arm and said, "Let's go!"

That's when I knew I'd done a terrible thing.

So I left at the urging of my friend, went home, and washed up with the garden hose in my backyard. I went inside and changed as quickly as I could. The doorbell rang, and I put my ear to the drywall to listen. I heard my mother's muffled voice.

"He's upstairs," she said. "I'll get him."

Apparently, someone in that scrum knew my name and had called the cops.

My mother called for me. It was time to face the music. I opened my bedroom door, and there she was, standing irate but voiceless. She whacked me across my left cheek really hard and said, "There's a policeman here to see you."

"OK," I said.

I walked like a defeated general down the hallway and spiral staircase. It took forever, it seemed, as a million thoughts filled my head: *Is he dead? Am I going to jail? And for how long?*

I reached the door. Behind the screen was a middle-aged cop, average size, but he could afford to miss a couple of trips to the doughnut shop. With his cuffs dangling in his right hand, he asked, "Anthony Costa?"

"Yes, sir."

The officer then turned me around, fastened the binders on me tightly, and said, "You're under arrest for the attempted murder…"

That's when it went dark. I blacked out upon hearing "attempted murder."

It was a fistfight, for Christ's sake, I kept saying to myself.

When the air cleared, I learned that in my rage, according to the witnesses, I had shouted more than once, "I'm going to kill you!" So in the eyes of the law, I tried to kill him. They were probably right. I was seething. I wouldn't have stopped had it not been for Mario. Perhaps he saved a life that day, because the kid did in fact make it. He lived.

I was still a minor and without any priors, so the judge gave me five years' probation and 240 hours of community service.

My mother wanted me out of the house—probably dead, too, but she never said so. My father was disappointed. Together they decided to give me one more chance.

As it turned out, the incident had a silver lining—one that would change my life for the better and for many years to come.

CHAPTER 6
MARIE

I spent the next couple of years at home with a muted mother and a father who was one tick away from giving up on me.

Nevertheless, during that time, I tightened a few screws and kept to myself for the most part. I even studied—enough to get by, anyway. I stayed out of trouble, and in 1957 I graduated from high school.

I was such a good boy that, after a series of letters written to the judge by my probation officer stating I had been reformed, my probation was commuted by a nice chunk, but not entirely. I still needed to complete fifty or so remaining hours of community service.

My remaining punishment was to be held at a minimum of five hours per week assisting the East Boston Boys and Girls Club in whatever fashion it needed me. *What a drag*, I thought, but it beat picking up trash on the side of random streets around Eastie and the rest of the city like I had been doing.

So I arrived for my first day and led myself to a glass partition, behind which a young girl was sitting pushing a pencil and shuffling papers in all kinds of piles. She was something, a picture of beauty, with long, curly dark-brown hair, olive skin, and a crazy-beautiful smile that could light up the darkest hour of night.

I approached the partition and knocked gently on the window to get her attention.

She asked, "Can I help you?"

I answered tentatively, "Yeah, I'm supposed to report here to do some, uh, volunteer work."

"Perfect," she said, "and your name is?"

"Tony Costa, miss."

"Please, call me Marie," she said. "Wait here; I'll get Cheryl."

"Thank you, Marie."

She spun out of her chair and vanished behind an open door.

Who the Christ is Cheryl? I thought.

About a moment passed before Marie reappeared from the mystery door with—I assumed—Cheryl.

She was a beast of a woman, a robust and balding specimen. Turned out she had the attitude to match. I cared little, though. I just wanted to do my time and get the hell out of there.

Marie introduced us. "Cheryl, this is Anthony—"

"Hello," I said. Ever charming and respectful when I needed to be, I extended my hand. "Pleased to meet you, Cheryl."

The fat moron never took my hand. She turned and said, "Follow me."

So I did.

She waddled through the corridors while I followed along through a regulation-size basketball court where a couple of young white kids were shooting around. Then on to the game room, which showcased a small TV, a Ping-Pong table, a pool table, and all sorts of fitness contraptions lying around on the floor. The bathrooms were bearable, but not ideal to squat in unless it was a dire emergency. The tour took us back to the front lobby, where Marie, again, was fulfilling some sort of clerical duties behind the glass.

"The courts sent you—am I right?" asked Cheryl.

"Yes, ma'am," I answered.

All the while I caught Marie throwing a glance my way here and there, followed by a playful grin, and so I returned a similar look.

Cheryl took notice and reacted.

"You are here to work," she said. "You are not permitted to do anything else, and that includes fraternizing with the employees. Is that understood?"

"Yes," I said without a hint of attitude.

The last thing I wanted to do was put myself in hot water again.

"Good," she said. "You can start by cleaning the bathrooms…and I want them spotless! Will that be a problem?"

"No, ma'am," I said.

"Good, because I would hate to tell Judge Carson that you were having a difficult time following my directions."

It's Judge Watkins, you fuckin' slob, I thought to myself.

"That would not be good," I said.

Again, I followed her, this time past the maintenance closet on the second floor.

"You'll find everything you need there," she went on. "I hope whatever it was you did, it was worth it."

And that was her parting shot before she said, "Ta-ta," turned, and walked away.

I let her lumber out of my sight before I began the trek to the maintenance closet. She was right. I found what I was looking for; in fact, the space was packed with every cleaning product from mops and rags to bug killers and air fresheners. I grabbed the mop and bucket, some sponges, and a plunger just in case I needed to stick it up her ass.

I was effective in cleaning. *The beast will be happy*, I thought.

The following day began with a pleasant surprise, as I learned that Cheryl had the day off, and my "assignments" were to come from Marie.

There she was, looking all pretty, like an angel, hair in a ponytail flopping about while she busied herself like a bee within her tiny glass enclosure.

I waved to get her attention. She raised her head, locked eyes with me, and smiled. Then she hoisted her index finger up and mouthed, "One second." I nodded. She placed a three-inch stack of papers firmly on her desk and then appeared through the door of her office.

"Tony," she said, grinning.

I said, "Hey, how you doin'?"

"I'm well, thank you," she said. "How are you?"

"I'm good, thanks." I asked lightheartedly, "So, we cleaning more shit today, or what?"

She giggled. "No, not today, but you did such a good job yesterday, even the janitor was impressed."

Taken aback, I said, "You have a janitor here?"

She snickered again.

"That was Cheryl's way of showing you who is boss," she said. "I doubt you'll be scrubbing toilets again."

"I guess that's a good thing, then, huh?"

Abruptly, Marie said, "Follow me."

She turned 180 degrees and led me down a corridor, through a wooden door, and down another hallway to the right. We stopped in front of another door labeled Gym.

"So," she said, "you're going to be here for the day, basically just keeping an eye on the kids, making sure they behave and put the balls and equipment back where they found them. It's not a bad thing either if you get involved in some of their games like basketball or dodgeball, or whatever. Sound good?"

I didn't listen to a word she said. I stared into her eyes with much purpose, enough to make her leery, I suspected, so without hesitation, I let my thoughts surface, and I said, "You're very beautiful."

She was flabbergasted and said, "Excuse me?"

"What…it was a compliment."

"I know; I just wasn't expecting it."

Following an awkward silence, she said, "Well," as she handed me a whistle, threaded on a cheap canvas necklace, "here you go. Call me if you need me."

I stood still and said, "I will. Should I call you at home?"

"Very funny," said Marie.

In the background, I heard the awful sounds of sneakers screeching across the floor, balls bouncing, and kids yelling.

"And watch out for Leon," she said. "He's quite a handful."

"I'm taking you out," I told her.

"Go!" she said sternly, but her body language gave me an inkling she was thinking about it.

"So, yeah?"

"Go," she said, playfully shoving me through the door, and then turned and walked away.

I held the door open with my left hand and said, "Yeah?"

"Yes," she said, turning back. "Now go work, please."

I finally let the door close.

I turned and witnessed the basketball court teeming with kids. They were yelling, fighting, and throwing crap everywhere. I blew the whistle. They dialed it down a notch, but that was it.

God help me, I said to myself.

Date night.

I took Marie to a Celtics game, immediately followed by a bite to eat on Hanover Street in the North End at a pizza joint my uncle Dom owned; it was his front—a way of demonstrating he was an honest, tax-paying citizen.

We showed up, and even from a good distance, we saw the line wrapped around the corner and down Prince Street, which was a block away. Even at that time of night, it was a typical scene after a Celtics or Bruins game because of the restaurant's close proximity to Boston Garden.

I grabbed Marie by the hand and walked her to the front of the line. There, Sonny, a very old friend of the family who worked at the restaurant, caught sight of us and waved us in.

I introduced Marie to him, quickly. Sonny then scanned the room and sighed, as the place was packed like a can of sardines.

Then he said suddenly, "Come with me."

We followed him through the maze of tables and booths filled with savagely hungry patrons until we came upon a small table occupied by an elderly man minding his own business taking down a slice of pizza and a coffee. Sonny grabbed two chairs from the back, placed them across from the old guy, and said to us, "Sit here."

I said, "Sonny…"

"Sit!"

Marie shrugged her shoulders and sat down, so I did, too.

The poor prick didn't know what hit him. He gave us a long befuddled look before he took his half-eaten slice of pie in his frail, quivering hands and continued like no one was watching. So Marie and I looked at each other and carried on like a couple on a first date as best we could.

It was a little uncomfortable at first, but once we settled in, it was OK. I took care of the old guy's bill, and Marie had a story to tell her friends and family.

With a couple of dates in the books, I braved the next move: for Marie to meet my parents.

I had already met her folks. They were off the boat from Sicily but were—good people and very friendly.

I told Marie my father was great, very welcoming and enjoyable to be around. My mother, on the other hand, was a little standoffish.

It was a Saturday around noontime. I planned on spending the day with Marie, so I went and picked her up and brought her back to the house. She was nervous, even trembled slightly in the car on the way over, but after a few words of false encouragement, she settled down.

My father answered the door with a grin, so I wasted no time in introducing him. It was nice. Dad even went as far as saying, "He's a good boy, you know?"

"I know," Marie said, as if she was relieved to hear it from someone so close to me. I saw that my mother had crept behind my father, and I took the opportunity to introduce her, too.

Ma said, "You know you're going to have your hands full with this one, right?"

Marie was in awe and speechless.

"Antoinette! Get back inside," my father said irately, as if she was a house pet that had gotten too close to the door.

My father's kind eyes turned back to Marie, and he apologized profusely before he told us to come in.

We sat at the kitchen table for a couple of hours while my father told stories about the time in World War II when he and ten of his battalion spent thirty days ashore on a desolate island in the South Pacific after their sub sank. No food, no weapons, "just the will to live," as he always put it. I had heard the stories a million and one times, so I tuned out. My mother said nothing and occasionally got up to sham us into believing she had some household chores to perform.

"She'll come around," I kept telling Marie.

I had a serious girl and a high school diploma but not a real solid job prospect. I decided to coast and stay at the gas station after I left high school, and so I did. I picked up more hours and subsequently worked through December of that same year for the same prick boss. But I knew eventually I'd have to become more than just a guy working on cars and pumping gas, especially if I wanted to keep a girl like Marie. Then, out of nowhere, my uncle Dom arranged a meeting from prison between a fella named Freddy K and me at the club.

He was an older gentleman, maybe sixty, who was heavily involved in the bootlegging business back in its heyday. He was a lifelong Bostonian with a ton of connections both in law enforcement and organized crime, which made me curious about this meeting.

It was a Tuesday, and when I got there, Freddy was in a hand in a card game. When he folded, he looked up, saw me, and said, "Let's go upstairs."

I followed him. Once in the office, he got right to it. "I'm going to get you a job on the waterfront."

"Doing what?"

"Whatever they tell you to do," he said.

"OK," I said.

Said Freddy, "I want you to go to the docks to the hiring hall and ask for Donny and tell him I sent you. He'll get you going."

"That's it?" I asked him.

"That's it, son."

"Well, thank you, Freddy."

"Don't thank me," he said. "Thank your Uncle Dom; he set this whole thing up. You're lucky," he went on. "Most guys need a father or a brother or whatever—someone who's already working there to get a union card. So you better not embarrass your uncle or me, understand?"

"Of course."

"OK, get outta here," he said. "I got shit to do."

So I left, excited and anxious, knowing I'd have a job, a good-paying union job that I couldn't wait to start…So I thought, until that momentous first day.

Nonetheless, I thanked the Lord that I had an uncle like mine, like Uncle Dom, who gave me the opportunity to jump-start a life that otherwise had become adrift, bleak, and without prospects.

CHAPTER 7
THE STORY OF FRANKY B

The year 1963 marked five years on the waterfront for me, and I loved every minute of it and for plenty of reasons, too: I made a nice paycheck, I had the cushiest jobs on the pier, and I met a lot of good guys, many of whom became close friends of mine for many years.

Franky Burk was one of them.

He was a veteran on the waterfront, a third-generation dockworker, who was respected as much for his seniority as he was for his vile temper. He was a big guy and strong as an ox. At nearly sixty years old, he was still knocking around guys half his age, and even the toughest longshoremen stayed out of his way if they knew what was good for them.

There was one warehouse on the docks that kept the shipments locked up. Product was loaded off the ship, onto the pier, and then into the warehouse until a truck came and offloaded everything to its final destination. This warehouse was also used for storing cargo that was to be loaded onto a ship and sent elsewhere.

Franky approached me one day in the warehouse at around three o'clock.

"Tony," he said, "I need you to do me a big favor and set aside one of the vacuums for me; I gotta grab one for my bitch wife."

"Sure, Franky," I said. "You got it."

"OK, good," said Franky. "I'll be back later to grab it."

"It'll be right in the corner in the first bay," I let him know.

"Thanks a lot, kid," he said and then walked about his business.

He wanted a vacuum, so he got one. A shipment came in that day, and vacuums were easy to "lift," as they were separated from one another on the pallets. So I grabbed one on the sly and placed it right where I told him I would. And, sure enough, at 5:00 p.m. on the nose, Franky returned, grabbed the Hoover, and carefully walked out with it, undetected.

As it turned out, that night he got into a fight with his wife before he even told her about the vacuum so he ended up leaving it in the trunk of his car.

A couple of weeks later, Franky walked into the hiring hall pretty hot. He made a beeline for a card game that I was playing in. He grabbed a guy—Harry—by the collar and told him, "Get the fuck up; I'm playing." Wisely, Harry gave up his seat without a fight. Franky took his place in the game, and so an eerie silence came over the group. Then I heard him say under his breath, "I'm gonna fucking kill 'em." Then he said it again: "I'm gonna kill 'em. Both."

He was fidgety. He couldn't sit still, and he was sweating like a pig on a spit.

Of the guys seated, I was probably the one fella there who could get away with asking him what his deal was without him flipping the table over, or worse. So I did; I asked, "You're going to kill who, Franky?"

Franky said, "My wife…"

"Your wife?"

As fast as he sat down, he got up and went outside to the yard.

"Give me a second, fellas," I told the guys in the game.

I followed Franky outside and caught up with him.

"My wife's been fuckin' around on me," he said.

"Jesus, Franky, I'm sorry," I said. "What happened? How'd you find this out?"

Apparently he got a tip from a bartender. He let me know that his wife had been frequenting a place called Neil's Tavern in Everett, just outside Boston, during daylight hours with the same guy a couple of times a week and that it had been going on for months.

The tavern was a seedy place, and unbeknownst to her, Franky had been well acquainted with the guy behind the bar, Jack, because the two of them had done time together in Billerica and had become pretty good friends. Even though

Franky's wife, Teresa, had met the guy in the past, she must have forgotten, or she would have chosen another place to spend time with her secret boyfriend. So the bartender never said a word and just watched her meet up with this clown two or three times per week around noon and then stumble out the door around three o'clock each time.

It wasn't until Franky went to the tavern one afternoon himself and grabbed a beer that he learned of his wife's indiscretions. Luckily, it was on a day that Teresa and her "friend" were not together in the same place, or it would have been a massacre. That afternoon Franky ran into Jack, and the two had a lengthy conversation, and it just so happened that it took place about an hour before he walked into the hiring hall hotter than a blowtorch.

In the yard, Franky said to me, "Someone's fuckin' going down for this one."

Oh, shit, I thought. *He's going to off his wife or the guy or both.* But I managed somehow to talk him down from murdering them to just dishing out a severe beating to only his wife's partner.

Just two days later, instead of going to the pier like his wife had assumed, he swung by my place and picked me up. We tailed the two of them back to Franky's brownstone on Main Street in Charlestown and watched them stagger into the building from a long day at Neil's. We parked directly across the street. Franky got out of his car and strolled around to the trunk, opened it, and with much pride, it seemed, took out a Louisville Slugger. He gripped the barrel of the bat with his left hand and closed the trunk with his other.

"Let's go," he said.

From what I understood, the bat was a hand-me-down from his father, Dickie. As a matter of fact, it was once used by the great Bobby Doer of the Red Sox. Dickie snagged it in spring training in 1933 after Doer took batting practice. When Doer was finished, he set the bat down against the wall next to the dugout, within reach of spectators. So Dickie took the bat when no one was looking and eventually gave it to Franky to display on his bedroom wall.

But Franky found other uses for it as well.

We walked into the building and waited at the bottom of the stairwell, which ran upward in a Z-shaped pattern. Franky's place was on the second floor.

I was nervous. We weren't there to steal a vacuum or a crate of booze; we were there to bust someone up. I knew it was going to get very ugly too, because that day Franky was a possessed man who was going to stop at nothing to punish this guy or both of them.

We waited patiently in a confined and brutally hot space. I often removed my hat and wiped the sweat from my eyebrows.

Then there was activity.

An elderly woman appeared from the only first-floor apartment, just a few feet to the right from where we stood.

Franky concealed the bat as best he could and engaged the old woman in conversation. Pleasant as a peach, he said, "Mrs. Walters, how are you, dear?"

She turned slowly, but quickly for a person of her age. She was hunchbacked, white-haired, riddled with bald spots, and draped in thin, veiny, pale skin.

"Oh, Franky," she said, grinning and tipping her bifocals to get a better look, "come here and give me a hug."

Franky obliged, with his right hand wrapped around her left shoulder and his left hand clinging to the bat.

"What are you doing here, just standing here?" said Mrs. Walters.

But he steered her off track and introduced us. "Mrs. Walters, this is my friend, uh, Greg...Gregory."

So I lowered my posture slightly, shook her hand, and said, "It's very nice to meet you, Mrs. Walters."

"OK," Franky said, "that's enough. You should get going, Mrs. Walters. Let me walk you outside."

"Well, OK, I guess," she said reluctantly.

Franky then took her by the arm and walked the old lady out the door. A few seconds later, he returned.

"The bitch never leaves the fuckin' apartment," Franky said, agitated. "And she picked today?"

I asked, "Gregory?"

"It's better that way."

It wasn't too long after when the real fun began. We heard a door open, Franky's door, but it wasn't in our line of sight. However, we could hear voices and some giggling from a female.

He whispered to me, "This is them."

I panned up to see a man of slight build, though pretty confident in his pose. He had a thin mustache and thick, wavy black hair. He looked weak, like the wind could blow him over.

Franky gave me a nod as if to say *this is him.*

The guy adjusted his coat and walked down the stairs unsuspecting and even demonstrating a little swagger, until his eyes met Franky's. He reached the bottom, but there stood Franky right in his way. He stopped abruptly and said, "You mind?"

Franky asked, "Was she good?"

"What?"

Just like that, the bat went up and came down tomahawk-style with blurred speed right into the guy's face, busting him open as he spun like a top. He fell, and Franky whacked him a half dozen times on his legs, back, and midsection, while the guy wailed out in pain.

With every blow, Franky grunted the words, "I! Said! Was! She! Good!"

Then, finally, some fatigue set in. That's when he took a moment and said to the guy, "I'm going to my car, but I'll be right back. You move, and this guy"—meaning me—"will kill ya."

But the guy was in too much pain to answer.

"Did you hear me?"

Then he mustered up the strength to nod.

"Good."

"Wait here," he said to me.

Franky stepped out, and I watched the guy. He was crouched in the fetal position, bleeding terribly, and barely making a sound when he wasn't crying like a baby.

About a minute later, Franky returned without the bat, but with a brand-new vacuum in his hand, the very one we took off the pier.

"Good boy," Franky told him.

Then he yelled up the stairs to his wife, "Hey, Teresa! Teresa!"

Within a few seconds, his wife opened the door to their apartment. She looked down the stairs in horror at the sight of her lover hunched over, crying tears of pain and bleeding everywhere. I didn't say a word, just looked on in astonishment at what had just taken place.

"Oh, my God, what did you do?"

Franky held up the Hoover and said, "I got your fuckin' vacuum, you fuckin' bitch!" and dropped it purposefully on the guy. He cried out one more time.

"You can use it to clean up this piece of shit," Franky said to her. "And by the way, if you call the cops, I'll kill ya! And I'll kill him. Understand me?"

Teresa froze.

Franky gave her friend one more kick to the stomach. He turned to his wife and said, "Really?" as if to say, *You chose him?*

He dropped the vacuum one more time on the guy, and then we left, and that was that.

Franky was confident that neither his wife nor the bloody heap he left on the floor would open their mouths. But the men in blue showed up down at the pier anyway about forty-five minutes after we left the scene. By that time Franky had washed up, changed, and had taken a seat in the hiring hall. I had joined him, and not five minutes went by before a couple of detectives walked in and took a jaunt over to our table.

"Here we go," said Franky.

He was just so calm, that Franky, answering each question. No hesitation in his voice. No fidgeting, and he maintained eye contact throughout the interrogation.

The guy asking the questions was big, barrel-chested, and square jawed, and he stood directly in front of his partner in such a manner as if to let us know *he* was in charge, not the little guy behind him or the guy he was interrogating. But it mattered none. Franky never flinched. And with every answer, he grinned ever so slightly; I was impressed.

Toward the end, the top dog indicated that it was a little old lady named Mrs. Walters who had said she saw Franky and a friend at the residence earlier today.

We exchanged a look.

"Wasn't me, Detective," Franky said.

Then the guy looked at me, but I remained stone-faced.

At that point we knew neither his wife nor her idiot friend chose to ID Franky, and without them, they had no case.

"That's all I got for you today," the detective said. He dropped his card, turned, and led the way out of the hall.

Once the cops left, Franky grabbed a paper, leaned back, and read like nothing had happened.

"I can't believe she said something," I whispered.

"Oh, yeah," he said. "I'm going to kill that old bitch when I see her."

Thankfully, he did not.

I felt for Franky, though. He'd doted on his wife, and for her to turn around and do something like that was rotten.

That night Franky went to his sister Joyce's place in Medford and stayed with her and her husband and two young boys for a week or so. Then Mickey and I helped him move into a small apartment just around the corner from the waterfront.

After the incident, I spent a little more time with the guy outside of work, hoping my company could soothe his anger. But there was something boiling inside of him, something preying on his mind, and I knew the slightest annoyance could represent a tipping point. And at that point, bodies could fly.

Then it happened.

Exactly one month to the day after he had beaten his wife's lover, Franky was at the pier when I saw him take a phone call from the business agent at around noon. Whatever the message was from the other end, it was concerning. He slammed the phone down and headed for the exit.

"Franky!" I shouted to him. "You need me?"

He reached the door, turned, and shook his head. He left, and I worried about him—and anyone who crossed his path in his fragile state.

That same day I left work around five o'clock, got in my car, and went home. I had a nice dinner before I settled in on the couch and watched President Kennedy give a televised speech. Then the phone rang.

I picked it up and said, "Hello."

It was Butchie, who said, "Franky killed a guy."

I was absolutely floored. I arched myself forward and leaned against the wall. I took a moment to process what he'd said.

"Who?"

"A guy who put his father in the hospital," he said. "It's a long story."

"OK," I said.

"I'll be by to fill you in," said Butchie.

Again I said, "OK."

Roughly twenty minutes passed before he arrived with the police report he'd obtained from a cop friend of his.

The call Franky took from the business agent that afternoon was from his sister, letting him know that his father, Dickie, had been in an altercation with his much younger neighbor over a simple noise complaint.

Dickie was sitting on his porch while the neighbor was working on his bike. A friend pulled up on his Harley, and the two began speaking. Then the friend flicked a cigarette on Dickie's lawn. So Dickie stood up, walked down his steps to his walkway, and asked the punk to watch where he tossed his butts. The neighbor intervened and told the old man to shut up and mind his own business. When Dickie threatened to call the cops, he likely sealed his fate.

Dickie was a frail man, slight in stature, who'd battled all kinds of illnesses, including two types of cancer: pancreatic and colon. He was in his early eighties when the incident occurred.

The neighbor busted through the gate and hit Dickie with a fist to the side of the head, easily knocking the old man down and out. The neighbor then got on top of him and delivered a few more blows before he got up.

The paramedics were reportedly on the scene quickly and were able to keep him breathing. When the cops arrived shortly thereafter, the neighbor and his friend played deaf and dumb, stating they had no idea who the perpetrator was but that they saw a couple of black kids suspiciously roaming the area just a few minutes prior to the incident. Unfortunately for the neighbor, for a brief moment Dickie was conscious enough in the hospital to explain the story, but only to Franky and his sister, who sat at his bedside. Moments later he slipped away.

Armed with that vital piece of information, Franky got in his car and left for the commonly quiet suburb of Melrose, Massachusetts, where Dickie had made his home for nearly thirty-five years. By the time Franky arrived, the commotion had ceased, of course, but it soon reignited when he banged on the neighbor's door. When the door opened, Franky asked for him by name; when he acknowledged it was him, Franky forced his way in, coldcocked him, and threw him against the wall. When he fell, Franky leaped on him and never let up delivering blow after blow to his face and head until he was first unconscious and then completely unrecognizable. For good measure, Franky took a lamp and slammed it on the guy's head.

It was only when he stopped that he noticed a frightened young woman curled up in the fetal position on the couch. She was frozen in fear. And by that point, Franky didn't care if there were witnesses or not; he turned toward the front door and left. Unfortunately, he had just gotten started.

He headed home, and while he was en route, the cops were heading to Melrose with an arrest warrant for the neighbor, not realizing they were about to come upon a body with a near-pureed head attached to it that had once belonged to the main suspect in Dickie's death.

Franky then left and headed to his former home to pay his wife a visit. He knocked on the door, but there was no answer, so he kicked the door in and headed straight for the bedroom, where he found her and the moron he had already roughed up under the sheets. He first dragged the guy out of bed and beat the hell out of him, and when he was done, he grabbed his wife and did the same to her.

Surprisingly, he didn't kill them.

When Franky finished up in the apartment, he went outside to his car, took his bat out, and demolished his wife's blue Ford. While he was smashing the car up, a couple of cops arrived at the scene and tried to take hold of the situation, but as soon as one got close enough, Franky dropped the bat, hit the cop with his fist, and then went after the other one to do the same. But the second officer was able to give Franky a good shot with the billy club, and it was enough to get him to the ground and cuff him.

The fact of the matter was, Franky had a tough exterior, but he was a tremendous human being, a kindhearted soul who would give you the shirt off his back. Truth be told, when I first began working on the docks, Franky was a guy who was mentioned often as someone I should latch on to as a friend and mentor. Unfortunately, when I started, he was doing a two-year stretch for an incident involving a guy he slapped around for running his mouth at a bar. He only broke his jaw, but the guy had a brother in the court system, so Franky got the maximum sentence.

Since he'd killed his father's neighbor, he was hit with a manslaughter conviction and received an eleven-year prison term and served eight. He did eventually make his way back to the docks, but only worked enough to be eligible to receive his pension for when he retired. When he did, he packed up and moved to Florida, and I never heard from him again.

CHAPTER 8
THE WEDDING

So I asked Marie to marry me, and she said yes. It was about time I popped the question. I was twenty-three, and with a few years on the waterfront under my belt, I felt stable and secure enough to be able to take care of her and our family once we decided to have kids.

We chose to have our ceremony on a Saturday at Sacred Heart on Paris Street, located a block from where Marie grew up. The church was old and gray; it reminded me much of the nuns who had taught me as a kid. The place was brightened, though, by the brilliant and colorful stained-glass pictorial windows and spectacular statues, which added just the right amount of mystique to the joint.

We had a problem, though: there was no air conditioning, and it was the middle of August. That posed a problem for many, especially the elderly. From my vantage point up at the altar, all I saw was a mass of unsynchronized handheld fans swaying rapidly back and forth and beads of sweat running down the cheeks of a lot of the guests. It was a friggin' sauna.

My kid brother stood with me as my best man. I had four ushers, including one of my oldest buddies, Mario, along with a couple of my cousins. On the other side, Marie had her older sister as her maid of honor and her three best friends from her childhood—all very attractive and of Italian descent.

I saw a handful of the guys from the waterfront sitting on the benches. They had dressed well, but they still stuck out like sore thumbs; they were gruff, and their massive arms were bulging out of their sport coats. Just a few of them—maybe four guys—took up an entire pew. Mickey was out there, but I couldn't see him. Butchie, too, was in attendance along with his date, whom I wouldn't get to meet until the reception.

Everything aside, it was, by far, the happiest day of my life. I don't think I blinked once after Marie began her walk down the aisle. I was afraid I'd miss the slightest glimpse of the beauty she was that day.

She wore a long white dress and a Spanish veil with a train. Her light brown hair dangled curls that draped alongside her angelic smile. As she made her way down the aisle, the guests gazed at her in awe, seemingly forgetting about the unnatural humidity suffocating the hallowed halls.

She stood in front of me, and I lifted her veil; I recall the difficulty in maintaining my awareness of everything else that was going on around me. I saw Marie and all her magnificence, and that was all.

It felt like it took forever before I finally was able to say "I do," and then I heard Father Andolini give the OK by saying, "You may kiss the bride." And so we made it official. We were married.

We broke our embrace to rousing applause, though I got the sense many clapped to the excitement of escaping the heat as quickly as possible.

The guests stampeded through the exit doors, while Marie and I brought up the rear. As soon as we saw daylight, my big aunt Janet pushed her way through the mob that began dousing us in rice and confetti. She grabbed Marie by the shoulders, gave her a quick kiss on each cheek, and said, "You look like an angel, sweetheart, but if I don't get me some water, I'm going to drop dead right here on the good Lord's steps—you understand, right?"

We then marched forward and quickstepped it through the line to the tan-colored 1957 Buick waiting for us at the curb. We darted in the backseat and closed the door as if we were fleeing an angry mob. Ready at the wheel was a longshoreman named Louie Di Stefano who moonlighted as a limo driver. I gave him a tap on his right shoulder to let him know we were ready to go, and then we were off.

The reception was held at a hall down the street, some five minutes away by car. It was small and tight, but it was fun. We had a band there that got everyone on the dance floor, including Mickey, who twirled his way around the place in, probably, the same tux he'd worn to his high school prom. He was trying every which way to score one of Marie's friends... but he didn't.

My uncle Tommaso—my mother's brother—was quite a character. He was shaped like a pear and soft as a grape. He caught up with me while Marie and I were making our rounds thanking everyone who came. "Look at you," he said, gnawing on a toothpick. "You got the nice job, the beautiful wife now; pretty soon you'll be having a few babies...there's hope for you yet, Tony."

I said, "Thanks, Uncle Tommy, I appreciate that."

Then he leaned in close and said, "If you need anything, you let me know. I know people—you know what I mean?"

"Thanks again, Uncle Tommy."

He raised his glass and said, "Congratulations to the both of you—*salut*!"

He was a nut. He knew no one, but by the way he walked and talked, you would have thought he was next in line to run the New England Mafia. No one took him seriously, though. No one.

Most of Marie's family was still in Italy, which made it an exhausting experience for her to meet some of my relatives, to say the least.

Finally, I caught sight of Butchie. It was great to see him among the commotion. Marie and I had found a quiet spot at the edge of the bar, so I waved him over. He walked hand in hand with his date.

Butchie introduced us. Her name was Caroline. She was a good-lookin' broad—a busty redhead from Dorchester and a little rough around the edges, I could tell, but very pleasant.

The four of us gathered and spoke.

Kiddingly, Butchie said to Marie, "You sure you know what you're doing with this knucklehead?"

"I sure do."

"Congratulations to both of you, then. We're very happy for you."

We thanked him for the kind words, and then he asked Marie, "Mind if I steal your new husband for a moment, darling?"

"I think I can let him go for a minute," said Marie.

"We'll be right back, I promise," he said.

Butchie and I walked off through the venue's double doors and outside to seclusion. We lit up a couple of smokes.

"They found Jimmy," Butchie opened with. "He was full of holes and dumped in the weeds near Castle Island—him and his wife, in fact."

"Jimmy G?"

"Yeah," he said, sounding disappointed.

"No shit! His wife, too?" I said.

"Yeah, they waited for them after he got out of the show in town. One of them crept up behind the wife and put two in the back of her head to shut the bitch up, while the other guy went to work on Jimmy."

"How'd you find this out?" I asked him.

He said, "My buddy who works down the precinct gave me a call this morning."

"So what's that mean for us?" I asked.

"We'll have to vote someone in at some point," he said. "Who, I have no idea."

"Jesus," I said. "I really liked the guy, ya know?"

"Yeah, Jimmy was all right."

"So, you next?"

"Next what?" He was surprised.

"You going to marry that broad inside?"

Butchie said, "Get the fuck outta here, man."

"What did I say?" I answered. "She seems like a nice girl." With the appropriate gesture, I added, "She's got a nice set of…"

"No, no marriage for me," he said. "Let's go back in and continue celebrating yours."

"OK. OK."

I took one last drag, tossed the butt, and started back up the stairs.

The party ended just before midnight, and that's when Marie and I went straight to our room at the Marriott Hotel in town.

No honeymoon, though. We wanted to wait to get settled before we planned any trips, which meant two days later, which was Monday, I was back on the pier working.

CHAPTER 9

THE WAY OF THE WATERFRONT

Life on the waterfront was special. We battled the elements when we had to. We took no shit from our coworkers because we couldn't show weakness; and the memos we wrote were written not with a notepad or yellow sticky, but with our fists, a bat, a club, or worse. In fact, if we had a union meeting, it wasn't unusual for a guy to be packing a gun to voice his opinions.

Bribes, kickbacks, and threats were a way of life on the docks, and that was the case for many years. That was the culture for anyone working in the International Longshoremen's Association, or the ILA.

How did it function?

It began with the clerks. They were the first to know about a shipment headed to the pier. They were called "checkers" prior to the sixties because they checked everything off the manifest as it was being offloaded from the ship to the dock. For instance, if five hundred cases of Johnnie Walker Scotch whiskey were supposed to arrive on pallets, the clerk made sure to check them by counting across and then down and then doing the math to come to a figure. Now, cases naturally went missing, but it was difficult to notice, because we could easily fill a pallet to make it appear it was full by simply excluding a small number of cases from the middle of the stack. And since the clerk only counted across and down, the missing booze would go undetected. Some guys took only a bottle or two out of a case, and if they did so, there would be no need to "dummy" the load.

The truth of the matter was, we stole, and we stole a lot.

There were guys who clothed and fed their families with the stuff that came into the docks. Tuna was one of the more popular foods to go missing; I mean, we took a lot of it. Some would have tuna for lunch and dinner, two or three times a week. And the clothes—shoes, pants, sweaters, you name it. We learned to convert the sizes to American when stuff came in from Europe, let's say. That was important. So a guy would bust open a box and take three pairs of sneakers for his kids and whatever else he thought would fit the family. So there was hardly a need to go out and spend our own money on certain items; it would have been foolish.

Other guys simply stole to fence the goods off.

Colibri lighters were expensive and went for around twenty-five dollars retail. The beauty of those lighters was that they came in boxes of a thousand, and the boxes weren't that big, so they were easy to move. We'd fence them to a guy in East Boston for one dollar each; then he'd unload them for ten or twelve dollars somewhere else. But the one thousand bucks we made was a pretty damn nice score.

So, some guys stole out of necessity, some to fence the products, and some just because they could.

One time I was approached by another longshoreman, Jack Kessler. He said he had a round twenty-five boxes of transistor radios tucked in the warehouse that he wanted us to take, but we had to move them quickly because they were going out on a ship within the day. So he had an idea to take the boxes and hide them in the Dumpster, and when the coast was clear, we'd take them out. We had a guard in on it, too. But no more than a few hours after we loaded the Dumpster, the friggin' garbage truck showed up. So we lost it, but the guard decided to tell the garbage man that he heard a rumor that there might be a bunch of boxes with transistor radios in them. And he essentially told him if the rumor was true, he could do what he wanted with them, which was fine, because at that point, we didn't care, the opportunity for us to make some dough off them was gone.

The following week, when the garbage man came back, he thanked the guard up and down because he'd taken the boxes, fenced them, and made a good amount of cash.

The guards on the waterfront were great guys and we, at times, included them on some of the product we took.

There were also the business agents who, more than likely, had very strong ties to the mob. They were in the hiring hall and took the phone calls from the shipping company letting them know a ship was coming in.

The business agent had a great gig when I started on the pier in '58. Shipping lines used to come in with, let's say, a load of perishable items; the business agent would let them know if they wanted guys out there to take the goods off the ship before they spoiled, it was going to cost them. If they didn't cough up the dough to the agent, the food would go bad. Simple as that. And the business agent knew the cargo because he had a copy of the manifest as well. The next thing the business agent would do was determine how many guys the ship needed for a job. Groups of twenty were called "gangs." But let's say only three gangs were needed; he'd tell the shipping company that they would need to pay for the three gangs, plus a handful of guys even though there was no real need for them. The company had no choice, so it paid the agent for extra labor, and the gangs went to work.

There was the stevedore, who was a longshoreman but also worked for the shipping company. He was the one who actually picked the guys that were going to work on any given day. So when the business agent told the stevedore that four gangs were needed, that's when the lot of the longshoremen faced for a job, hoping they got picked for a day's work. If not, they'd come back the following day and try again.

And you did not mess with stevedores; they were the toughest guys on the pier. Some of them were gunmen, in fact, and they had to be to deal with disgruntled longshoremen on a constant basis. Just like the business agent, the stevedore was almost always connected to organized crime. The job itself, though, was tops on the waterfront. Here's why:

Let's say a ship was scheduled to come in on a Monday and needed to be worked on for three days. The stevedore would get a full day's pay for that Sunday, even though the work wouldn't begin until Monday and would end on Wednesday. If the ship left Wednesday night, he got paid for Thursday as well. He'd get the "day before" and "day after" pay. So, five days' pay for three days of work.

Now, let's say another ship docked on Thursday and needed two days of work. He'd get his "day before" pay, even though he was already getting paid on the previous ship. His paydays would overlap, so he could conceivably get paid for nine or ten days or more in a week. All of that was on top of his base pay. In the fifties it was maybe twenty-five dollars per day.

The stevedore was also the guy who picked out the longshoremen while they faced for work. So he'd stand there and call out names, and each guy who stepped forward received a button. Whoever received buttons—which represented work for that day—would then, in turn, give the stevedore one or two dollars to consummate each day's pay. But once containers came into play, the system that allowed the stevedore to collect his payoffs all ended. The feds became wise to the corruption, and they invaded New York City. Once that happened, Boston had to reform to prevent the same thing from happening, so the stevedore was no longer able to collect from the guys picked to work. Plus, there was a fear that if the feds came to Boston and took a close, hard look at what was going on, they might eliminate some of the jobs benefitting from the system.

But a stevedore back in the forties or fifties made a fortune. With twenty guys in a gang, if only three gangs went to work at $2 per guy, that was $120 per day (all cash) from kickbacks. He'd then kick back half the money to the two business agents, who would split the dough and take $30 each. That was a smart thing, because it was the business agents who recommended which stevedore was going to work with the shipping company scheduled to come in. At the end of the day, he'd pocket the $60 on top of his ship pay, plus a few bucks from each longshoremen picked to work, and in that era, that was a lot of money.

On the other side of the coin, at times, naturally, some of the longshoremen would have to kiss a little ass to get work, because they were only making $3 per hour to begin with. Still, bringing home $120 wasn't too bad on a forty-hour work week when you consider that most people in the workforce were only making around $75 per week. And each guy got paid every day at the end of his shift, which turned out to be a problem for some of the men, as a few enjoyed hitting the local bars and strip clubs as soon as they had the money in hand. In some instances they'd disappear for a few days, at times causing some of the wives to come down to the waterfront looking for them.

Now, most of the stevedores were good guys. More times than not, if they'd see a few longshoremen in a barroom, the stevedores would buy them a round or two. From a stevedore's point of view, he had to also keep the peace, so the gesture was a way of keeping the men happy.

And when the stevedores' and business agents' pockets were full, the rest of the cash funneled to the president of the union, who was typically affiliated with organized crime. In 1952, it was a guy named Billy Stone, who was well connected to an outfit out of South Boston and a proven street thug.

He was an Irish guy, and it's important to note that most of the guys on the waterfront were of Irish descent, with a few Italians like me and no blacks.

From what I understood, Billy grew up in New York until his teen years, when his family relocated to Boston. Butchie, in fact, knew the guy from the old neighborhood despite the age difference. Billy was well aware of Butchie and his propensity for violence, so when JR got him on the waterfront, it seemed like a perfect match. Billy became president and had Butchie, a loyal crony who gave him the little muscle he needed to begin his reign.

Unfortunately, in 1956 Billy succumbed to a pair of shotgun blasts through his midsection as he exited a bar in Charlestown, paving the way for Jimmy G to take over at that time until his untimely death.

Containers didn't come into play until the late 1960s. Prior to that it was cargo ships, but once the change began to take place, the ships—which were much smaller—were being converted to container ships. Eventually bigger ships were built to accommodate the transformation.

The advent of container ships brought a dynamic alteration of the everyday duties performed by longshoremen. Gangs went from twenty guys to sixteen, and each had a gang boss. The business agent kept the records of which gangs got what work and what days, and that was important because he was the one who determined how many gangs were needed for the job. The formula was simple: the gangs that had the lowest number of hours for that week were called first, and then the next lowest would be called second, and so on. Many times there'd be several gangs on a job, so it worked out well. Other times guys had to face for a job in front of the stevedore. It was a fair system by all accounts.

The new gang system eliminated the opportunity for the stevedores to take advantage of the kickbacks they had so often profited from, so it was a pretty big blow to them in that regard.

When a container ship came in, here's how it worked: there were the "upmen" on the ship who would unlock the containers from the top and "downmen" who would be responsible for unlocking, or unlatching, the containers from the bottom. The containers are latched down as a way to stabilize them to prevent them from crashing into each other or tipping over while on the high seas.

Typically, there were four downmen and three upmen pulling the pins. Once the containers were unfastened from the deck—which took a mere thirty minutes or so—they were ready to be lifted by the cranes. When everything was completed, let's say at 8:45 a.m., the gang boss would tell the longshoremen that he needed two downmen and one upman to stay, just in case a few of the pins were not actually taken out properly.

"Whack it up yourselves," he'd say.

Whoever was able to leave was told to come back by four o'clock in the afternoon, because that's when we'd be unloading.

Containerization also offered a new method of stealing.

Every now and then, a forklift operator would lift a container and intentionally bang it against the side of who knows what—maybe another container—but he'd dent the thing so bad that he'd put a hole in its side. Once that happened, the entire load was considered damaged. The agent of the ship then called the insurance guy, who would deliberately give us a two-hour head start to get in that container and take whatever we wanted before he even showed to survey the scene. The insurance reps, at least the ones I knew, were really great guys. Once we took what we wanted, whatever was leftover went to auction at another pier.

The shipping companies also got in on the act.

These companies paid for the rental of the containers along with the total weight of the contents inside. So, let's say eight hundred cases of whiskey were put into a container, and it weighed roughly forty thousand pounds. That's what the company put on the manifest: forty thousand pounds. What they would do next was try and stuff another two to three hundred cases into the container, because they weren't paying for the extra weight anyway. The only problem was that at times the companies got greedy and loaded the containers to the point they couldn't handle the weight. And in some instances, the bottom gave out, and product was lost either on the ship or on the dock. At that point a cleanup crew was dispatched to handle the mess. But when it worked, shipping companies saved thousands upon thousands of dollars every year just by adding some extra weight to the containers.

And with containerization becoming the main method of transporting product, the cranes needed to make the transition from motorized engines to electric.

One time we had an engine in the warehouse just sitting there untouched for nearly two years. It was two years old, so nearly brand-new, and was worth around $90,000, and it was the same kind of engine a boat could use. So, me and a couple of other longshoremen were going to take it, because we knew a guy who would buy it for $45,000 and throw it right in his boat. He was going to save money, and we were going to make it. But just as we were getting ready, a guy from the Port Authority came in, questioned why the engine was even there, and then decided to sell it back to the company that made it to recoup some of the money lost.

That was a tough pill to swallow, because it would have netted us $15,000 each; a nice chunk of change for doing almost nothing.

That was the system when I started, and if a guy balked or squawked at any of it, the stevedore would handle it.

CHAPTER 10

FOR PETE'S SAKE

"I threw him down the stairs," I recall an older, weathered gentleman with a rasping voice telling Uncle Dom as I sat at the top of the club stairwell eavesdropping. I was nine years old.

"Is that right?" my uncle said, chuckling.

"A quarter of the way down, the guy's shirt gets caught on the railing, somehow stopping him from hitting the bottom," the older guy went on. "Can you fuckin' believe that?"

"So what'd you do?"

"I said to the guy, 'Hold on; I'll untie you.' So I walked down the stairs, ripped his shirt free, stood him up, and threw him down the stairs again."

They both laughed, and I couldn't help but find it amusing myself, even at that age.

"The guy went ass over teakettle all the way down that staircase, you know, at that bowling alley over in Malden—you know how long that thing is…"

"Oh, yeah, sure I do," said my uncle.

"That was it. He didn't get up for a few hours, but a week later or so, he had the dough, so that was a good thing."

Who was this person telling the story? I wondered.

His name was Pete Arrio; he was one of the more distinguished members of the club and a bookmaker who grew up in the projects of Eastie. He had a short fuse and more scars than a bare-knuckled boxer from all the scraps he'd been in. My uncle often boasted that Pete was one of toughest guys he'd ever met. He wasn't someone you'd want to cross, even in his twilight years; it was best to stay on his good side.

At the ripe old age of seventy-two, he knocked out a prison guard when he heard he'd been disrespectful to Pete's wife when she came to see him while he was away in the federal prison in Danbury, Connecticut, on gambling charges. Right in the visiting room, he excused himself from his wife and attacked the guy, roughing him up pretty good.

The guard got off easy, though. If the fight had been in the street, Pete would have killed him.

Conversely, as much as he had a penchant for snapping at the drop of a hat, on most days, the man was a gentle soul and would give the shirt off his back if he deemed you worthy.

When I was just a kid, maybe ten years old or so, he'd often give me a few bucks, five or ten dollars, and send me down to the corner store to pick up a few sandwiches for the guys at the club, and he'd always let me keep the change. Or if it was his wife's birthday or their anniversary, he'd send me to the flower shop to pick out a nice arrangement and card for the Mrs., and again, he'd let me keep the leftover cash.

It was November 1964 when I learned Pete had passed away of a sudden heart attack, and suffice it to say, my heart filled with sorrow. It was a devastating blow to many, including all the members of the club, and it showed.

The funeral home was packed. It was moving, seeing the scores of people showing up to pay their respects to a man who had made his reputation on the streets but had also given back to his community so generously. I saw guys in shackles who were escorted by cops and allowed to attend and pay their respects.

Pete had donated to the Boys and Girls Club, the local recreation center for troubled teens, and a slew of charities. As a result of his connections to many of these organizations, at the service I ran into a childhood friend of mine named Joey Federico. We had gone to elementary school together, but I hadn't seen him since then, because as soon we finished grade school, his parents packed everyone up and moved to Medford. The reason he was at the funeral was because he'd worked at the recreation center in Eastie, where we grew up, so he was paying his respects to Pete, who used to drop by once in a while just to see how everything was going. In doing so, they had developed a rapport, so there we were, together again.

It was nice to see him. We struck up a conversation, and I learned he had submitted an application to become a police officer in Boston but hadn't heard anything in the few months since he applied. My uncle Dom knew a captain at one of the precincts, so I told him I'd ask him if he could somehow contact him and maybe ask if he could move Joey's application to the top of the pile. He was so appreciative, and I said to him, "Just doing a favor for an old friend."

That was it; I only asked that he let me know if it worked out or not.

Now, since Pete could no longer extend his gratuities personally, he still had some unfinished business left on the table—his betting book. And it was a big one.

Pete had employed ten guys who were taking action for him, all within the Greater Boston area, including a pair of longshoremen—Ray Donahue and Dickie Smith. I thought nothing of it until I received a visit down on the waterfront from a midlevel gangster in the New England outfit informing me that my uncle Dom would love it if I paid him a visit in the can.

"Really?" I said, sitting behind the glass partition with the receiver in hand, holding it to my ear in the visitor room at the Walpole Prison.

"Sorry, kid," Uncle Dom said, "but I had no choice. You're the only one I trust who can run Pete's operation for now."

"For now?" I said.

"It's just temporary," my uncle went on. "Pete had a good book, one that a lot of guys would love to get their hands on. I had to, uh, you know, how do you say it?"

"Nip it in the bud?"

"Yes, right, nip it in the bud."

"By passing it off to me…"

"Yeah," he said. "What the fuck do you think I'm talking about here?"

"You know," I said, "I think this is gonna be pretty good, actually." And I went on, "Marie and I could use the dough, and I think we're going to have kids…soon anyway."

"Good!" said my uncle. "The guys under you will do the work; you just have to make sure no one's fuckin' with them or you and that everyone gets paid. You make a few bucks, you go home to your pretty wife, and life is good."

"For how long, now?" I asked again.

"Two years, tops. Then Benny will be out, he'll take it over, and that will be that. You remember Benny, right? The guy with the fruit carts downtown?"

His name was Benny Carbone, and I knew him, but not too well. He had the fruit cart in the North End, but he also had an Italian restaurant in Somerville with his brother Salvi where he conducted a lot of his illegal businesses, including loan-sharking and gambling. Benny was also a member of the Mafia.

I remembered eating at the restaurant as a kid; the food was fantastic.

"I do, yes," I told my uncle. "Good guy."

"Benny's good people," he said. "So give it a shot. If you get used to it and you like it, maybe you and Benny can partner up; I don't know. That's something you and him can discuss later on."

"We'll see," I told him.

"And, kid..." he said.

"What's that?"

"Don't fuck this up."

"I won't," I said. "Come on, what's the worst that can happen?"

By his expression, I gathered something bad.

"I'll be careful," I said, "and by the way, can you do me a favor? I got a friend who's trying to join the force in Boston; he put in his application but hasn't heard anything. Can you talk to someone over there and help him out?"

"Yeah, I'll see what I can do. What's his name?"

"Joey Federico," I said.

"How do you know him?"

"We went to school together...he's a good kid."

"I'll figure something out."

"I really appreciate it," I told him.

It was the last thing I expected, to have this new job. Truth be told, when I had a moment to digest it all, I became a little anxious. I wasn't too keen on the headaches I was about to endure taking over that business. Chasing deadbeats who couldn't pay, managing ten other guys, balancing the books, and overall immersing myself in the culture of organized crime just wasn't my style—or at least it hadn't been since I was a headstrong teenager with something to prove and nothing to lose. But I knew the money was going to be good, and that fact outweighed the risks.

When I went home, I explained to Marie I'd be working more—nothing to worry about, but I would have to be away from home a little more. I also assured her it would not impede our plans for the future. She wasn't thrilled, but since I was planning on using the club's office anyway, she knew she could get in touch with me quite easily, because I made sure she had the number there.

The way it was to work was that at the end of each night, I would record each guy's figures for that evening, plus the take from the previous night. Again, I had ten guys on the payroll. Some bookies had more, some had less; regardless, it was going to be a project, especially for someone like me who had never "really" taken action before.

To alleviate some of the pressure, I enlisted the help of Butchie in case I ran into any problems; he could end them very quickly. Additionally, we were now about to become employees of the Boston Mafia, which meant a certain amount of proceeds would need to be kicked up to the guys in the North End. So, in fact, it was a good thing that Butchie got involved, because I could have him make the drops, since he knew a lot of those guys anyway.

During the early stages of the operation, things were running smoothly, more so than I'd expected. It was a pleasant surprise, especially considering we'd just moved out of football season and into baseball season, when, historically, bettors seem to almost level off or at least make up some of their losses from the previous football season. That meant less chasing and more paying out, but despite the trend, we were doing well. I was pulling in a few thousand on a good month, and with the fall season around the corner, I started to rethink my stance and consider making this new business part of my long-term ambitions if Benny was so inclined to allow it.

But I wasn't there yet.

Because as predicted, things did in fact get interesting, and on many levels. The relative ease in which we functioned at the outset would soon become a thing of the past.

But on a very positive note, I received a call from Joey Federico letting me know he was accepted to the police academy.

CHAPTER 11

ONE BIG ACTION

We dealt with a pretty standard clientele, which was made up of anyone from corporate bigwigs, contractors, and restaurant owners, to athletes, a lot of blue-collar workers, and even some local politicians. I didn't care about anyone's name or occupation; as long as everything ran well, I was happy.

And it did until I hit my second baseball season—I got a call at the club from one of my bookmakers named Nick Cohen, a construction worker from Revere.

"I got an issue, Tony," he said.

"What's up?"

"I got a guy with a big nut, over twenty g's, and he's been giving me the song and dance for like a month now." He went on, "At this point, I feel like there's not much I can do, so I wanted to let you know."

"Not for nothing, Nick, but what'd you let him keep going for?"

"I know, Tony; it was stupid, and I'm sorry."

"Who is he?" I asked.

"That's the thing," he said. "His name is Jay Granger. Heard of him?"

"The ballplayer?"

"That's the guy, yes," Nick said. "I think that's one of the reasons I let him continue to bet."

"No shit, huh?" I asked him. "How'd you hook up with this guy?"

"My idiot brother works in the locker room over there at Fenway," he said, "and started shootin' his mouth off, sayin' he could lay some real action…turns out the guy is a degenerate who loves to gamble."

"Second base for the Sox, right?" I asked.

"When he's playing, but he's a fringe guy…rides the bench a lot," he said. "Anyway, he bet heavy and lost, then tried to make it back, of course, and took another beating. I just figured 'cause of who he was that he had the money."

"No, I understand, Nick. It's OK; this shit happens."

"So the guy racked up a bill, and now he's havin' trouble comin' up with the dough," he went on. "What do you think?"

"Butchie's a big fan; he's going to love this one," I said.

Right away, Nick got nervous.

"You're not thinkin'—"

"No, no," I said, "Just meeting him alone; Butchie will be excited. I couldn't give a shit, personally, but I'll set up a meeting with this Jay, on the pier, though, to discuss his problems."

"That sounds great, Tony," said Nick, "and sorry again."

"Don't worry about it; it happens," I assured him once again.

This was just the kind of stuff I loathed, but at the same time, I knew it was a common type of bullshit that took place in the gambling business.

I called Butchie to let him know the "good" news, and he was as excited as a pig in shit.

We picked Monday, May 24, 1965, since the Sox had a scheduled off day. That was important to me because now I could set up the meeting at a reasonable time so Marie wouldn't become concerned.

I told Nick to tell his brother to set it up, and he did so without a problem, for that evening at eight o'clock.

Monday.

Butchie took his position just to the right of me, with a Louisville Slugger by his side, hoping to have it signed, while I sat at the desk assuming a more authoritative role.

We waited in the office that Ray and Dickie used until we heard a knock at the door. Butchie was giddy. Again, I didn't give a shit.

"Come in!" I called out.

The door opened slowly. Nick came through first, then Jay.

"Fellas," Nick said.

Butchie, all smiles, nudged his way off the wall and approached them.

"Jay Granger," he said, shaking his hand like he was meeting the pope. "I'm Butchie. I'm a big fan."

"Thank you, Butchie," he said in a thick, southern drawl. "I really appreciate that."

Nick then introduced Jay and me.

Jay was a little guy, not too old, maybe twenty-eight or so, but not an ounce of fat on him. Weak handshake, though, probably due to some nerves.

"Have a seat," I told him.

"Thank you."

I'd say for a good twenty minutes, all we did was talk baseball, and no one was more excited than Butchie. Jay actually took him through an at bat he'd had against Whitey Ford in the World Series when Granger played with the Dodgers. I admit it was intense and surreal, but as entertaining as it was, I wasn't going to let this guy talk his way out of his debt, so I put the brakes on "story time."

"So," I said, "you're into us for a good chunk, huh?"

That's when the room went silent.

"Yes," he said. "And let me just say it certainly was not my intention to get to this point, sir."

"It never is," I told him, emotionless. "And call me Tony."

"Yes, sir, Tony."

"Just Tony," I replied.

"Yes, of course, Tony," he said.

Then it got weird. He went on in a cocky manner, "You know, I bet with a couple of fellas out of Revere, I think it was…let me off the hook without paying them, and I have to say that the generosity that these boys exuded was simply exceptional."

Butchie and I exchanged a look, and I noticed his expression turned from warm to very cold and stiff.

I was so taken aback by the notion I was surprised I didn't reach over the desk and rip his face off. But I kept it together…not like it mattered. Butchie, ever so graceful, took the bat that was resting against the wall, and with his fists joined in a grip, came down hard on the desk like an ax splitting wood—bang!

"Whoa! Whoa! What are we doing here?" Jay shouted.

"Let me tell you something, Jay," I said calmly, as I leaned forward. "You're not in Revere—not even close. You're on the waterfront, and down here we have our own set of rules, and they don't include giving breaks to redneck, fuck-face ballplayers from Hokeytown who couldn't hit a beach ball with a fuckin' paddle."

Trembling, Jay said, "I'm really fuckin' scared, Tony. I'll get the money, I promise!" As he looked back at Nick, Nick looked away like he didn't see a thing.

Butchie removed the bat.

"Twenty thousand dollars, Jay," I said. "That's a pretty big nut. How do you intend to pay us?"

"I know, and I'm sorry," he said. "If I could just get a little more time?"

"But you've been given enough time already." I took a deep breath. "But I think we can work something out. Most of us I assume are fans of the Sox here, so we'd hate to have Butchie put you on the disabled list permanently, if you know what I mean?"

"I do."

"So here's what we're going to do," I said. "We want tickets."

"You want tickets?" he asked curiously.

"Shut up," I said. "And I want autographs from all the best players, including Ted Williams—"

"He's retired."

"That's your problem," I said. "He fishes every day we hear; find out where and get it done."

Butchie gave him a stern look.

"I'm sure someone can get a hold of him for me," Jay said.

"That's the spirit," I went on. "And Benson and Lee... and who's that big bastard at first baseman?"

"Foster," Butchie answered.

"Foster, yes. Nick, how old is your boy?"

"Nicholas is eight."

"And a bunch of souvenirs for Nick's boy," I told him.

"I guess that all sounds good," Jay said.

"Good." To Butchie I said, "You good?"

"Yeah...I'm good," he said, presenting the bat in a much more congenial fashion. "He can actually start by signing this."

"Do you have a pen?" a jittery Jay asked me.

"Here you go." I tossed him a pen I'd fiddled with throughout the duration of the meeting.

"To Butchie," he instructed.

Jay paused. "Looks like there's some red smudging here."

"Go around it," Butchie said.

So he did.

"That brings us to the money," I continued. "I think we can all walk away happy with a figure of…$15,000, and we'll give you another month to get it. Sound good?"

Jay nodded and said, "That sounds great, sir…I mean Tony, really great."

"We'll be looking for those tickets," I said.

He stood up to leave, while Nick opened the door behind them. Butchie, in fact, followed them out and gave Jay advice on how to hit a breaking ball. And then his voice trailed off along with everyone else's.

Jay came through with the tickets, with a pair to each home game for the remainder of the season, and considering it was only May, it was a good deal. We gave a lot of them away to some of the guys on the pier and delivered several more to the pediatric units at the Mass General Hospital.

Despite the charitable outcome Jay unwittingly brought to the table, I spent a good amount of time reflecting on my role in all of it. I had played the part well that night, like the man in charge—I had to—but I began to feel the very real effects of the bullshit of keeping this business going. Up until then it had been a cakewalk.

Notwithstanding the cash flow coming in, I felt that when Benny did finally reconnect with me, maybe it would be a good idea to simply hand him over the keys to the operation and just walk away. It was something to think about at the time.

Then it came about; an incident that proved to be more than enough for me to close the book and never look back.

It was a nightmare.

CHAPTER 12
RED HEAT

Marie was spending most of her days scowling at the paper before giving our real estate agent an occasional ring to get the latest updates, if any, on houses that might be on the market in the city. She was hell-bent on finding a house before we started a family, and with the extra cash I was making with my side business, we could expand our options by spending a little more dough on something if we really liked it.

It was tedious for her, and on most nights when I came home, it was quite obvious, sometimes painfully obvious, given the way she snapped at me over the littlest things, such as failing to remove my boots on the doormat or shaking my snowcapped hat and wetting the hardwood floor in the hallway. In either case, I'd get a good tongue-lashing. However, one particular night I got a little more.

I was at the club when I was coaxed into playing another hand of poker. I knew I was playing with fire, but I'd already taken a good chunk of cash from a couple of the guys, so I felt a willing approach was the right thing to do.

"Deal me in," I said with a purpose.

A collective sigh of relief swept the table.

After just a few hands, I had mentally checked out and found myself tossing hands away without even looking at the cards. Finally, I got to the point where I didn't even give a shit. It was eight forty-five, well past the time when I should have been aware that Marie was likely stewing over a cold dish of ziti and veal cutlets.

So I got up. "I'm out, fellas," I said to a round of brief, but intense, mocking. "I'll catch up with youse later."

Roughly twenty minutes later, I arrived home and put the key in the front door. The jingling must have caught Marie's attention, because I distinctly heard the footfalls of Italian clogs pounding the hardwood floor and getting louder as they neared. The quick steps were accompanied by a few curse words, undoubtedly aimed at me. So I braced myself when I opened the door, slowly and carefully.

There was Marie arching her right arm back and firing a baked potato at point-blank range, striking me in my right shoulder. And then another and another. I crossed my arms in front of my face in self-defense, and judging by the cool temperature of the potatoes, they must have been sitting out for quite a while.

I yelled, "What the hell are you doing?"

Then, I couldn't help but laugh.

"I had dinner ready at five thirty, and now it's cold!" she yelled.

I played coy and asked, "What time is it?"

"You know what time it is, you asshole!"

Marie was a pistol. She had a petite frame, but a hair-trigger temper prepared to go off in a split second.

"Come here," I said.

"Get away from me."

I grabbed her, brought her close to me, and hugged her until she calmed down.

Then I explained to her, "Yes, I was at the club, and a game went a little longer than I expected. I won a few hundred bucks from the guys, so I couldn't just leave. I'm sorry; it won't happen again."

I still felt compelled to ask her, but in a cautious tone, because I knew better, "Have a tough day or something?" as I released her from my embrace.

"Not me—we," she said.

"What are you talking about?"

She gestured to an open envelope on top of the kitchen table. I reached for it, picked up a notice, and began reading. It was a summons to appear in court. We would be defendants in a civil lawsuit brought by one Harry Douglas for "failure to follow through on a purchase of a residence."

A few months back, Marie and I had agreed to a price on a home in Somerville, a small single-family about twenty minutes from the pier. But the inspection was not to our liking, and we canceled the deal. Unbeknownst to us, the selling agent failed to mention our cancellation to the sellers, who just assumed their home would be sold before they purchased and moved into a new property. When the sellers finally did become aware of the truth, they took action against the agent. The agent, in turn, filed a suit against us, claiming we did not have sufficient reason to back out.

Hell or high water, there was just no way I was going to allow that scumbag to hang a lawsuit over our heads while we searched for a home. There was just no way.

With the stresses of bookmaking piled on top of that bullshit, my blood started to boil, but I kept it together in front of Marie, because she was in panic mode, and it showed.

"Tony, we can't buy a house if this doesn't go away. And even if we fight it, it's going to cost us thousands of dollars. What are we going to do?"

"I'll figure it out," I said to her, but with little conviction. My thoughts immediately ran down the path of trying to come up with a quick and easy solution.

It didn't take long.

Pat "The Wall" Kelly, a.k.a. Wally, stood a mere six feet tall and came in a tad over 450 pounds. We knew that because the only way to get an accurate reading of his weight was to get him on the meat scale down at the butcher's warehouse. He lay down on it like it was a hammock, and then we saw the arrow spin like a top until it rested just past the 450-pound marker. *Even the arrow was out of breath*, I thought at the time.

Wally had gotten his nickname by putting a guy through drywall when he heard someone put his hands on an elderly woman who lived across the street from him. He knocked on the suspect's door, and when it opened, Wally grabbed the guy by the neck, punched the hell out of him, and then tossed him through drywall. On the other side of it, a few laborers stood in amazement at two things: the fact that someone had thrown another human through the wall they had spent a couple of weeks putting up, and the large mass that was Wally offering a look that said, *If you have a problem, I'm here now.*

They didn't, and Wally left quietly.

As tough and imposing a fella as he was, Wally was the type of guy that made you think he was the best friend a person could have—if he was on your side. If he wasn't, it was best to stay far away from him.

I was on his good side.

I caught up with Wally in the hall sitting by himself wolfing down a twelve-inch Italian sub. I walked up to him and said, "I need a favor."

"OK," he said. "What kind of favor?"

"*That* kind of favor."

"I'm in. Should we ask Butchie?"

"No," I told him. "I don't need to bury anyone—just scare them real good."

"Then I'm your guy," he said.

I stalked that bastard, Harry, for a few weeks so I wouldn't make a mistake by beating the shit out of the wrong guy. Of course, I knew his name already, but I learned much more during my recon missions. He lived alone in a small brown beach-cottage-style house on a quiet street in Saugus. He drove an old, rusted-out red Chevy Corvette with a vanity plate that read, "REDHEAT." All signs pointed to a guy with a small prick who got off on screwing people in business.

This Harry even looked like a rat, with his big, bushy toupee stapled to his melon, a pointy nose, and pencil-thin arms and legs. Truly, based on looks alone, he deserved a beating just for the way he carried himself.

I'd seen enough, so I invited Wally to come with me to visit the guy at his home one evening after work.

As far as I knew, the weasel had no idea what I looked like. I rang the bell. I saw Harry take a good look at us both through the long single-pane window on the door, but he gave Wally a double take, like most do. He slowly opened the door about six inches.

"Can I help you?" he asked.

I said, "Yes," and told him who we were looking for, and he replied with, "Well, that's me. What can I do for you?"

That marked the end of the small talk.

I stormed in, with Wally following behind, turning sideways so he could fit through the door. We began demolition work to his place using Harry's head. We bounced him off a couple of walls and then let him lie there for a minute or so to catch our breath. In that minute he said, "Take whatever you want, but please don't kill me!"

We stood him up and pasted him against a wall. I introduced myself and then wasted no time in unleashing the verbal threat that if he didn't drop the suit, me and "this guy here"—meaning Wally—would come back to finish the job.

Wally played with his mind a bit and began to insist we kill him right then and there, but it was just a game. I was confident the weasel was going to do the right thing and drop the suit as fast as humanly possible.

As soon as I got home, I listened to a voice message on the answering machine from Harry's attorney stating he had dropped the case.

Wow, I thought. *That was a hell of a lot faster than I ever expected.*

Marie was ecstatic. I was, too, seeing her that happy.

Eventually we bought a modest single-family with an average-size backyard right in East Boston, about ten minutes from the pier. The house had a fireplace along with a grapevine in the backyard, so we loved it instantly.

These things happened. I wasn't a gangster and never wanted to hurt anyone, but I always clung to the notion that if a person or persons threatened my family, there was no limit to what I would do to protect them. I never believed otherwise.

It was my paternal grandfather, Joe, who exemplified this more than anyone.

Before he ever stepped foot on Ellis Island, he had been a carpenter in a small town in Sicily named Augusta. After a man in the town got rough with his sister, Margaret, he had put his hammer down, taken his shotgun, and blasted the guy twice in broad daylight not three steps from his front door.

Soon, it would be my turn. I would cross over a line, a forbidden boundary, and when I did, I would never be the same again.

CHAPTER 13

It'll Be Cheaper to Kill Him

My bookmaking operation was running smoothly again, with the only hiccup being Jay Granger's attempt to weasel his way out of his debt, and that ended up turning out pretty good for us.

Then arrived the day when Carmine came around to shake things up a bit. He was Pete's nephew, a no-good junkie lowlife who had the gall to stake a claim to his late uncle's business—now my business.

I had a history with the kid before he was put away for petty theft and drugs.

Just a few years before he passed away, Pete had asked me for a favor: to have Carmine's car disappear so he could collect on the insurance on it. Given my admiration for Pete and his close relationship with Uncle Dom over the years, of course, I agreed to help him out, even if it was for his pile-of-crap nephew.

In most cases such as that, guys would just roll the car out to the pier, drop a flare in the backseat, and leave while the vehicle was being barbequed. But I had a friend, Timmy, who ran a warehouse full of cars waiting to be chopped up. So, I figured, *why not give Timmy a little business at the same time I'm helping this piece of shit?*

Now, of course, when you're dealing with a crumb like Carmine, you just know something could go wrong, and so it did. I got a call from Timmy letting me know that a police captain in the Boston PD had tipped him off that a couple of unmarked cars were ready to pounce on Timmy as soon as he moved Carmine's car.

Why?

Because that idiot Carmine told a friend, and then word got out where his car was…The whole thing was a disaster. The location of the car was pinpointed rather easily, and now it was just a waiting game. Timmy wasn't going to touch the car, but fixing this thing was going to take some work by the cop, some by Timmy, and some by me.

So we met in a private room at the back of a restaurant called Dolce Vita in East Boston. The original plan was this: the cop was going to dismiss the tail for as long as it took to dismantle the car and dump the parts quickly before anyone knew what had happened. But instead, after the tail was removed, I drove the car out of the warehouse to a side street nearby and left it. *Fuck him*, I said to myself. Carmine was shit out of luck, as there would be no insurance payout, and he was still stuck with the car. Furthermore, when I explained the situation to Pete, he gave his nephew a few slaps, accompanied by a warning that he'd kill him if he ever embarrassed him like that again.

But now that Pete was gone, Carmine saw a chance to make a move on his deceased uncle's operation, as if he had the brains to know what to do with it.

So there he was, fresh out of Billerica Corrections and somewhat clean, when he showed up at the club one afternoon looking for yours truly. But I wasn't there, so he started calling and leaving messages, threatening to kill me and everyone in there if he didn't get what he wanted.

I sat down with Butchie and asked for his advice in handling the situation. Not surprisingly, over a coffee and Danish down at the pier, he said matter-of-factly, "I'll kill him."

"Is there perhaps another way we can handle this?" I asked. "It's just that it's Pete's nephew—"

"*Was*," he interjected.

"I realize that, but—"

"But what?"

I said, "I'd just feel bad, that's all."

Butchie took my sentiment as a joke, but it wasn't. I loved Pete, and if I could get away with not taking his nephew out, I'd be happy about that. So I had an idea to go to Walpole to see my uncle Dom and get his take on the matter.

That was a mistake.

Less than twenty-four hours later, I was sitting in the visitation room behind the glass across from my uncle.

He was aging quickly, I noticed, and seemed bitter, at least judging by his demeanor. Prison wasn't suiting him at all.

Still, I opened up with small talk, but that went nowhere in a hurry when, after thirty seconds or so, he said, "What do you need, kid?"

I was taken aback and now felt a little less bad for him, but I went on anyway, "There's a situation."

"What kind of 'situation'?" he asked smugly, causing my blood pressure to rise by the second.

"Pete's nephew has become a problem, and—"

"And what?" he interrupted. "You afraid to get your hands dirty or something?"

"I thought maybe you could—"

"What do you want me to do?" he said. "I'm in here—you want me to call his mommy and have her tell him to knock it off? Handle it yourself, because I can't wipe your nose every time you get in a jam! That's what your idiot friend, Butchie, is there for, ain't he?"

He'd never liked Butchie for some reason. Maybe because he wasn't Italian, or perhaps he saw him more of a renegade who lacked the respect of authority. Whatever the case, no sooner had he finished his sentence than I stood up holding the receiver, and in windmill-like motion, I whacked the glass, dropped the receiver, turned around, and left.

Things only got worse when Carmine came into the club one day with a shotgun, shot up the ceiling, and once again threatened to kill everyone, starting with me, if I didn't get in touch with him.

Until that point, the only issues I had dealt with were guys paying late or having to dish out some dough when the bettors had a few good weeks, but nothing like this. I needed to act.

To avoid a bloodbath, I suggested to Butchie paying him off with a lump sum of $25,000. Butchie scoffed at the idea, stating that the bum would blow it all in a month on hookers and LSD, and he would be right back in the mix, stirring up more shit.

"It'll be cheaper to kill him," I recall Butchie saying.

I hated to admit it, but he had a strong point. As I sat there listening to him, on the inside, I was cursing my uncle for putting me in this position. There was nothing I could do, however; I was in it, and there was no way out, not with this bullshit going on.

I told Butchie I'd take it under advisement, but I knew what was going to happen, and I was sick over it. It was the only way to rectify the problem. The kid had to go.

That evening I didn't sleep a wink.

I met Butchie the following evening at the office at the club. After we shut down the books for the night and all the business was accounted for, we began planning Carmine's execution.

Ideally, staging it as an overdose seemed the most plausible, even prophetic in a sense, but the trouble this kid had caused warranted a much more meaningful and statement death. So Butchie decided on a setup in which the kid would be told he was getting the business and a $25,000 gift as a show of respect for his late uncle. I asked that he be popped just a couple of times in the chest if possible, so he could at least have an open casket for his mother.

"There won't be anyone in the casket, Ton'," he said. "This kid is getting chopped up."

"Jesus Christ, we really have to do it that way?"

"Yeah, Ton'," said Butchie, "we really have to. And what do you care, anyhow? It was only his nephew, and he couldn't stand the junkie prick."

"At this point, I don't even care. I just want this thing behind me as fast as possible. We'll do it your way."

"Good," he said.

We had the *how*, and then we needed to figure out the *where*.

The club was an option, but we'd have to kill him and then transport his body away from the scene, and I didn't want to turn the place into a massacre; it wasn't fair to the rest of the members—it wasn't their problem. The docks, of course, were an option, but I didn't want to bring any unwanted attention like that. However, the main office was there, and it could be viewed as a credible meeting spot, since he'd think he was getting a tour of one of his new workplaces. After some discussion, we both decided the waterfront was the best bet.

We now had the *how* and the *where*; it was time for the *when*.

We knew we couldn't waste much time. The kid was unstable, and if he felt we were stalling, he might take another shot at the club, and what's worse, I might actually be there if he did.

The club he could access with ease, but the waterfront he could not, which was why Carmine decided to send his message to the club. Down on the pier, he would have been killed on sight or soon after. Sometimes I wish he had tried to find me on the waterfront; it would have made my life a lot easier. But the stupid bastard didn't.

Just as I was about to throw out a suggestion, I heard Gus downstairs calling my name.

"Tony!"

So I yelled down, "What is it?"

"Your honey is on the phone!"

It had to be important, I thought. So I went downstairs and took the call. It was Marie, and she was in hysterics. She went on about how she'd received a few menacing calls over the course of two hours or so from our "friend." According to Marie, he'd said he was going to kill her—and, of course, me and anyone close to us. I told her not to worry as best I could and that I'd be right home. I hung up and walked back up the stairs to where Butchie was still sitting.

"Everything all right?" he asked.

"He's dead; we do it tomorrow," I said.

"I'm free," Butchie replied.

"Good."

I raced home, and when I got there, Marie had calmed down considerably, thank God.

"Are you OK?" I asked.

"Tony, what's going on?"

"It's Pete's nephew," I said. "He thinks I owe him money or something; he's out of his mind."

"Who is Pete?"

"Pete," I said. "Uncle Dom's friend who passed away like a year ago."

"OK. Well, do you owe him money?" she asked.

"No, of course not," I told her. "The kid is a stone-cold junkie who's looking to borrow some cash, and now that Pete isn't around, he's going to everyone. He came down to the club and got rough with a few of the guys, so I intervened. But don't worry about it; I'll take care of it."

"Well, you'd better!"

I had no reason to be upset with Marie. I knew the business came with some unpredictability, but I had always assured her it was risk-free, that nothing would ever compromise her or my safety.

This was bad.

The following morning, I ran into Mickey and told him I might need him for a favor that night. I had asked Butchie about it, and he was fine with it. If we followed through with the plan, I'd have Mickey as an extra set of eyes just in case. Surprisingly he didn't ask any questions. He just said, "No problem."

When I saw Butchie on the pier a little later, he came up to me and whispered in my ear, "The kid took the bait" and kept walking.

I had no choice but to tell Mickey what the deal was and give him the option of coming along or hanging back. But he was in.

That's when I knew I was in for one hell of a night.

CHAPTER 14

HELLO, CARMINE

Wrap a cord around his neck, chop him up, bag him, and then bury the kid in a pre-dug hole Butchie had prepared for occasions like the one we had. The makeshift grave was in a wooded area off the highway in Medford about one hundred feet from the edge of the Mystic River.

It was still light out, and even as the day turned into night, the eight o'clock hour in mid-August offered no cover—a fact that only heightened my tension. So I watched every tick of the clock until the sun ducked beneath the horizon and disappeared, taking the light with it.

That was my cue, though. That's when I told Marie I needed to take a ride to the club to retrieve some paperwork I'd left behind. She wasn't thrilled, but I had no choice.

So I left my house and headed right for the pier.

I felt some jitters on the ride over, but for the most part, I was OK. When I drove by, the gate was already open. The pair of guards who were supposed to be working had taken a few hours off at Butchie's request. He often took good care of a lot of those guys anyway, with either cash, broads, or product off a ship.

So I pulled around to a side street and parked off waterfront property. I walked back toward the gate and looped around until I arrived at the entrance, which was connected to a longer brick structure used for storage of smaller equipment and supplies.

There I saw Butchie's blue Ford pickup parked right out in front, so it seemed likely he was OK using his vehicle to transport the body. Mickey took a cab there, like he did wherever he went because he wasn't allowed to drive.

I walked up the iron-rusted staircase hugging the brick structure. I took a pause when, from a distance, I noticed Mickey waving, letting me know he was at his post as the lookout. He was shivering from the cold and smoking a butt but looked ready to go otherwise. I waved back and continued on up. I got to the top, turned the doorknob slowly, and walked into what was essentially a waiting room before I actually made it to the office, which was behind the next door. To the left there were a couple of folding chairs, a chalkboard with work assignments, and a message board on the wall with essentially the same info. To the right were a few black-and-white photos of past longshoremen for no other reason than to spruce up the room, which would otherwise be an eyesore to the common person. One of the photos, in fact, was of former heavyweight boxing champion, James J. Braddock of New Jersey, who had worked on the docks in New York as a longshoreman.

But what stood out to me that time was a sheet of plastic rolled tight about five feet high and leaning against the corner just to my left as I walked in. I only saw it after I closed the door. The plastic would be shielded if the door remained open. But Carmine, who was going to be sawed into several pieced on it, was going to be escorted in by Butchie anyway, and he'd never see it; he'd likely walk right past it and notice nothing in his drug-induced haze.

I approached the office door, gave it a couple of knocks, and then turned the knob, walked in, and saw Dickie just finishing up recording the day's action. Butchie was already there shootin' the shit and appearing as peaceful as a pipe.

I was hot, my core temperature was rising, and I began to perspire—that's when Butchie hurried things up.

"You all set, Dickie?" he asked.

"Yeah," Dickie said. He rustled some papers, stuck them in a notebook, and said his good-byes. "We're all good here."

The two of us were left alone.

"Are you OK?" asked Butchie.

I lied to a degree and said, "I'm good; let's do this."

"OK," he said with a noticeable air of doubt and then left the office—I figured to grab a smoke.

I sat alone, and in my solitude, I came to the realization there was no viable way to prepare myself for what was going to happen that night. And so I became less anxious due to one undisputable fact: we really had no choice. We had to take that kid out, or the ordeal would continue to escalate. And if something ever happened to Marie as a result of my passiveness, that was something I could not live with. That's what gave me the strength to bury the cocksucker.

Still, I was feeling a lot of different emotions. I was pissed at my uncle, anxious about cutting limbs off another human being, and now having strong reservations about maintaining my responsibilities as a bookmaker. In fact, I knew the first chance I had to get rid of this job, I was going to take it—but that opportunity wouldn't come until Benny was paroled, so regardless of what happened that night, I'd have to wait at least a little longer.

The door reopened. "Where's that fuckin' idiot Mickey?" asked Butchie.

"He should be outside; I saw him when I came in."

"Fuckin' guy," he said.

"He's probably taking a piss or something."

"He better not fuck this up, or I'll put him in the ground, too," said Butchie.

Involving Mickey was my idea. Butchie could do without him, and before a wiseass comment came out of his mouth, I decided to move. I went to the safe, counted out $25,000, put the cash in a paper bag, rolled the top to close it, and placed it on the floor behind the desk, just to the right of where I'd sit.

Then we waited and waited...and waited some more, and more, until 10:30 p.m., when the phone rang. Butchie answered.

"Don't worry about it; take your time," he said. "We're here...we got the dough."

But when Butchie hung up the phone, he breathed a sigh of uneasiness.

"He's not alone," he said. "He's bringing his cousin, Paul."

I asked, "He knows something's up?"

"Who the hell knows?"

"So now what?" I asked.

Butchie shrugged his shoulders and casually stated, "I guess Paul's gotta go, too. It's too bad; I liked the kid."

"That *is* too bad," I said.

"It's his own fault for running around with this lowlife piece of shit."

"How do you even know him?" I asked him.

"His family got that bakery called Giovanni's down there on Broadway in Southie. I used to go in there and shoot the shit with him. Nice kid."

"I know that place," I said. "Best pastries around, I love it there. Marie and I head down there whenever we want to grab something good to go with our coffee."

"They got good stuff; there's no doubt about it," he said. "Just plan on them being closed for the next few days or so. They're going to be mourning."

As we were talking, I could see that Butchie was deeply pondering what to do with this new variable that needed to be accounted for. Paul posed a wrinkle that we had to iron out.

"Any ideas?" he asked.

I thought for a second. "We're going to have to separate them, I would assume?"

"Yeah…I don't know," he said. "I'll have to draw Paul outside somehow, whack him, then come back and take care of 'idiot Carmine'—but how?"

After we'd spent only ten minutes trying to hash out a backup plan, a pair of headlights approached and then turned into the docks and steered toward the office. That's when Butchie picked up the phone unexpectedly and made a call. To the person on the other end, he said, "It's me. Can you send someone down as soon as possible? White, black, send a fuckin' Eskimo—I don't give a fuck. The gate will be open."

He hung up the phone.

"What's going on?" I asked.

"I'm going to lure him outside with pussy."

Butchie then went outside to greet the pair and escort them in, per the original plan.

About five minutes later, I heard pounding on the door, and then it opened.

"Look who it is," Butchie said grinning.

I stood up and said to the two of them, "Gentlemen, I'm Tony."

Paul was the first to step forward and introduce himself. He seemed like a polite kid, clean-cut, too, so I wondered why he was hanging around his "piece of shit" cousin, who looked like a fuckin' walking corpse. Carmine was so thin and disheveled looking, but calm and composed, no doubt from the hit of whatever it was he'd taken on the way over.

We stood for a moment, an uncomfortable second or two, when I broke the ice. "Have a seat, guys."

They both sat, and the two looked around curiously, probably wondering where the money was, but before they had a chance to inquire, there was a knock at the door.

CHAPTER 15
Good-Bye, Carmine

Both Carmine and Paul pivoted quickly; Carmine spun around, and both placed their hands to their pistols, which were tucked into their jeans.

"Relax," Butchie said. "We thought it'd be nice to provide a little entertainment for the evening to settle everyone down."

Butchie opened the door, and in came a scantily dressed blonde, long haired and busty and made up like a Barbie doll in a tight blue dress.

Judging by Carmine's and Paul's expressions, the move seemed to work. The two were disarmed, literally and metaphorically. Sensing their weakness, the young lady seductively approached Paul and asked, "Who's first, huh? You?"

Paul turned to Carmine for approval, and he reluctantly gave it.

"But hurry up," he said.

"No problem."

"She should be done with all two inches of you soon anyway," Carmine said.

There was a collective chuckle.

So Paul, the broad, and Butchie walked out and then closed the door. Carmine and I were left just sitting there and neither looking to provoke any real conversation. Finally, he said in a drawn-out, lazy voice, "So you got that fuckin' money? I gotta be somewhere."

I took a moment only to envision reaching over and ripping Carmine's throat out, but that would have thrown the plan out the window, and who knows what kind of chaos would have ensued then?

"Yeah, you got it," I said as I reached down and grabbed the bag.

"Hey!" he shouted, again going to his pistol.

"Relax," I said and brought the bag up and dropped it in front of him. "You might as well count it while your buddy is out doing his thing with the broad."

"It's cool," he said. "If it ain't all there, I'll come see ya."

"Suit yourself."

Carmine just sat there and held the bag tightly to his chest like an infant would its favorite blanket. Then an eerie quietness overcame the office. It was quiet, too quiet. In fact, if it weren't for a horn from a large vessel blowing through the harbor from time to time, there would have been no noise at all. Unfortunately, the unnatural silence went on for a good ten minutes.

Then, "Hey, what's the deal with these guys? They comin' back, or what?" Carmine asked.

"They're probably enjoying it too much. You know how it is. Let me call them; they're a couple of offices down."

I was getting nervous. This was part of the plan that hadn't been completely hashed out. Butchie was supposed to get rid of the girl, kill Paul, and then come back and wait for Carmine to leave.

"Yeah, right."

Just then the phone rang. I picked it up. It was Mickey calling from another office. "We're good," he said.

I said, "OK," and hung up the phone.

"They're outside," I said, "if you're not sticking around. They'll be right through the door you came in."

"I'm not stickin' around."

With that, Carmine stood up with the bag glued to his torso.

"Come back tomorrow, and I'll introduce you to a couple of the guys, and they can get you up to speed on everything."

"Yeah, sounds good."

Carmine turned and headed for the door. He opened it and then paused suddenly in bewilderment. After he took just one step, he obviously realized the plastic cover that was laid out before him had not been there when he came in, and more importantly, his cousin Paul lay dead on it. I saw a hand holding a gun protrude from the doorway by Carmine's left ear. Before Carmine had time to panic...*Bang!* His brains splattered all over the room. His body collapsed immediately and thudded to the floor.

Butchie then appeared in the doorway. Looking even more puzzled than Carmine had, he turned, looked at me, and said, "Wow, he's still holdin' the fuckin' bag. Come here; check it out."

I wasn't really in the mood to play games, but I got up anyway and walked through the door, and to the right was Carmine's mutilated head, barely attached to his neck, and his arms still wrapped tightly around the bag.

"Wow, you weren't shittin'," I said. I was, in fact, really surprised.

Butchie reached down, pried the bag away from Carmine's dead limbs, and said, "Come on; you can't take this where you're going."

"Where's Mickey?" I asked.

"He's outside keeping an eye out," he said. "Let's go grab him."

We exited the lobby, closed the door quietly, and walked down the stairs. Suddenly Butchie stopped and listened carefully, finally realizing that Mickey was in the backseat of Butchie's pickup getting a blow job from the hooker. So Butchie raced down to the passenger side, where Mickey's head was, and pounded on the window five or six times. The two in the truck were visibly startled and began to gather themselves as quickly as they could.

Through the window Butchie yelled, "Nice fuckin' lookout you are, you stupid bastard! Get dressed and get inside!"

The hooker, with clothes hanging off her, got out the opposite side and scampered off; then she stopped and turned back to Butchie. He fanned a few hundred bucks he got out of his pocket and handed the money to her. She then resumed her gallop out of the pier.

Mickey was still a bit untidy when he got out of the truck. Butchie looked at me in amazement, as if to say, *How stupid can someone be?*

We let Mickey head back up the stairs first, while Butchie and I grabbed a couple of saws out of the back of the truck. Then we heard Mickey yell, "Oh!" He ran back outside the door and vomited over the railing.

"Go up there and control that son of a bitch," said Butchie.

I raced up the stairs, and before I could say anything, Mickey heaved again, took a moment, and then insisted he was ready to go. He wiped his mouth and went back inside.

There were two bodies in the lobby because Paul had never made it outside. Apparently, he'd naively thought his "relationship" with Butchie was enough to keep him out of harm's way, so he'd let his guard down. The broad had walked outside, and as soon as Butchie had good position on Paul, he had wrapped a telephone cord around his neck so tightly he couldn't make a sound. He'd lain there dead the entire time Carmine and I were in the office. I was simply killing time with him so Butchie could then grab the plastic tarp, lay it out on the lobby floor, and quietly place Paul on it. Butchie had remained on the other side of the door until he heard the phone ring. That was his cue. Mickey, at some point after he'd made the call, had walked back to the office and seen the broad and decided to have a little fun. I'd had no signal to rely on, so I'd had to time it right. And I had.

Now, though, we had two stiffs to dispose of, so we went to work.

The first to be filleted was Paul. Butchie did most of the cutting, while I did some but also helped Mickey fill two double-wrapped, heavy-duty black plastic bags with the limbs.

When the first bag was full with what was left of Paul, Mickey took it outside and dropped it in the back of the pickup. But before he took the first bag out, Butchie asked him sarcastically, "Think you can handle that?" Mickey just nodded and went about the task.

Then it was Carmine's turn. While cutting him up, Butchie took a look at his face and said, "You know, his face looks pretty good for a guy who just got whacked in the head. The rest, not so much, but the face…we could have had that open casket after all, had we went with your plan."

I gave him a good, long, and vile look after that comment. That's when Mickey returned.

He reacted to my expression and said, "What, I was just saying…"

"Let's just finish up here, please?"

"Yeah, yeah," he said. "I don't see you cuttin' anything."

"I have my talents," I said. "And this ain't one of them."

Butchie pointed to Mickey. "So what's his?"

Mickey looked at me and waited a second for an answer, so I said, "He's a good friend."

"Done here," Butchie said. "Load up the bag."

We packed it tight, and then Mickey delivered the second bag and just stayed in the truck. He was sick, but quite honestly, I wasn't too far behind. I felt a couple of fleeting bouts of nausea and held it together, but it wasn't easy.

With Mickey completely limp and useless just sitting in the truck, Butchie and I balled up the plastic tarp and tied it with some thin rope. After we gave the walls a quick wash, the place was looking good. I grabbed the tarp in two hands; Butchie opened the door and gestured back that the coast was clear.

So with no one in sight, we made for the truck. With Butchie in the lead, we exited the lobby and walked down the stairs, trying not to make a sound. I dropped the plastic in the back of the truck, draped the cab with a thick black cover, and then hopped in the passenger seat. Butchie was driving, with Mickey sitting in the middle, nearly catatonic, and I was in the passenger side.

Butchie started the truck and eased ahead, lights off, as quiet as could be. At that point, if anyone had tried to stop us, Butchie would have just run them over. As it was, there was no need. We rolled to the gate. I got out and widened it enough for the truck to get through and then closed it after it did. I got back in, and we left. The guards would lock the gate when they got back from their extended break.

In that truck you could have cut the tension with a knife. I could tell Butchie was disgusted with Mickey. For a moment I thought he was going to put a blade in him for the way he'd acted.

It was 2:00 a.m. We drove from the waterfront to Medford, and no one said a word. We didn't have to. Butchie knew the way, and he wasn't much for talking at that point, so we let him be.

We arrived at the river. There wasn't a soul in sight, and I breathed a sigh of relief. We took a turn off the paved road and drove into the woods until the brush was too thick to go any farther. Butchie put the car in park and said to Mickey, "Watch the truck."

The two of us went around the back to the cab and lugged it all: Butchie had the two bags, while I grabbed the bloody tarp and a shovel. We walked about fifty feet or so before he slowed down and then stopped. Then we stood over the hole. It was plenty big enough, so we tossed the merchandise in, and then I started shoveling the dirt back on top. With everything in the hole, there wasn't much room for the dirt, so it didn't take me too long to cover everything. The rest of the muck I just tossed aside, patted it a bit, and that was all. We walked back to the truck, got in, and left.

We dropped off Mickey first; I had a sense that Butchie wanted to talk about his erratic behavior, and I was right. Butchie went on to say that he was worried about Mickey, not about his well-being, but at the prospect of him cracking under the pressure if the cops were to approach him about what had happened that night.

When a guy like Butchie begins to worry about such things, it's a serious thing.

"Mickey is solid," I told him. "He wouldn't squeal."

Maybe not to the cops, he wouldn't, but what about to an acquaintance or some street hooker who decided to suck the information out of him? I thought. It was a notion I kept mum on, because if Butchie had such an idea in his head, there would be no turning back. Mickey would be a goner.

It was roughly three in the morning when we finally pulled up to where my car was.

"Get some sleep," Butchie said. "I'll catch you tomorrow."

"Yeah, you, too."

I got out of the car, and as soon as I found my keys, Butchie drove off.

A few minutes later, I pulled into my driveway. I walked up the stairs and into my home as quiet as a mouse so I wouldn't wake Marie, who was a heavy sleeper anyway. I headed for the bathroom first to wash the dreadful reminders off my body of what had happened earlier. Then, I crashed on the couch. I lay there fixated in deep thought, with nothing but the worst recollections of that night swirling around in my head.

I came to the sad realization that it was plausible that Mickey, at that moment, could have been dead. Butchie very easily could have dropped me off and gone right over to

Mickey's and rung the bell; once Mickey opened the door, Butchie'd pop him a couple of times, and no one would ever know who did it. Well, I would. It'd take nothing for Butchie to transform his relationship with Mickey from quasi friend to loose end.

Eventually I did close my eyes, and when I awoke, it was a new day, though I picked up where I left off, wondering about Mickey's fate, so I gave him a call.

Thank the Lord, he answered.

CHAPTER 16

IT'S A BOY!

It had been nearly eighteen months since we gave Carmine and Paul their dirt naps, and though initially I had a tough time with the whole thing, I learned to put my feelings aside in favor of a more positive and healthy distraction: Marie and I decided to start a family.

It was late afternoon on April 23, 1967. I was at the club playing whist with three other guys when the phone rang. My partner in the game, dim-witted Jimmy Hillis, put his hand down and got up to grab the call.

"Hello," I heard him say. "Who is this?" Then he looked in our direction and said, "He's in a hand right now. Can you give him a call back, darling?"

"Who is it?" I shouted back.

"It's your wife," said Jimmy. "She's having a baby."

I sprang from my chair, ran over and grabbed the phone from Jimmy, and asked him, "Are you an idiot?"

He shrugged his shoulders.

She was going into labor, she told me. I hung up and told the fellas I had to leave.

Jimmy said, "What about the game?"

I didn't have time to respond to the idiot. I took off like a bat out of hell and headed straight for my house, bypassing all rules of the road. I ran in the house, and there she was, sitting on a kitchen chair, holding her belly, and wincing in pain.

"I got you," I told her.

She clung to me as we walked back to the car. I set her in the front seat. She was—well, by all accounts, she was sweating like a pig but handling the pain like a champ; better than I could have.

I sped through the city traffic like it wasn't there and got to Mass General Hospital on the other side of town in under five minutes.

I pulled up to the curb, and while I moved quickly getting Marie out of the car, a nurse seemed to have been close enough to realize what was happening. So I was joined by a helpful woman, and the two of us helped her into a wheelchair. I was never so frightened in all my life. I told Marie I loved her and kept pace with her until I was instructed to take a seat in the waiting room of the maternity ward.

I sat there an agonizing hour before another nurse came out and told me Marie was ready to deliver and asked me if I wanted to be there with her.

"Of course," I said.

So I followed her through a couple of corridors and into a room. They suited me up in scrubs and led me behind the curtain where Marie was bracing for the birth of our first child. I held her hand, and she held mine back so tightly I thought I was going to lose it. Then, under the direction of the doctor, she pushed and pushed and then screamed, and then she pushed again until we heard the cries of my baby and a nurse shout, "It's a boy!"

Marie just fell back, crying; I kept her hand. It had all happened so fast.

"It's a boy," I whispered to her.

"I know, Tony," she said. "I heard her, too."

"OK," I whispered back.

After all the hoopla, we both got to hold little Anthony Jr. as he slept. I remember cradling him in my arms and saying, "I'd do anything for you, you know that? Anything…"

It was the greatest day of my life.

CHAPTER 17

THE BOOK IS CLOSED

It was the spring of 1968.

still wasn't talking to my uncle, and I honestly did not give a shit. I was too busy with a toddler at home, working on the pier, and still taking action. That's right; I was still a bookmaker, because Benny, who was supposed to be my replacement, ended up doing another three goddamn years for witness tampering in another trial that had nothing whatsoever to do with him.

Though there'd been no real bumps in the road since we'd sent two in the ground, mentally I was done—emotionally exhausted from all the bullshit, and if Benny didn't come out soon, I thought, I'd have to explore another exit strategy.

In July of that same year, on a night like any other, I was in the office at the club balancing the books when I heard the soft creak of footsteps climbing up the stairs. I got up, a bit guarded, as I wasn't expecting anyone. I knew Gus had gone home, and no one else ever came up unless it was an emergency. So I called out, "Hey, who is it?"

After one last step, an old, bald, wrinkly guy poked his head from the staircase and said, "Is this how you treat all your friends?"

His voice was grating, his back was hunched, but boy, was it good to see him!

"Benny!" I shouted. I ran over to him and grabbed his hand to help him up that last step. I was excited. I hadn't seen him in twenty-some-odd years, but I was even more thrilled that I knew I'd be giving him back his bookmaking business.

"Jesus Christ," he said, "did you add steps to this fuckin' place while I was gone?"

I was all smiles and said, "It's great to see you, Benny."

"You, too, kid. Now get me a seat—that was a heck of a journey I just took."

"You want to come in the office?" I asked him.

"No, out here is fine."

So I grabbed a couple of chairs, and we sat next to a small round wooden table.

"Are you here to square everything away?" I asked.

"Only if you want me to, kid," he said.

I was all too happy to let him know the business was all his.

"Good," he said. "Anything I should know before I jump back into the shit?"

"What did my uncle Dom tell you?"

"A lot. He said you got your hands dirty a few years back."

My expression said it all. It brought me down.

"I'm sorry about that, kid."

"It's OK, Benny," I told him. "There was nothing anyone could do."

"Listen, kid," he went on, "this shit ain't for everyone, so you have nothing to be ashamed about. I don't even know if it's for me, for Christ's sake."

"Why do you still want to do it, Benny?"

"Because," he said, "unfortunately I belong to another club that ain't so forgiving when you want to get out—you know what I mean?"

I nodded.

"But you," said Benny, "you have no business getting involved in this shit. Get out now while you can. You married?"

"Yeah," I said, glowing now, "married to a great girl… got a little boy at home, too."

"Then that's all you need," he said. "And how's the waterfront treatin' you?"

"It's good, real good," I said. "No complaints here."

"I'm glad, kid," he said. "A lot of guys would kill for that job; remember that."

"No, I know."

"That was a nice thing your uncle did for you, getting you that gig."

"I know."

"Listen," he said, "I don't like to meddle in anyone's business—I really don't—but don't you think it's time you took a ride to see your uncle…show your face over there?"

"Yeah, we'll see," I said in a dismissive manner.

"Hey, you do what you want; I can't make you do anything. But if there was one thing I learned in the can, it was, boy, did I miss people on the outside. And I know you two had a little something there, and things got a little ugly, but I guarantee you he misses you."

"So, uh, how is he?"

"He's a miserable, old cocksucker, same as always," Benny said.

I smirked. "I guess he would be."

"Well, he's only got a few years to go down there, so we'll see what happens," said Benny.

Then he got up slowly to his feet and said, "I bid you farewell, my friend. I just wanted to come up and see how you are doing. You're doing good. I'm proud of you. Do me a favor and tell the guys I'll be seeing them soon, would ya?"

"The guys"—he meant the other bookmakers working under him.

"That's it? You're leaving already?" I asked him.

"Yeah, I got a lot of stops to make, unfortunately. It's what I gotta do."

"You take care, Benny."

We shook hands, and that was the end of his visit.

He gave me a lot to think about that night, but mostly I was relieved I was done with the bookmaking business.

I knew I would miss the income—that part would sting a bit—but at least I could see Marie and Tony Jr. (which was what we'd decided to call him) more often, and as an added bonus, I'd rid myself of the headaches of taking action.

The next thing I did was pick up the phone and call Butchie. I told him the news, and he was more than fine with it. He wasn't as involved as I was, and he didn't make the cash I did either.

The only thing left to do was to start living my life on my own terms, or, as Frank Sinatra put it, "My Way."

If only it were that easy.

CHAPTER 18

THE CALM BEFORE THE STORM

I took Benny's advice, and so I went to see my uncle inside. I mean, I loved the guy, but I was bitter, because as much as I was grateful for the opportunity he had given me to work on the waterfront, I was too upset over his lack of support during that fiasco with Pete's nephew. But after so many years of not speaking, getting that good talking to from Benny convinced me to cast all animosity aside and go to Walpole, and I was glad I did.

He was happy to see me.

We took a walk around the yard and caught up. He remarked a few times that I'd grown up so much since the days I ran around in the streets, getting into trouble with him or at my own will.

He looked pretty good, too, and he wasn't shy about saying it.

"I look good, don't I?" he said, bending his back to accentuate his now smaller belly.

"You look great, Uncle Dom," I said. "You really do."

He knew he'd get out eventually, so he'd started taking care of himself by walking more in the yard and dabbling in the gym they had set up there. It was small, according to him, but he didn't need much but a place to lift a few light weights and move around a bit to get his heart rate up.

"It took some time, but I finally got used to this dump," he went on. "But it's not a place you ever want to be in. Take it from me, kid."

"I know, Uncle Dom."

"Good," he said. "How's the waterfront these days? Good?"

"It's good…busy."

"How long you been there now?"

"Over ten years now," I said.

"Any regrets?" he asked.

"I don't think so, no."

I spent a good hour with him, and when I walked away, I was encouraged that we'd rekindled the relationship we'd once had before he went away.

As for me and my own future outside of the rackets, well, I was a family man. A doting husband and father, happy as the day was long. Nothing mattered more.

In the fall of 1970, we were blessed with the arrival of my daughter, Isabella Antonia. With two kids at home and a mortgage, I took up as much work as I could down at the pier to support my family.

Still, though, the kids had it pretty good. We spoiled them, in fact. During Christmas and birthdays, the toys piled high to the ceiling, and every summer we rented a cottage for a week or two down in Cape Cod.

My parents, for a while, were still going strong and remained in East Boston in the home I grew up in. It was a thing for the old greaseballs back then to get a home, raise a family, and never leave.

We remained close, though, and they had a great relationship with my kids, which meant a lot to Marie and me.

Each and every weekend, we had our Sunday dinner together at their house, with a few mixed in at ours. But no matter where we ate, no meal was too big for my family. We always had a couple of types of pastas, meatballs, veal and chicken cutlets, salad, and an antipasto. It was like Easter every weekend.

My brother, Tommy, was around here and there, but he enjoyed the single life, so he mostly did his own thing. He was a good-looking guy with a great job and lived alone; I could hardly blame him. He, in fact, started working down on the pier with me, though not as a full-timer. He was a proud Boston firefighter, but in his time off, he used to visit the hiring hall and face for a job to grab some extra cash. And he did a good job. Most of the time he was either driving cars off the ships that were headed for the dealerships, or he was driving a truck or forklift in the yard.

I remember a time he was trying to back a box truck up against the warehouse, but it took seven or eight times to get it up straight. When he finally did, a bunch of us gave him a standing ovation.

He was a good sport, and the guys loved him, but he wasn't a longshoreman. He was a great firefighter, though.

Things started to go south when my mother, who'd been battling several ailments including respiratory disease and heart disease, had to go in a nursing home, causing my poor father to sell the house we'd grown up in. The "home" sucked my father dry, so my brother and I often pitched in to help with the cost.

As a result, the noose around my wallet began to tighten its grip even more.

Overall, life was still pretty good, though it would have been nice to have a few more bucks in my pocket. Then the Lord decided he would intervene…just not the way I expected.

In May of 1974, Tony Jr. received his First Communion. We had a big bash back at the house that included our family and friends and a few of my son's friends from school and their parents, along with Father Donovan, the priest who ran the service that day. We had an interesting conversation.

"This is quite a celebration you have here, Tony. Everyone seems to be having a wonderful time," Father said.

"It is," I said, "and thank you very much for coming. I know Tony Jr. is excited that you're here."

"Oh, well, I wouldn't have missed it for the world. And it's a beautiful day out; look at this sunshine," he said as we both gave a quick look up, squinting for a moment.

"Yeah, I think we lucked out with the weather."

"How's it going down on the docks, Tony?" he said.

"It's going pretty good, Father. Thank you for asking." I went on, "How's the, uh…how's your thing going?"

"Well, Tony, I'll be honest with you," he said. "Life in the parish could be better. The people these days just don't have the faith anymore, not like they used to, anyway. It's a real shame, Tony. A real shame."

So I said, "I'm sorry to hear that, Father."

"Yeah, I know," he said. "Like I said, it's a shame." He went on, "The truth of the matter is, when attendance is down, so are the donations coming in, and eventually so are mine—you know what I mean?"

"I do, unfortunately," I said as I became curious as to where this was headed.

"And so, Tony, if you could lend the father a few bucks, I tell ya I'd really appreciate it," he said. "And I'll pay you back, as God is my witness. I'll pay you back with interest, in fact."

"Father," I said, "with all due respect, are you out of your fucking holy mind?"

"I realize the timing isn't perfect on my end…"

"So this isn't about the church," I said. "It's about you?"

"I suppose it all depends on one's point of view."

"There's only one point of view, Father," I said. "How much do you need?"

"Two thousand dollars should cover it," he said to my surprise.

"Should cover what?" I asked.

"The thing of it is, Tony, I sort of owe a bookmaker downtown, and he said if I don't pay him by Monday, no amount of praying is going to bring me back from where he'll send me. Can you believe that, Tony? Threatening a man of the cloth like that?"

"Yes," I said, "I do believe it!"

"Listen, if you don't have it readily available, I understand. Perhaps you know someone down on the waterfront who can help me?"

"You don't want those animals on your back either," I said. "It's not the money, Father—I'll give you the dough. It's just...I can't believe what I'm hearing."

"You'll be happy to know I would never steal from the church."

"Thank you. I feel so much better now, Father," I said sarcastically. "But you came to me instead..."

"Among others," he said.

I hung my head in disgust. "Father, if I help you out, you gotta promise me you won't gamble anymore, please?"

"Oh, I promise, Tony. This is it for me. After tomorrow..."

"Tomorrow?" I said. "What's tomorrow?"

"I kinda already placed a bet for tomorrow, and you'll be happy to know I wagered on our very own Boston Celtics to win the NBA championship!"

"This is really happening," I said.

"I'll tell ya, Tony, that Dave Cowens and John Havlicek, they're something, aren't they? They're going to beat those Bucks, and if you were wise, you'd place a wager or two on that series."

I was speechless.

Then I said, "Father, wait here."

"Of course."

So I ran in the house and went to my bedroom and into the closet, where I had a safe with some cash and a revolver. I spun the dial a few times, opened the safe, and counted out $2K, bundled it tight with an elastic, closed the door, and went back outside.

I had just a few hundred bucks left in there, but it was money that Marie wasn't aware of, or counting on, so at least I didn't have to worry about that. I was generous to a fault and always had a hard time turning people away; whether it was letting them borrow a few bucks or doing a favor for someone, I could always be counted on, and I took pride in that.

"Here," I said, handing him the wad cautiously, "here's $2,000."

He took it and quickly put it in an inside pocket.

"You tell no one, you understand me?" I said.

"Of course. God bless you, Tony. God bless you," he said over and over.

"Yeah. Yeah," I responded. "This is a onetime gift, understand? You don't have to pay me back."

"I understand, Tony."

"And don't you say 'God bless you' again, or I'll knock the Lord off your goddamn shoulders. Don't!"

He nodded and said, "Now, I'll still see you on Sunday, yes?"

"Please get out of my sight right now," I told him.

He was smart and walked away.

Mickey, who was also in attendance, approached me eating a piece of cake and said, "What's up, Tony?"

"Do you believe this cocksucker priest just borrowed two thousand off me?" I said.

"You're shittin' me," he said.

"I wish I was," I said.

"Hey, you gotta try this cake; it's delicious," Mickey said.

"Yeah, in a minute," I said, still agitated.

"So where's Butchie?" he asked.

"I don't know; I invited him, but he's been a flake lately."

The relationship between us had shifted dramatically. Though we considered ourselves very good friends, Butchie was still out there looking to make that big score he always wanted, whereas I was focusing more on taking care of my family.

The rest of the day was a lot of fun, highlighted by the performance of my buddy Louie Di Stefano, the same guy who'd driven Marie and me in the limo the day we got married. Louie showed up dressed like a clown to entertain the kids. He was nuts. Despite him half-assing the costume, which was really just a painted face and a mesh trucker's hat, I was grateful he came. He blew up a few balloons and chased the kids around, and they had a blast.

And then a pony showed up. I didn't have a big backyard or anything, but we didn't care. Especially when we saw the look on each kid's face when my father escorted the thing into the yard by its reins. He put every kid on the saddle and gave them each a ride around the small rectangular plot. I felt bad for my father; he worked his ass off walking around all day. Nothing took a bigger beating than the grass, though. Between the hoofprints and the amount of shit that came out of that goddamn animal—it was astounding!

Overall, it turned out to be a great day. It was a lot to clean up, but worth every piece of crap I disposed of.

And the Celtics beat the Bucks in seven games, so at least I knew at the time the good father wasn't in imminent danger. In fact, I heard he lived a pretty long life, beyond the age of ninety anyway. And as far as I know, he never placed another bet.

Yeah, life was good. If only it had remained so. But instead I learned the hard way how an old promise could result in some real tragic consequences, ones I would never recover from.

CHAPTER 19
THE NEXT CRIME OF THE CENTURY

It was January 1975, and by that time the feds had already put the clamps down on any efforts made by longshoremen to conspire and extort the shipping lines. The straw that broke the camel's back was when a shipping company called Universal Shipping kept showing up on the docks with fresh produce but was unwilling to pay the business agent his tribute. After enough of its deliveries went bad on the ship and became unsellable, the company went out of business.

So, the government, after already putting the screws to New York during the sixties, had then focused its efforts on Boston. It had launched an investigation and found enough dirt to overhaul the system, regulate how shipments made it to the docks, and ensure they did in a timely fashion.

And whose ass did that burn as much as anyone's?

Butchie's, because by that time he had become a business agent, and without the stevedores making the extra dough on kickbacks, that meant he wasn't able to take advantage of the position the way former business agents had in the past. Then, one day he came across an opportunity that would shake the foundation of the waterfront for many years to come.

Out of the blue, Butchie approached me in the hiring hall and said, "Meet me at the bar after you're done today."

It took me by surprise, to say the least, considering that his tone and demeanor signaled, at least to me, that something concerning was going to be the topic of discussion.

"I will," I said. "Everything OK?"

"Couldn't be better, my friend. Couldn't be better."

With that, he walked away but not without my curiosity piqued at a high level.

When he said "the bar," I knew what he meant, so I headed straight to Rick and John's place—only at that point, it was just Rick's; John had passed away a few years earlier of a heart attack, I had been told.

When I arrived, Butchie was sitting by himself in a booth, gripping a beer and seemingly in deep thought until he saw me. He motioned to me with his free hand to come over, and so I walked over and sat with him.

"What's up?" I asked him.

He put his beer aside and wasted no time getting to the point. "I got a tip from Kevin…something big is going out on a ship, something huge, and I'm going to take it before it leaves the pier."

Kevin Manning was the clerk and a very close confidant of Butchie at that time. Each had ties to organized crime, and not surprisingly they had several mutual acquaintances as a result, both Irish and Italian.

"Take what?" I asked him.

"Gold," he said, "a ton of it, maybe twenty mil, all of it shaved, no bars and coming in on a truck."

He then removed a crumpled-up piece of paper from his jacket pocket, placed it on the table, and smoothed out the wrinkles as best he could.

I saw that it was a manifest.

"Now look," he said as he scrolled his finger down the left edge of the document to a line that showed a delivery from Trans-Global Shipping. "Look at that—you know what they ship?"

"What do they ship?"

"They ship gold, motherfucker, gold to and from Europe, Asia, Africa, wherever—to all the scumbag brokers all over the place. This one is headed to London. Now pay attention."

His finger kept moving. Under the "Merchandise" header in the middle of the paper, I saw that it read "Currency," and under the "Package" header all the way to the right, it read, "3 Units—weight 7,500 lbs."

In 1975 the price of gold was around $160 per ounce. Times sixteen ounces per pound, it was $2,560 per pound, which meant roughly $18 million of metal was leaving the pier.

"You want to steal it?" I asked him.

"What else am I going to do with it?" he said. "Listen, my guys down in the North End are going to take it and ship it to Sicily or some shit, where they're going to melt it down and sell it to whoever—I don't know, and I don't care. All we have to do is put it on a truck while it's sitting in the warehouse all by its lonesome. Then we'll bring it to a garage owned by a guy named Phil—he's part of 'the outfit'—and he'll take care of the rest. Our cut would be fifteen percent."

"*Our* cut?"

"Yeah, that's right," he said. "You and me, and whoever else we get to help. I'm thinking six guys…Kevin is happy with a small cut just for giving us the tip. We'll give him twenty-five thousand. Or something."

"You want to steal seventy-five hundred pounds of metal from the rest of the world? You think they're not going to be watching that thing like a hawk every second it sits on the pier?"

"First of all, we're not stealing from the rest of the world, probably just one country or business or something, and their shit is insured anyway. No, we're taking it from Global. Secondly, maybe they will be watching it; maybe they won't be," he said, "but this is it. This is what I've been waiting for all these miserable years on the docks, and I'm not going to let the opportunity pass me by. So I need to know if you're in or you're out, because I'll be honest, judging by your tone, I get the feeling you're going to need some convincing here."

"I got to be honest with you, Butchie—"

"Please do."

"This isn't my thing anymore. So I'm out," I said. "I'm sorry, but my life has changed. I don't want any part of this bullshit. I'm ready to coach my son's Little League team, for Christ's sake…this is…this is just too much."

"You're out?"

"I'm out."

"So I'm supposed to do this alone?" he said.

"Alone?" I said. "Butchie, you'd need those other guys involved at the very least just to account for the extra security that might be there. And what's the date on this thing?"

I gave the paper another glance.

"You have three weeks to plan this thing," I said.

"I can get a team ready—that's not a problem."

As he talked, I kept looking at the manifest and shaking my head. Then I put it down. I could tell that my noticeable disinterest was getting under his skin, but I didn't give a shit.

"I'm sorry," I said. "You have my support; you know that."

"What the fuck does that mean?" he said, more agitated now. "You gonna stand off to the side and clap your fuckin' hands while we take the shit?" And so he clapped his hands to mock me.

I just sat and took it all in while he ranted. Then I said, "I'm going to get the fuck outta here, man."

"Go ahead," he said. "Go home. Just remember you promised me, right here in this place, that if I found a nice score, you'd be all fuckin' shits and giggles and help me take it. That's all I'm saying."

"What?"

"You remember the first time we came in here all those years ago," he said.

"I don't know about the 'shits and giggles' part, but I was eighteen fuckin' years old when I said that. What the fuck did I know? I'm thirty-five now, and I don't want to look over my shoulder the rest of my life wondering when the feds are going to bust in my house and raid the place. I got a family now to think about, too."

"Fuck that. You got a short memory, you know that?"

"How so?"

"Didn't I help you when I wasted that junkie kid and his cousin? Wasn't I there for you when your own uncle turned his back on you? If it weren't for me, who was going to have your back? You weren't going to ice those guys." He went on. "How about all those cushy jobs I set you up with on the waterfront—and still do, as a matter of fact. Did you ever stop to think about that stuff?"

"And I appreciate all of that; you know I do."

"I'm starting to wonder if you really do," he said. "Look, I can get guys to help me out here with this thing, but you're the only one I trust with my life if shit goes down. I need you for this…please." Then he leaned in and said, "This, my friend, is the next crime of the century."

"That's what's causing my hesitation."

"It's a lot of money."

"It's a lot of risk," I said.

"If we don't do this, someone else will," he said.

"Then let them."

"What's it gonna be?" he asked me again.

"I don't know," I told him.

"No, I need to know. Planning begins now. Are you in, or are you out?"

"Then I'm out."

"Then you can go."

So I got up, left, and went home.

The following morning I went to work. There was one ship, but my gang wasn't called, so I faced for a job. The stevedore, Mitch Kelly, never even looked in my direction. No doubt, it was the work of Butchie. He was being petty about the whole situation, but nonetheless, for the first time in a long time, I didn't work.

I didn't want to go right home, so instead I went to the club and hung around, played some cards, and shot the shit with the guys. Then, when I'd had enough, I left and got home just in time for dinner.

After we ate, the kids ran off and watched TV, while Marie and I cleaned up. I was quiet, and she took notice.

"You OK, honey?" she asked.

"Of course. Why?"

"You just seem…off. Everything OK at work?"

"Everything is great, babe; it couldn't be better," I assured her.

"I have to show you something."

And by her expression, I just knew it wasn't good. So she reached up to the cabinet above the dishwasher, opened it, pulled out a letter, and handed it to me.

"What's this?" I said.

"It's another bill…from the nursing home."

So I opened it and nearly passed out when I did. I sat down.

"It's twenty-five hundred dollars!"

"Tony, we can't keep this up. I know it's your mother, but we have to figure something out."

"We got this today?"

"Yeah."

"Does my brother know?" I asked her.

"I don't know."

I stood up and punched a cabinet, putting my fist halfway through it. Marie gasped, and then my son ran in, scared.

"What was that?" he asked us.

"Everything is fine, honey," Marie assured him. "Go back and watch TV."

And so he ran off.

"Did you really have to react that way with your son in the next room?" she said.

"No, I didn't. I'm sorry."

"Can you pick up more hours at work?" she asked.

"I can try, but…"

"But what?"

"Things might change down at the docks. I might not be working quite as much."

"Well, why? What happened?"

"Nothing," I said. "It's this whole thing with Butchie. We got into it, and that's it, so things might change."

"That's no kind of answer, Tony."

"What do you want me to do, huh? Want me to get another job? A part-time job? Tell me!"

"Don't put this on me!" she yelled back. "You do what you have to, because we can't keep going on like this!"

"You know, Marie, you're really pissing me off right now."

"You know what, Tony? You don't worry about a thing, 'cause I'll get a job. I'll have my mother watch the kids or one of my friends. I'll figure it out."

"You're not getting a job; I'll handle it."

"You will?"

"I will," I said, "but for now, I just need you to get the Christ off my back."

"Fuck off, Tony."

And she stormed off.

None of this was fair. I had no bad habits. I hardly drank, I had no gambling problem, and I didn't do drugs or sleep with other women. I was a family man who cut some corners in life, but apparently it wasn't enough. I was overcome by fury after the argument, so I grabbed my keys and left.

"Where are you going?" Marie asked.

"None of your goddamn business!" I said.

I felt terrible for the kids. We never argued, and if we ever had a disagreement, it was settled peacefully. But when it came to money, as for most couples, things could get ugly.

But I also had other things going on that she didn't know about, and that was my conversation with Butchie. Along with the storm brewing inside me, I was letting some guilt seep into my system.

It was true: Butchie had done a lot for me and never asked me for anything in return. Even when I'd told him we were done with the bookmaking operation, it hadn't bothered him in the least. The guy never complained about anything.

Maybe I did owe him. But what he wanted was a little more than a favor between friends. It was to aid him in a serious felony. One that would, at the very least, bring enormous attention to the waterfront. And worse, if I got caught, I could potentially lose everything: my job, my house, my family, my freedom—everything.

It had been a long time since I'd done anything out of the way. And believe me, I'd fought the urge; there was no question about that. But I was too settled in my daily life, Marie and the kids were happy, and money was never really an issue, not until that point.

What weighed heavily on my mind was that Butchie was going to do it, with or without me. And if something happened to him and I wasn't there to help, as he always was for me, I wasn't sure I could live with that.

I talked myself into putting one foot in and one foot out.

I still had my reservations, and I had as many doubts that we could pull it off. Because I believed wholeheartedly that the gold would be guarded by a small army of trained men packing some real heat. So I wasn't convinced we could actually put the plan in motion.

I also didn't like that my loyalty was being called into question. Where I should place it was a real question for Butchie, not me. Because, again, what he had asked of me perhaps stepped over the bounds of true devotion to a friend, considering the potential risks involved.

God help me, I thought. Because in the end, as in many times in my life, I regrettably let my anger get the best of me.

So where did I go?

Straight to Butchie's. I parked out front and waited for him, as he wasn't home yet from the bar. When I saw him pull into his driveway, I got out and met him at the base of his front stairs. He was surprised, naturally, and glassy-eyed, no doubt from a few extra pops he'd had at the bar after I left.

"What do you want?"

"You're going to need a lookout, I would imagine," I said to him.

"Yeah, I'm gonna need a lookout," he said. "Don't break my balls; are you telling me you're in now?"

I nodded. "I'm in."

"Let's go inside," he said.

We sat across from each other at his kitchen table and began a lengthy discussion.

"I want to be out of the way," I said. "I'll give you my eyes, but that's it. Agreed?"

"Agreed," he said.

"What if the warehouse is under heavy surveillance?" I asked him.

"We'll turn around, head right back here or to a bar, have a few beers, and call it a night."

"No one gets hurt," I said.

"No one gets killed, if that's what you mean," said Butchie. "It's tough to pull things off like this without dishing out a few bumps and bruises—you know that."

"OK," I said, "and when this is all over?"

"I'll never ask you for another thing."

"I gotta be outta my fuckin' mind," I said.

"But you're definitely in, right?"

"I'm in," I said, "but under one more condition."

"Name it."

"I want Mickey involved," I told him. "I know how you feel about him, but he's a good friend, he understands loyalty, and I know he could use the dough."

"Absolutely not," he said. "I can't afford to have him fuck this up. Look, he's a good guy, I'll give you that, and I respect that he's your friend, but I can't do it, not this time. If you want to take care of him out of your cut, by all means, but I can tell ya that once I bring up his name to the others, they could back out, and I can't have that. I need you to understand that, Ton'."

I gave it a moment and thought about his words and came to the conclusion that I wasn't going to change his mind, so I wasn't going to fight it. Instead, I held tight to the notion that if we pulled off the job, I'd take care of Mickey by giving him a few bucks out of my end, which he would greatly appreciate anyway.

So I said, "OK."

"OK?"

"I'm good with it."

The bastard smiled for the first time that night, because we had a heist to plan that was to take place in just three weeks, which was the last week of January.

"Now," I said, "the rest of the crew…who'd you have in mind?"

CHAPTER 20

THE RECRUITS

Tuesday, January 7, 1975.

"We could have wiped our asses with a sack full of twenties and still lived a pretty good life with that take," Sammy said in his thick brogue as he sat across from Butchie and me at the Hilltop Tavern in Chelsea around eleven o'clock the following morning.

The burly ex-marine was rough around the edges, half shaven and gray whiskered, pretty tall—he stood around six foot even—and always looked at you with an intensity as if he was going to knock your head off your shoulders if he didn't like the next thing you said.

They'd grown up together, Sammy and Butchie; Sammy left to go back to Ireland with his old man to run a family-owned tavern outside Dublin. But it wasn't enough for him, so he worked his way on to a ship, and when it docked in

New York, he got off, hitched a ride to Boston to surprise his mother in Southie, and stayed with her until she passed away of cancer. Butchie set him up on the docks, where he worked as a mechanic for a couple or so years until he left to join the marines. He did a couple of tours in Nam but never came back to the waterfront.

Butchie always referred to him as his cousin. And I could see the closeness between them, as well as the trust.

Sammy went on, "But we were speedin' down the parkway, eh, when my driver, my fuckin' numbskull idiot brother-in-law, slams on the fuckin' brakes, givin' me and the guys in back a heart attack…ready for this? To let a fuckin' flock of geese cross the fuckin' road! The pigs were a mile behind us, but far enough for us to lose them and get to the garage. So I'm hittin' him and yellin' at him, 'Go! Go! Go!' But the son of a bitch wouldn't go! So I raised my pistol to his fuckin' head, and the cocksucker still wouldn't step on the gas. I'm telling you both, till this day I wish I'd pulled the trigger; I wouldn't have given a fuck what my wife thought or if I did a life sentence for it, either, I can promise you that."

"So what happened?" I asked.

"The motherfuckin' cops had us surrounded a few seconds later," Sammy said. "I just looked and looked at him. I thought I was in a fuckin' nightmare. And he kept apologizin' and apologizin'…'I couldn't hurt the fuckin' geese,' he kept saying. I rotted five years for that fucker. We called him Goose while we served together in Plymouth."

We couldn't help but laugh, and Sammy understood. He couldn't have made that story up if he tried.

"That's quite a story," I said. "One for the ages."

"One my favorites," said Butchie.

"So, what do you two got for me, huh?" Sammy said. "Because I'm done with banks."

"No bank," Butchie said. "I got a tip. We have something going out—it's gold—and we're going to take it. Over seventy-five hundred pounds of it being shipped overseas."

Clearly very curious now, Sammy said, "Gold, eh? You have my attention now, cousin."

Butchie leaned in for emphasis. "The manifest has it going to London, England."

"Is that right?" said Sammy.

"That's right."

"Going to a country full of pussies, ya know?"

"Yes," said Butchie. "Now, you remember how to drive a forklift? You were pretty good at it back in the day."

"Ah, yes," Sammy said. "Still good. Still good. But…"

"But what?" Butchie asked.

Then Sammy burst into a fit of laughter. Butchie and I exchanged a look.

"What the fuck is so funny?" Butchie asked.

"Well," Sammy said after he came back down and caught his breath, "you don't think they're going to be watching their precious metal with one hundred men or better?"

"Perhaps, but I'll take a handful of good longshoremen in a battle of wits on the docks any day. That's our waterfront, and no one knows it like us, especially the three sitting right here."

"If there's one hundred men, we're not going through with it anyway," I said.

Butchie said, "We'll see."

I shot him a look.

Sammy deliberated and then turned to the bar and shouted, "Three whiskeys, please!"

"Coming right up!" the white-haired barkeep yapped back in a sarcastic manner.

"What else can you tell me?" Sammy went on.

"I may need you to rough up a guard," Butchie said.

"What else?"

"It's a lot of weight, so we'll need something sturdy to take it out, but I don't have time to talk about that right now. I just need to know, are you in, or are you out?"

Sammy pondered the question and then abruptly slammed both his hands on the table. "I'm in!" he shouted. "I was in when the two-a-ya sat down, but I wanted us to share a fuckin' drink—if it ever gets here."

Just then the barkeep waddled the shots over on a tray, while Sammy gave him the stink eye. "For Christ's sake, my nana moves faster than you, and she's been in the dirt for thirty fuckin' years!"

"This guy's a wise guy, huh?" the barkeep responded. "He's three cents short of a nickel, and the other two cents went broke."

"Get outta here, old-timer," Sammy said, "before I put you right next to my nana."

It was harmless banter between the two. When the old guy walked away, we saluted and took the shot down.

"So," Sammy said, "when's the truck coming in?"

"The twenty-ninth."

Counting with his fingers he said, "That's less than three weeks."

"That's right," said Butchie.

"That's three fuckin' weeks."

"I'm well aware, Sammy."

"Then we better get goin', eh?" he said.

"We're moving as fast as we can. We gotta see about a couple of other guys. But let's meet at the club in Somerville two nights from now on Thursday at eight," said Butchie. "Remember the club? We'll have everything ready by then."

We shook his hand, said our good-byes, and thanked him.

It was our intention to secure everyone on that day. I went along because I wanted to see the group Butchie had in mind as a way to put my mind at ease—to feel more comfortable about the operation.

Our next stop was to see Wally, but we knew he wasn't down at the pier, so we went right to his home in Dorchester, where he lived and took care of his mother. But first we called him from a pay phone outside to make sure he was there. Butchie made the call, spoke briefly, and then hung up the phone and said, "He's expecting us."

We hopped in Butchie's truck and drove off.

When we arrived, we pulled into the only open space in Wally's driveway, next to his brown Buick. His front yard seemed to have been neglected, and the front of his green-vinyl, two-family home had turned gray.

I rang the bell and was greeted by Wally. A little head jerk told us to come in. We did, and he led us to the kitchen, where Butchie and I sat down.

"Try to keep it down; my mother is taking a nap."

"Of course," I said.

"Can I get you guys anything?" Wally asked.

But we were good. "No, thank you," Butchie said. "We don't have a lot of time."

Wally sat down and said, "So, lay it on me. What's so important?"

"I got a fix on something big. I got the tip from Kevin; then I saw it on the manifest—seventy-five hundred pounds of shaved gold headed to London to be melted down."

That's when I zoned out and started to feel anxious. Till then, in the back of my mind, I still hadn't believed it was going to happen. But the meeting with Sammy made it real for me. And Sammy and Butchie were no joke. They weren't the type of guys to back out of something that they felt was well worth the risk. When they decided to do something, you could bet your ass they'd get it done—or die trying.

I came back into mental focus when I heard Wally say, "I'm in."

"You sure?" I asked. "That was a pretty quick call on your end."

"That's a lot of gold," he said.

I said, "Yeah, but—"

"But nothing," Wally interjected. "Look at this place. I can't keep up with it, and I got a mother with one foot in the grave who, on most days, forgets she gave birth to me or worse—she wishes I was dead. I can't keep taking off work to take care of her, and the state ain't kickin' in like I thought it would. So, yes, I'm in. Just tell me what I'm doing; I imagine we don't have a lot of time."

I shook my head. "Truck comes in three weeks; it gets shipped out on the following Monday."

"What's my role?" Wally asked.

"I'll need you in the warehouse," Butchie said. "In case we need to move the chests by hand once they're put in the truck. And we might have to again when we make the drop. Now, can you make it down to the club Thursday night around eight?"

"I can make it," he said.

"Good," Butchie said, "real good."

That day was a whirlwind because we needed to act quickly to secure a team; given the time constraints, four guys was pretty good, I thought, but Butchie wanted two more to feel better about everything.

So we continued to look, and we had to hurry, because every minute counted.

It was the seediest place I had ever been to.

Connor's Basement was a bar—a stone-encased, dust-filled hole in the earth in Charlestown. But it was roomy, with a basement, naturally, designed as a makeshift fighting ring for dogs, and it allowed for twenty-five to thirty spectators hooting, hollering, and rooting for their prize hound to tear out the throat of another.

It wasn't my thing, but we were there for another purpose, and unfortunately it came at a time when a match was about to begin.

Downstairs was where we saw our guy—Connor Haggerty, a former longshoreman, now bar owner and dog-fighting promoter. He sat on a stool at the counter holding a leash connected to a fierce-looking pit bull with more scars than a whipping post at a southern plantation. A private match was about to ensue between Connor's pup and a Rottweiler being readied by a guy whose name I'd never heard before

Connor asked us to wait a second while they let the dogs go in the middle of the floor. So they did, and it was a spectacle; in no time, blood was spilled. Each dog vied for the other's neck to bite down on until Connor's dog had an opening and lockjawed the other in its jugular and wouldn't let go. Connor tried to pull his prize pup off, but the bastard wouldn't give. It got to a point where Connor was punching his own dog in the back of the head until he released the thing.

It was gruesome. The rottie couldn't get to his feet. Once Connor had his pit at bay, the other guy handed over some cash, then picked his dog up and cradled him, and carried him up the stairs and out.

Connor took his dog and put him in a cage while we spoke.

"Hey, it's good to see youse. What brings you fellas here today, huh?"

"Listen," Butchie began, "we don't have a lot of time, but a truck is coming in with a lot of gold in two days, so I'm trying to put a team together to take it…Interested?"

"Whoa, fellas. I'm flattered," he said. "but I have to ask first; what would I be doing in this venture?"

"I need you to help take care of a guard," Butchie said. "Just disable him, nothing more."

"I can do that," he said. "Just how much we talkin'?"

"Seventy-five hundred pounds, give or take."

"I'll take." Connor said followed by a burst of laughter. "You got a plan?" he asked.

"We'll hash it out Thursday night at the club in East Boston. So, you in? I don't mean to rush you, but time is of the essence—you know what I mean?"

"When?" asked Connor.

"In three weeks."

"Yeah, sure, let's do it," Connor said. "I think it's about time I got out of this racket anyhow, ya know?"

"Great," said Butchie.

"So, what's your dog's name?" I asked Connor.

"Penelope," he answered. "Wanna pet her?"

"No, I'm good, but thanks anyway."

"Sure. Hey, you guys want a drink before you go?" he asked us.

"No," Butchie said, "we're in a hurry, so we'll see ya tomorrow, OK?"

We shook hands.

"I'll see you gentlemen later," Connor said.

Five down, one more to go. When we got out to the sidewalk, Butchie said, "I'm going to get Sally, and that'll be it."

"Sally?"

"Yeah," he said. "I'll go see him alone. He lives a couple of blocks from me."

Salvatore "Sally" Rego was a longshoreman who had been on the pier for just a couple of years. Prior to that he was knee deep in rice paddies fighting in the Vietnam War. He was a tough bastard and a capable human when having to handle a high-pressure situation, assuming the war didn't scramble his brain none.

Although neither Butchie nor I had much of a relationship with Sally, we both understood him to be a solid guy. Still, though, the choice to have him on board struck me as a bit odd, and the only conclusion I could come up with was, if shit got bad, Butchie wanted an experienced gunman there as insurance.

"Go for it," I said. "Mind taking me home?"

"No, not at all," he said. "I'll just fill you in with the rest tomorrow or Thursday when I see ya."

"Sounds good."

And then he took me home.

CHAPTER 21

THE PLAN

Thursday, January 9, 1975.

We all came separately.

Sammy, Wally, and I arrived at the club promptly and headed upstairs. There was Butchie, leaning over the pool table with the blueprints of the waterfront and a few papers scattered over the plans. There was no doubt by the look in his eyes that his head was in the game. It was all or nothing.

"Where's Sally?" asked Butchie.

We looked at one another dumbfounded.

"Anyone speak to him?" I asked.

Same reaction from the group.

That's when we heard footsteps coming up the stairs, which caught our attention. But when the door opened, it wasn't Sally; it was Gus.

"What do you want, Gus?" asked Butchie.

"I spoke to Sally," he said. "He's in Rhode Island, locked up."

"What the hell do you mean, 'locked up'?"

"He beat the shit out of someone down there on the beach, so they locked him up and threw his dog in the next cell." He went on, "So he wanted me to tell you he is very sorry, but he will not be making dinner tonight."

"Why didn't you give me the phone, Gus?"

"I don't know!" he said. "He hung up, or we had a bad connection or something."

Butchie hung his head in defeat.

Gus left, and no sooner did he make it to the bottom of the stairs than the office phone rang. We all looked sharply at each other, before Butchie took it upon himself to head into the office and shut the door. The office phone naturally had a separate line, so the hope was that Sally had dialed upstairs as well to speak to Butchie directly.

He returned visibly disappointed.

Butchie said. "Sally is out."

"What do you mean, he's out?" asked Sammy.

"He's out, and that's that," Butchie said. "He's not interested, and I don't have time to change his mind."

Connor said, "We're going to need another guy, Butchie, just in case security is tighter than we want."

"You think I don't know that?" he snapped back.

Wally said, "Connor has a point, just saying."

I stood still. Quiet. Waiting for Butchie to raise the white flag, scrap the whole idea, and admit it was crazy to start with. Then, in an unbelievable turn of events, Butchie looked at me and said, "What about your buddy?"

"What buddy?"

"Mickey," he said. "He doesn't have to do anything; just stand there on the roof with a radio and let us know if he sees anything."

"I thought that was my job?"

"Not now," he said. "Now I'm going to need you on the pier with me."

You could cut the tension with a knife. All eyes were on me, waiting for an answer, because, ironically, at that point the entire operation hinged on my willingness to change my role and include Mickey, a guy who no doubt was expendable, if you asked Butchie. But he wasn't to me. To me he was a friend, and one who'd been there with me since the day I started on the waterfront.

"I'll call him," I said.

And so I did. I left him a message and told him to come to the club and that it was important.

Thirty minutes or so passed before Mickey appeared, but since he would take over my role as lookout, we felt it unnecessary to wait for his arrival.

Let the games begin.

Here's the plan we devised: Facing the front gate, directly adjacent to the left of the warehouse, was a construction site that had all the equipment we needed to haul the gold away. Butchie and I were going to steal a heavy-duty truck of sorts.

Then we were going to wait for the signal from Connor that he and Sammy had the guards bundled up (however many there were) and a call from Mickey that the coast was clear from his view. At that point we were going to drive the truck through the gate and into the warehouse.

Though Wally seemed like the logical choice to subdue a guard, or perhaps two, we feared that because of his massive frame, the guard might actually be able to identify him or at least give a description that could lead to direct questioning of Wally by the cops later on. We didn't want to take any chances, and Sammy and Connor were more than capable of handling the task.

Now, with the truck missing from the construction site, it only made sense that suspicion—or at least some of it—would fall on the company that owned the truck, which was Borelli Construction.

The warehouse doors were operated electronically, but Butchie was going to handle that by cutting the wires the day of the robbery so we'd have easy access to the back door without tripping any sort of alarm. Plus, the door being "fixed" was closest to the street.

The guards? That was the million-dollar question that wouldn't be answered until the first night the gold sat in the warehouse. The state police or the local cops were the two logical choices to watch the warehouse—but only if Global decided to hire them for the detail. We doubted very highly that some candy-assed security company had manpower or the balls to stop us, so we weren't particularly worried about that. But once we figured what the deal was with that, we'd assess the risk on moving in on the warehouse. Otherwise, we just needed to worry about the waterfront's security, which was a pair of guards—one in the booth and one on patrol—and there would be no reason to suspect it was going to be any different the night we chose to make the move. The idea was to subdue one of them, tie him up, and then lock him in the security booth while the other was on patrol. Once the guard was taken care of, and we got the OK it was clear, it was show time.

Sending that signal was Mickey's most important job. Beyond that, all he had to do was watch from above and alert us if anything looked out of place. We could station him very easily on the roof of an apartment building that gave him a perfect aerial view of the yard and both ends of the warehouse. Butchie had the master key to the building in case he needed to bring a broad there on the sneak. All he had to do was to ask the "super" what place was vacant, and he'd walk right in.

"You do not move from that spot, understand me?" Butchie said when Mickey was caught up to speed.

Mickey nodded like an obedient child.

The same day the gold was to roll in on the truck, Butchie was going to make sure at least one of us had a hand in unloading the gold off the truck to get a good look at it. Butchie was going to remain in the office since he was a business agent.

Now, the *how*.

The warehouse was massive, and we anticipated the gold being hidden securely, but as long as one or more of us were responsible for taking it off the truck, we were confident we weren't going to walk around like the blind leading the blind searching for it. Once we located it, Sammy would then do his thing on the forklift, load it onto "our" truck, and drive through the back end of the warehouse and into the street on our way to Phil's garage. It shouldn't take more than fifteen minutes to lift three chests carefully from one spot and place them gently onto the truck. If our time estimates held true, that gave us ample time to get in and get out before the second guard came back around and noticed his friend bundled up.

"Wednesday and Thursday of that week, Sammy and I will be on the roof after dark watching to determine what security will look like," Butchie said. "If all goes well, it's a go for Friday."

"Does anyone have any questions?" Butchie asked.

There were none.

"Don't forget to dress warm," Butchie said. "OK, we still have nearly three weeks, so enjoy them. We'll reconvene one more time only, in the apartment building the night we make the move. Sound good?"

Collectively we agreed and one by one began to disperse, except Mickey, who was ushered into the office by Butchie, who then closed the door.

Ten minutes, if I was to guess, they sat in there, and it made me nervous as a bastard. I could only assume it was less of a pep talk and more of a series of real threats to Mickey in the event he screwed something up.

I knew Butchie hated him, but he also had no choice. Mickey was the last option—the only option on such short notice—if he wanted to pull that thing off.

Mickey's job was simple, so I felt pretty good about him being included. Directly across the street from the warehouse was that apartment building. It was six stories with a roof and a three-foot wall bordering its edges for protection in case an individual slipped or something; they wouldn't just roll over the edge. It also afforded enough height for someone to crouch down and look over the edge through a pair of binoculars, which was all he needed to do. Look and report—that was all. When it was over, he could go home and wait for his cut to come at some point. And no weapons, not for Mickey. There was no reason.

When they finally came out of the office, everything seemed fine. Butchie patted him on the back, and Mickey was all smiles; the meeting had gone well from what I saw.

"I'll see ya later," Butchie said to him.

"You got it, boss."

Mickey left, leaving the two of us alone.

I wasted no time in asking. "What'd you say to him?"

"I just said, 'Be ready'—that's all." Noting my expression, Butchie said, "Hey, you wanted this."

"That's right," I said. "I did."

"OK, listen, I know you're mad at me, but I promise after we do this thing, you'll be the happiest guy in the world. You'll have it all."

"I thought I already did."

"Not yet," he said.

"Look, I'm gonna go," I told him.

"You don't want to grab a bite to eat or something? Some Chinese?"

"Nah, I'm good," I said. "I better get back to Marie; she's probably getting nervous, and I don't want to push my luck after the last time with the potato thing."

"What are you going to tell her in a few weeks?"

"I'll figure it out. I'll use the club or something—I don't know," I said. "I'll see ya."

So I left, wondering how in just a couple of days, I went from an unassuming longshoreman with a wife and a couple of kids to a guy conspiring to steal millions from God knows who with my bare hands and thinking I was going to get away with it.

I needed help. I was stuck in this mess, and I wasn't getting out, but I needed to talk to someone about it. As far as I knew, there was only one person who would understand my problem, and by luck alone, he was out on bail and resting at home.

I was going to see Uncle Dom.

CHAPTER 22

A VISIT TO UNCLE DOM

My uncle Dom was let out of prison just a few days prior on Monday, but with a number of stipulations: he needed to meet with a parole officer once a week, he couldn't leave the state of Massachusetts, and he couldn't have any contact with anyone on the list he was given of one hundred known members and associates of La Cosa Nostra—a.k.a. the Mafia.

Needless to say, his life as a thug for "the family" for all intents and purposes was over.

So if I was looking for comfort leading up to the big heist, perhaps another person might have been a better choice, considering he likely was not in the best of spirits. But I had no one else; he was it. I was planning on going to see him anyway after he was out a week or so and had settled in at home.

He lived in a middle-class residential neighborhood littered with two- and three-family homes, beeping car horns, cracked sidewalks, and young kids running around or riding their bikes. My uncle's house was a double-decker Victorian with white vinyl siding and a rusty gate: it was modest in size compared to his neighbors' but had a manicured front lawn. It was occupied only by him and Jeannine—his longtime girlfriend—with the top floor and attic used for storage. And it was old, a family construct dating back to the first automobile.

I trotted up the stairs and rang the bell. I was greeted by Jeannine.

"Tony, it's so good to see you," she said excitedly.

"It's very nice to see you, Jeannine," I said. "Is my uncle in?"

"Of course," she said. "He's right inside. Won't you come in?"

"Thank you."

Always so polite, that Jeannine. She'd had it tough growing up in the projects of Somerville. Her father lost his life in World War II, and her mother passed away of cancer before Jeannine's sixteenth birthday. For nearly three months, she was homeless, until she found a job as a waitress in a local chain restaurant and never left. She maintained a foothold there and eventually became a manager. That's where my uncle had met her some twenty-odd years ago.

She was a sweet lady. Even when my uncle was doing his time, when I saw her at a wake or wedding, whatever the case was, she was always very kind and never brought up the problems my uncle and I had.

I stepped in cautiously, because considering my uncle's predicament at the time, he was capable of anything from a warm embrace to a lead pipe across my forehead. I'd seen him deliver both, and up close.

From where I was standing, I could tell the inside of the house hadn't changed—not since I was a kid anyway. The fixtures were old, the furniture was still blanketed in plastic, and every space on the wall held a picture or object depicting our Lord, Jesus Christ. In front of me, to the left, was a long staircase covered with the same light-brown shag rug I used to trip on going up and down the stairs when I was growing up. And to my right about five feet from me was the living room. That's where Jeannine headed. I removed my cap and then paused in the hallway and waited for her to let my uncle know I was there. I heard whispers, and then she reappeared.

"He's right in here," she said.

So I crept in, turned a slight corner, and there he was, lying down on his couch and watching a black-and-white telecast of *All in the Family*. My presence did nothing to divert him from the show until—referring to the TV—I said, "You know, they sell these in color now?"

His eyes shifted in my direction, emotionless. "Well, look what the cat dragged in," he said.

"May I sit?" I said.

"Do what you want; I don't care."

Yeah, he was miserable, so I proceeded cautiously.

I took a seat in an armchair covered, of course, in plastic, and in between us was a wooden coffee table. On it was a tray with a cup of water, some pills, and a small bowl of half-eaten soup of some kind.

He looked OK—healthy, anyway, but tired. He found the strength to muscle his way into an upright position. He picked up his cup, took a sip from his shaky hand, and placed it back down.

"You sick or something, Uncle Dom?"

"Nah, just a cold, I think. I don't fuckin' know," he said. "I saw your father last week…he came by. He looked good—better than me, anyway."

"Yeah, he's doing OK," I said.

"He showed me a picture; you got a nice family…the boy and the girl and all."

"Isabella and Tony Jr., yes."

"Your boy got his dad's temper?"

"I think he does, yeah, but he's a lot smarter than I am."

"No shit," he said jokingly.

He turned his attention to the TV and then said, "I like this guy Archie Bunker; he's a funny bastard."

"He sure is," I said. "Listen, Uncle Dom—"

Cutting me off, he said, "If you think I'm looking for your sympathy, you can go fuck yourself…government telling me I can't talk to my own friends—bunch of bullshit."

Just then Jeannine entered the room to ask if I wanted anything.

"I'm OK, Jeannine, thank you."

To my uncle, she asked, "And you, dear?"

Using his thumb and forefinger for emphasis he said, "How about a little cup of tea, sweetheart?"

"Sugar?"

"Two," he said.

She left the room.

He said, "It's tough to get good service around here, you know what I mean?"

I chuckled and then said, "She's a good woman."

"She is, she really is."

"So, I got something going…and I wanted to talk to you about it."

"Whatta you got goin' on—aches and pains? I got this gout thing in my foot now."

"No, it's nothing like that."

"Well, spit it out then, kid."

So I told him, "Me and a few of the guys are looking to, uh…take something big off the pier, in a couple of weeks, in fact…something very big," I said.

Jeannine walked in, dropped the cup of tea in front of my uncle, and asked, "Anything else?"

"No. Leave us."

And she did. She spun around and left.

"How big?" he said, propping himself up a little more.

"Well, it's gold, a lot of it, close to twenty mil, and it belongs to…I don't know who, and I didn't want anything to do with it, but Butchie, you know—he has a way—"

"He's an idiot."

"Yeah," I said just to be agreeable.

"Well, you sure you want to do this?" he said. "I mean, this is big-time stuff you're talkin' about here. Everything else you've ever done is chump change compared to this."

"I know," I said, hanging my head. "Honestly, Uncle Dom, I don't know what I'm doing anymore. I guess I thought maybe there was something you could say to make me feel better about the situation, become I'm nervous as hell about it."

"What can I say, kid?"

"I don't know; you're right," I said.

"You can always back out. That's always an option."

"I wish it were that simple, but I dragged someone else into it."

"I see."

"Yeah."

"Is it the money?" he asked. "You and Marie having problems?"

"No," I said. "Well, we do OK. I mean, we've had some obstacles to overcome, but money will never really be a problem as long as I'm working."

"I guess all I can say then is be careful," he said. "I mean, I don't know what you were looking for here; I still think it's your choice. Butchie is a big boy—he'll handle it."

I said, "We'll see."

"So, when is this thing happening again?"

"Two weeks."

"And who else is involved?"

"I guess it doesn't matter."

"Well, look," he said, "I wish there was something I could do or say to make you feel good about it; just know I hope everything works out, and I want you to be careful. That's a lot of gold that's going missing, so people will be looking for it, you can mark my words."

"I'll be expecting it for sure."

"You better," he said.

I said, "Hey, maybe I'll come by with a present after it's all over."

"You keep that shit away from me. They'll lock me up for another twenty years."

"Yeah, I should have thought of that—sorry," I said.

"Anyhow, how's that jerk-off union leader you got over there?" he asked me.

"Jake?"

"Yeah, that's right, Jake. How the Christ did you ever elect that Irish prick?"

Jake O'Sullivan.

He was, in fact, our union leader, and a crooked son of a bitch, as it turned out. He'd had some connections with the Irish gangs in Southie back in the fifties, so for a period of time he was somewhat liked by the guys on the waterfront. Jake also owned a couple of strip clubs on the north shore, which also made a few of the guys tolerant of him.

My uncle had grown up with him but never liked him, and he'd had a few run-ins with him in the past, which typically ended with Jake getting slapped around a bit. At this point he was nothing more than an incompetent drunk, and he was absent for most of the union meetings, with our vice president, Nicholas DeMaria, holding court.

Nick was a good guy and a hands-off leader, though. We liked him. But Jake, he was something else. I'd had an altercation with him on the pier only a year prior.

We'd had a large shipment of Swiss watches come in that he had a particular interest in. So he stumbled over to the container drunk as a skunk, where me and a few of the guys were unloading them onto a pallet set to be driven off in a truck the next day.

"Be careful with those boxes," he slurred.

I shot him a look of death. He gave it right back to me and continued to watch us through his blurred vision while smoking a butt, balancing himself against which way the wind was blowing so he wouldn't tumble on the gravel. Then he took his cigarette and tossed it at my feet, so I straightened myself up, looked at him, and said, "Watch where you throw that thing, will ya?"

"What'd you say, Costa?"

"I said watch where you throw that thing!"

So he approached me, got in my face, and said, "You got a problem with me, Costa?"

All the guys stopped working and stood in awe as Jake and I had our standoff until one of them got between us and played the part of peacemaker.

Then Jake opened his big mouth and said, "You're soft, you know that, Costa? You're soft!"

I just nodded and smirked. The guy wasn't worth my time. I could have dropped him before he knew what was coming.

So nothing happened. The idiot finally retreated, and we continued to work.

I never took shit from no one, especially not an old, drunken fool like Jake O'Sullivan. No one, in fact, ever took him seriously.

The problem with Jake was he didn't know his place. It didn't matter if a guy was a union leader or not, he had no control over the longshoremen, and if he tried to demonstrate authority and it got out of hand, someone would just put him in the ground, simple as that.

Truth be told, I think his contempt for me had begun long ago, likely due to the tumultuous relationship he had with my uncle.

"This is his last year, and we'll vote someone else in," I said.

"Tell him I said hello, would ya?" asked my uncle jokingly.

"Yeah, sure," I said. "Is he on the list?"

"What list?"

"The list of people you can't speak to," I said.

"What are you, fuckin' nuts?" he said. "He's on a lot of guys' lists, I'm sure, but not that one. You know what I mean?"

"Yeah, I most certainly do," I said. "Listen, I'm going to go."

I stood up and said, "I'll see ya in a few weeks."

"Good luck, kid."

"Thanks."

I said good-bye to Jeannine and left.

All I could do was go home, be with my family, and pray that by the time the robbery came and went, everything would be OK.

CHAPTER 23

THE ARRIVAL

January 29, 1975.

I drove at a snail's pace on the way to work, but it still felt like I got there too soon.

I pulled into the pier, and right away I could see the mayhem unfolding beyond the gate. The waterfront was flooded with guards from private security companies from all over town, plus local and state police were there keeping a close eye on everything we were doing, and I mean everything!

We couldn't go to the bathroom without a guy with a badge peeking over our shoulders checking to see if anything suspicious was falling into the bowl beyond our own urine. It was a real pain in the ass.

"You got a problem?" I asked one of the cops as he stood behind me while I took a piss in a stall. "You need a sample or something?"

Other guys were yelling, calling them faggots and exposing themselves to get a rise out of them. Anything to make them uncomfortable.

It was right around ten o'clock when everyone began to stir. I saw a bunch of badges walk toward the warehouse. All eyes, including law enforcement along with us longshoremen, were zeroed in on a box truck slowly making its way into the yard and through a side entrance of the warehouse. The security guards were like a pack of hyenas around a dead carcass.

"Take it easy! Take it easy!" A representative from Global called out as he maneuvered his way through the crowd and into the warehouse, as Wally and I looked on from just outside the main entrance. The rep unlocked the back of the truck, and there they were—three good-size black chests sitting at the tail of the cab and ready to be moved.

Butchie had already let the gang boss know who to grab to work in the warehouse. Then he called out, "I need those half-dozen guys, and that's all! Let's go!"

That meant Wally and I and four others. Mickey was on a ship unlocking pins.

So we went to work. Wally, the others, and I cleared out some room in the warehouse and then Dougie Brennan got in a forklift and one by one took the chests off and stacked them in a corner.

I worked on the pier most of the day directing the loads as usual, and I helped out some of the mechanics, as they were shorthanded. I was done right at five, but it was at that very hour that the strangest thing happened relative to what we had planned. The waterfront completely cleared out. There were no more local cops or staties or any type of security personnel outside of two guards responsible for the entire waterfront. The only ones left were a few straggling longshoremen itching to leave the pier and head home or do whatever it was they did when they finished up. Everyone was gone. It was so bizarre that I couldn't help but stand and do a 360-degree turn to make sure I wasn't imagining anything. But I wasn't, and that only meant one thing: if the waterfront was going to be cleared like this the next couple of days, this heist was on.

God help us all.

CHAPTER 24
THE DAY OF

Butchie had reported back with a phone call late on Thursday, the night before the robbery. He said only one thing: "It's a go."

Friday, January 31, 1975.
I awoke that morning like it was any other—to the sweet sounds of my daughter objecting to the way Marie brushed her hair. Tony Jr. was sitting quietly eating his bacon and eggs, while I just lay in bed with my arms crossed behind my head, thinking deeply about what a spectacle the next twenty-four hours might be. I got up fifteen minutes earlier than usual hoping to spend some extra time with the kids before they went outside and waited for the school bus.

I sat at the kitchen table with my son. "Are you ready for school there, champ?"

"Homework is done, bag is packed, Dad," he said, rolling his eyes, but I got a kick out of it.

"Your birthday is coming up in a few months; did you figure out what you want yet?"

And he screamed, "Red Sox!"

"Whoa, take it down a notch, uh?" I said, "You want to go to the Sox game? I think we can manage that."

My daughter then raced into the kitchen, and I grabbed her and set her on my lap. "Hey, no kiss for the old man?"

"Sorry, Daddy," she said, and she gave me the cutest peck on my cheek.

"That's more like it. Did you eat breakfast?"

"She had an English muffin earlier," Marie said.

"That's a good girl."

Tony Jr. was done with his food, and the two of them headed for the front door, so I followed. I crouched down, hugged them both tight, and said, "I love you so much."

"OK. OK," my son said, trying to unlock himself out of my embrace.

Then my daughter opened the door, turned around, and said, "We love you, too, Daddy!"

"Bye-bye, sweetheart!"

They ran to the sidewalk and waited for the bus. I just stood there and watched until it came.

Marie took notice of my behavior and said, "You feeling OK, babe?"

"Yeah, of course. I just felt like I should spend more time with them in the morning. They're gone all day, ya know?"

"Well, they'll be back soon enough, and you can have them all to yourself."

"What do you mean?"

"I got a hair appointment at six; I thought you could watch them until I got back."

"What time are you getting back?"

"I don't know," Marie said. "Seven thirty? Eight? You got somewhere to be?"

"No, I mean, you know how it is…"

"If you have somewhere to be, just tell me, and we can get a sitter for a couple of hours, but I'd like to avoid spending the money if we don't have to."

"No," I said adamantly, "no sitter; I want to watch them. The only problem is I might have to shut the club down tonight…Gus hasn't been feeling too well."

"That's fine, whatever you have to do, as long as I can have one night where I can get home and see the kids ready for bed, bathed and all."

"You will; I promise."

"But Tony," she said. "You have to stop agreeing to things like that just to make others happy. Think about yourself once in a while, would you?"

"Of course," I said. "Last time, I promise."

"OK, then, you better get in the shower before you're late for work."

"Yeah, heading in now."

I gave her a kiss and started to get ready.

I wasn't on the pier ten minutes when Butchie caught up with me. He said, "Everything good?"

"Everything is good."

"Because I already cut the wire to one of the warehouse doors on the side," he went on. "I figured, why meddle with it while all these cops are standing around? I got here early and took care of it. They won't even know which one it is."

"OK," I said. "Listen, what time were you thinking tonight, because I got the kids until around eight?"

"That's fine; do your thing," he said. "I want to wait till dark anyway, and we'll have to set up Mickey on the roof first. So even if you came after eight thirty, that works for us. We're going to meet in the apartment building. I'll grab us a few sandwiches so we can eat something quick, and then it's game time. Sounds good?"

"Sounds good to me."

Listen," he said, "you're ready for this, right? Because there's no backing out of this thing now. Everyone is ready, even that half a retard Mickey."

"I'm good, I promise; I'm ready to go," I said. "And could ya lay off the guy? Without him there'd be no guarantee we could do this thing."

"All right, all right, I'm sorry," he said and then walked away.

Myself, I was doing OK. Like he said, there was no backing out, so what could I do but stick to the plan and hope for the best? These guys I was with, the crew we'd put together, they knew what they were doing, so I at least felt better knowing that.

"Then I'll catch you later," he said. "OK?"

I hated to admit it, even to just myself, but with more pieces to the puzzle in place and without incident, I was starting to become somewhat excited, which was a feeling I'd never seen coming. I'd only felt anxiety, anger, and contempt until that point.

CHAPTER 25

PHASE ONE

I got home around five twenty, and the kids were already fed. Ten minutes later, Marie left for her appointment.

While at home, the kids essentially took care of themselves, which was nice. Tony Jr. sat quietly at the kitchen table and did his homework until around seven thirty, while Isabella watched an hour of Bugs Bunny and then asked that I read to her in the parlor as she sat Indian-style on the end of a couch we were sharing. And I did. After thirty or so minutes, her eyelids started to get heavy, so I began getting her ready for bed.

My daughter was quickly sound asleep. My son finished his homework and sat me in the parlor and watched *Happy Days*, one of the more popular shows in the seventies.

Then the phone rang, so I got up and answered it. It was Butchie.

He said, "Meet us at the building across from the pier in apartment 4A."

"OK, I'll be there."

So that was it, really, as far as the conversation went. I hung up the phone, went back to the couch, and continued to watch TV with my son.

At roughly seven forty-five, Marie came through the door.

"Hey, the little one is in bed," I told her.

"Great."

She continued to the bedroom, so I followed her.

As she changed into more comfortable clothes, I asked her if it was OK that I took off, but I could tell by her body language that me leaving was still not sitting well with her.

"Go ahead," she said, "just don't make it a late one, OK?"

"Yeah, I'll do my best."

"I wonder, Tony, maybe you have another one on the side or something."

Here we go, I thought to myself. At the hairdresser's, the girl cutting her hair had probably got her all riled up about me going out, so now, of all nights, I had to deal with another argument on my way out the door.

"What are you giving me shit for, Marie?" I said calmly. "I'm not fuckin' around. Sometimes the guys need me and I don't want to let them down."

"What about when I need you?"

"I'm always here for you and the kids; what the hell you talkin' about?" I said.

"No, you're not," she said. "You're here, you're there…I don't even know why I'm arguing with you, just go."

"I'm not screwing around, Marie."

"Just go, please."

Quite honestly, I didn't want to go anywhere, but I was stuck, so that was that.

When she left the bedroom, I went into my safe for no other reason than to grab my revolver. I went downstairs, outside, and to the car and placed it under the driver's-side seat and then went back in the house to say good-night to my son and good-bye to my wife.

I first dropped by the club and said hello to a few of the fellas, stood over a card game and watched a hand, and then left.

The ride to the apartment building was similar to my commute that same morning. The twenty minutes it took to get there felt like five, and I was a nervous wreck on the inside, but cool as a cucumber on the outside.

I actually parked a good hundred yards away on a road situated in back of the building and far enough away so that from where I stood, I couldn't even see the waterfront. It was a good walk, but I didn't care. In case things went bad, I didn't want my car anywhere near the scene.

So I walked around to the side of the building and through the unsecured front door, right up to the fourth floor to apartment 4A, and knocked three times. Butchie answered and pulled me in.

All the guys were there sitting around a table, all so calm and collected. In the middle of the table lay a pile of black ski masks. Butchie reached in and tossed each of us a mask, one by one.

"OK," he said. "Let's all head up to the roof and take a look at the layout one more time from up there."

We all marched up to the top of the building and found a perfect spot for Mickey to stay put and watch. But first, Butchie peered through a pair of binoculars to give himself one last look from above. Then he passed the binoculars to me, and then I passed them along to Wally, and so on until we all got a turn.

"It is fucking astounding, ain't it?" Butchie said. "All those goddamn cops checking out at five o'clock and leaving this place all to us, three straight days. Stupid."

But Connor had to say it. "It's not a trap, is it?"

"It ain't a trap," said Butchie with some oomph. "Sammy and I sat up here the last two nights and didn't see nothin', no one but the two guards."

"I'll tell ya what, if it is a trap, I'm fuckin' shootin' my way out—that's a promise," Sammy said.

Said Butchie, "Just focus on what we know, and right now we know there are two guards down there we have to take care of, and that's it." He went on, "Right now there's only the one jag off in the booth. The other one is out there somewhere patrolling. When the second one comes back and relieves the other, that's when Mickey gives the signal, and that's when we go in and tie up the new guy in the booth. If the last two nights were any indication, the guard on patrol will head straight to the edge of the pier, then into the maze of containers away from the warehouse. We'll have about an hour before he gets back, so we have to move quick. I'll hot-wire one of the box trucks I saw down there. Connor is going to let Tony, me, and Wally know when the guard is bundled up, and then the fun begins. And don't forget to cut the phone wires in there, too."

Then he turned to Mickey. "You stay here and just watch. If something looks out of order, radio us; otherwise, once we leave with the gold, I'll see ya tomorrow. Understand?"

"I got it," Mickey said.

"Good," said Butchie as he handed him the radio.

"We're going to sit here and wait until they make the handoff down there, and then we'll go into the construction site and wait again until they make one more switch. So we're looking at around eleven o'clock as a strike time." He continued, "Now, just in case something goes wrong, my pickup is parked on the side street to the right of this building. I can fit three. We're getting in and going, and going fast. If you got your own car, even better, use it. And remember, whatever happens, we go to work tomorrow like nothing happened—got it?"

Of course, we agreed collectively. Then we sat around and waited while Butchie kept a close eye on the guards. Then he simply said, "Let's go," which meant the guard on patrol had come back and relieved the other guard, who sat in the booth.

Butchie handed Mickey the binoculars and said jokingly, "Don't lose these; they're expensive."

"Promise."

"We can't all go at once, so I'll go first, then Connor, Wally, Sammy, and Tony."

With that, Butchie said, "See you on the other side, gentlemen."

Connor followed a few moments later, and then Wally and Sammy left a few minutes apart. I was left alone with Mickey.

"You know, if we get all this money, I can go back home to Maine, marry my Betty, and leave this place," said Mickey.

"Betty?"

"Yes," he said, "she's my one and only…we write to each other, and I told her once I saved enough dough, I'm going to go home and marry her."

"For Christ's sake," I said. "How long have I known you? And I'm just hearing about this lady friend of yours?"

"Some stuff I like to keep on the down low, you know what I mean?"

"Fair enough," I said. "You got a picture of this broad?"

He dug one out. It was a black-and-white photo of a pretty brunette, all dressed up in some sort of long gown fit for a fancy ball.

"She's very pretty," I said, handing it back to him.

"Thank you. You know, if I never end up with her, Tony, I mean…I won't die a happy man, ya know?"

"You'll be fine," I said. "You won't die of a broken heart; I won't let ya."

"I may not die of a broken heart, Tony, if I don't marry her. But when I do finally go…I'll have one."

"Let's stay positive, OK?" I said. "We gotta focus here. We'll worry about the women later. In fact, I better go."

"Go ahead, before Butchie has a heart attack," he said.

And we both chuckled.

"We don't want that," I said. "OK, I'll see you tomorrow, I guess?"

"I'll see you tomorrow, my good friend. And good luck."

"You, too."

We shook hands and parted ways. To this day, I wish I'd stayed up there.

CHAPTER 26
PHASE TWO: THE UNDOING

I took the walk from the apartment building and went diagonally across the street to the left, where the construction site appeared unfenced and unattended. I took careful steps, as it was dark out and I didn't want to make any noise. I heard their voices, though, so headed in their direction until I saw them all congregated outside a big white box truck.

"OK," Butchie said, whispering, as soon as I walked over, "we're all here. I've been eyeing this truck for a couple of days now. This is the one. I'm going to get in it now and take care of the dash."

Just as he walked around the front of the truck, Sammy lit up a cigarette, but Butchie wasn't having it.

"No smoke," he said. "I don't want anyone on the other side of the fence knowing we're here, understand? And keep your fuckin' voices down."

Sammy then gently dropped the butt on the ground and extinguished it under his boot. Butchie continued on and popped the lock on the driver's-side door and went to work. While he was doing his thing, I tried to break up the monotony.

"How's your pup, Connor?"

"She's dead."

"Oh, Jesus, I'm sorry," I said. "It's been just a few weeks. What happened to him?"

"It's OK, ya know…no matter who you are, there's always someone bigger and stronger, and so another dog came along and got the best of him."

"Well, I'm sorry again."

"No problem; I really appreciate it," he said.

After a bit of silence, Connor said, "It's a beautiful night, ain't it?"

"Oh, for Christ's sake," said Sammy. "I can't listen to this fuckin' puppy dog and ice cream talk. I'm going over to the fence."

We found it amusing. But Sammy put his mask on and walked away to where he and Connor would eventually cut the fence to get to the security booth.

"It sure is," I said to Connor. "Any plans for the weekend?" I asked him.

"Nah," he said. "Are the Celtics in town?"

"Um," I wondered. "I thought they were on the West Coast or something."

"Maybe the fair or something," he said. "Is the fair in town?"

"No fairs in this friggin cold," I informed him.

"I'll tell ya," he went on, "I'd like to grab this broad I met at a coffee place and take her out somewhere. A fair would have been nice."

"Maybe in the spring," I said.

"Take her to the track," Wally said.

"The track?" asked Connor.

"Yeah," Wally said. "The track ain't a bad idea. You can watch the dogs run from inside, have fun placing a few bets, have a few cocktails and then leave and take her out to a nice dinner."

Connor said, "My dog just died, and you want me to see dogs run? I can't disrespect her like that."

"It was just a thought," said Wally.

"You should see the way that broad looks at me, though," Connor boasted.

"You?" I said jokingly.

We laughed collectively.

We spoke for a while, and it was good. It took the edge off—for me, anyway.

Then Butchie returned.

"What time is it?" Butchie asked.

"Nearly eleven, according to my watch," I told him.

"OK," he said. "Let's keep quiet over here; better yet, Connor, head over to Sammy, it's getting close to that time anyway. The three of us can sit in the truck."

"You got it, Butchie," said Connor as he put his mask on.

"You got everything?" asked Butchie. "Rope? Tape?"

"Sammy's got it on him," he said.

"OK, good," said Butchie.

But just then the call came over the radio from Mickey.

"They made the switch."

Connor picked up his pace.

"Copy," Sammy responded.

Then Sammy and Connor, masks donned, cut the fence, walked into the yard carefully, and disappeared into the night. Butchie, Wally, and I sat in the front seat of the truck in silence.

About five or so minutes went by, and another call came in, this time from Connor.

"Guard is down; gate and warehouse are open."

"Copy," Butchie responded.

"Goddamn, those boys are quick," said Wally.

"All clear from the roof," said Mickey.

"Let's roll," Butchie said.

And roll we did. We maneuvered out of the dirt-paved construction site and went left, and then we took another quick left through the main gate and one more left until we reached the side of the warehouse where the door wire was cut. That's when Butchie went a little farther and then backed the truck in safely with the help of Sammy, who was already inside.

We got out of the truck and met with the others, all five of us, but there was no time to waste.

"Where is the guard?" Butchie whispered.

"Taking a nap," Sammy said.

"Good work."

We all began to look for the chests, and it didn't take long before we found them, considering Wally and I had been there when they were unloaded.

"There they are," Butchie said.

Behind them, ironically, were a dozen or so vacuum cleaners—made me think of Franky.

"Connor," Butchie said, "go stand at the other end of the warehouse and make sure no one is out there on the street. I don't trust that idiot on the roof is going to see everything."

So Connor walked off toward the street side of the warehouse, stood, and watched. Then Butchie handed me his flashlight and told me to keep the light on him. I did. He knelt down with the crowbar in hand and wedged it into a crease in one of the chests. He strained a few times until he popped it open. We both gave huge sighs of relief. Despite the time constraints we faced, we couldn't help but stare at the magnificent sight of this chest filled to the top with shiny flakes mixed with gold dust. Then, out of nowhere, Wally grabbed hold of Butchie's head and gave him a big kiss on his cheek. We all laughed.

"Get off me," Butchie whispered hard and then threw Wally off him. "Let's load it up."

Sammy hopped in the forklift parked fifteen feet or so across from the chests and waited for Butchie to tell him it was OK to turn the key.

But first, Butchie went back and opened the back of the truck, and when he did, we saw that the truck already had some equipment in it, including a couple of jackhammers and several parts to build a scaffolding. Still, though, there was plenty of room to fit the chests; the problem was, would the truck be able to handle the weight?

"Should we unload the truck first?" Wally asked.

"No," said Butchie, "there's no time."

That's when Butchie gestured to Sammy as if he was turning a key to let him know to punch it.

So he did, and ever so carefully, Sammy maneuvered the forklift and caught the first pallet perfectly, raised the chest up, turned left, and headed straight for the truck. At that point, even with Sammy moving so slowly, we still had plenty of time to grab all three.

It was a perfect lift and drop into the truck.

"Get the next one," Butchie said.

"Hold it," I said.

They all froze and looked at me sharply.

"What is it?" Wally asked.

"The weight," I said. "I'm wondering if we can even get another one on here."

"We have to," Butchie said.

Wally gave it a good look and admitted, "You put any more in there, and I could run faster than you can drive it. What if we leave and come back?"

"What are you, stupid?" Butchie said.

Wally just shrugged his shoulders.

All the while Sammy waited as we discussed the issue.

"Let's try," said Butchie. "If it doesn't work, it doesn't work. But we're lookin' at a hefty pay cut here if it doesn't."

"Butchie," I now pleaded, "we won't make it out of the warehouse if we add any more weight to this thing. We either unload their shit, or that's it."

Butchie thought for a few seconds.

"Can you guys hurry up and make a decision?" Sammy interjected from the forklift. "The guard is goin' to come back, and we're all goin' to get caught with our dick in our fuckin' hands."

So Butchie said, "Give me a hand with this jackhammer."

I leaped up and took the hammer with his help and handed it to Wally, who placed it on the floor and off to the side. Then we brought the second one down the same way and left it with the other.

"There," Butchie said. "We're back in business. Wall', I need you here to help me move the chest a bit."

Wally struggled to get his weight on the truck, but he managed to climb in, though it didn't matter. It was then that a call from Mickey diverted our attention.

"Hey, guys?" we heard.

So I ran to the front seat of the truck and grabbed a radio.

"What is it?" I whispered.

"The other guard…he's getting close to you," Mickey said.

"Turn off all the radios now," Butchie said.

"Copy," I replied back to Mickey and then turned off the radio. The rest of the guys did the same with theirs.

We all scattered except Butchie; he walked over to one of the warehouse's side doors and peeked through one of the fogged-up windows. After a moment he said, "He's walking this way." So Butchie ducked behind something and then ordered us to do the same. I watched everything unfold from behind the rear of the truck on the right side. From there I saw Butchie pull a gun from his backside and ready it just below the window. That's when I noticed a silhouette of a man, or at least an image from his neck up, walk slowly and curiously just outside along the side of the warehouse. Then he turned the corner, and as he did, Butchie followed him from the inside of the warehouse and kept pace. When the guy reached the front entrance, he took a couple of steps forward, cupped his hands to his eyes to make blinders, and looked inside.

It was intense. All this guy had to do was just attempt to lift the door latch from the ground, and he was a goner. To do so he needed a key, and the only place to get one was at the security booth. But he didn't have to. I saw the guy turn in the direction of the security booth, and my heartbeat skipped into a frenzy. Then, with his back to us, we heard a pop and saw blood splatter lightly on the window! We scrambled, Butchie unlocked the door and lifted it open, and there was Mickey, with a pistol resting at his side, and a guard wailing in pain from a gunshot wound in his back. Mickey's eyes were as wide as the craters on the moon. He'd shot the poor guard.

It was apparent the guard had made it a point on that night to check on the warehouse before he reached the outskirts of the yard where the containers were. We were fortunate he'd never checked on his buddy, though, who was likely knocked out cold. Nonetheless, the guy was on the ground, on his front side and bleeding profusely. We were in shock. Then Butchie went for Mickey's gun, took it away from him, and gave him a vicious openhanded slap, knocking him to the ground. In effect, the slap brought Mickey back to earth from his catatonic state.

"If we get out of this OK, I'm going to kill you," Butchie said. "And what are you doing with this piece?"

Mickey couldn't gather himself enough to answer.

I was sick to my stomach. I didn't want anyone hurt, and I felt this guy was sure to stop breathing at any moment.

Then, "Butchie, please," Mickey said in a terrified voice.

But he tuned him out and walked back toward the truck. "The decision's been made; let's go," he called out.

Wally, Connor, and Sammy followed.

"I'll get in the back," Sammy said.

"Mick," I said, "what was that? You were supposed to hang back and just watch. Nothing more. You didn't need to bring the piece."

Mickey stuttered, "I kept calling you…you didn't answer. He was going to ruin everything, Ton'."

"No, he wasn't," I said.

Butchie called out, "Let's go!"

I shook my head in disgust and turned around. I took a couple of steps but stopped abruptly when I realized Mickey hadn't moved a muscle. So I turned around and said, "Mickey, let's go."

He took one step in my direction, and that's when the real nightmare began. The guard he'd shot wasn't dead. I noticed his arm was slightly elevated from his seemingly lifeless position, and he was pointing his pistol in our direction. I heard the gun cock, and I shouted, "Mickey, watch out!"

He turned his head toward the shooter, but it was too late. We heard, *pop!* He was shot in the right side of his chest by the same guy he'd put down.

I rushed to Mickey. He was on his back and gasping for air. Blood was streaming out of his chest like an oil spill from a tanker.

"Mick!" I called to him. But he just stared at me like I was a ghost, and he was shaking, coughing up blood.

Butchie rushed over to the guard with his gun drawn and fired a shot and hit him. While keeping the gun on him he said, "Leave him," but he relented when I gave him a stinging look.

"Get him up, then," he said.

So I did; I put Mickey on my shoulder and got him upright. I could feel the warmth of his blood running down my neck, back, and front side—a feeling I'll never forget it.

The original plan was to have Sammy drive to Phil's garage with Wally and Connor, and Butchie and I would follow in his pickup. Now it changed.

"Bring him to my truck; I'll be there in two minutes," Butchie said. "I need to clean this place so it doesn't attract anyone till morning." Then he turned to Sammy and said, "I need you to take the truck and go to the drop; we'll meet you there later. Don't move from the place."

"Understood," Sammy said.

I took Mickey and essentially dragged him from the warehouse, across the street, and to the truck. We left a trail of blood from the pier to the car. I held him with one arm and opened the passenger door with the other. I placed him inside, and then I got in next to him. I took my mask off and my jacket and applied both to his wound to try to stop the bleeding, but the sucker wouldn't stop. All the while I kept talking to him, telling him everything was going to be OK and to hang in there and so on. And at the same time, we waited for Butchie to come back…and waited.

CHAPTER 27

STAY WITH ME

Finally, after four or five minutes—though it felt more like an hour—Butchie arrived, jumped in the driver's seat, and drove off in a hurry.

I sat in the back seat of the truck with Mickey lying across my lap; he was bleeding profusely. It was everywhere. I could feel my socks getting soaked from the flow of blood leaving his body.

I kept talking to him, saying things like, "Stay with me" and "Everything's going to be all right," but he looked bad—real bad, though I wasn't giving up on him.

Butchie—on the other hand—was focused on the wheel and taking sharp turns and speeding through stop signs and traffic lights until he stopped short on a curb on a side street in Charlestown off Main Street.

"Where are we?" I asked.

"House call," said Butchie.

The resident was an acquaintance of Butchie's. An unlicensed doctor who was always on call for matters such as this, for people who needed urgent care but could not afford to go to a hospital and face questioning regarding why they were hurt in the first place. So, to go undetected, people saw this guy, and a few others just like him around town.

He lived in a brownstone a block over from the Bunker Hill Monument. Butchie bolted out of the car and ran around to my side, opened the door, and helped prop Mickey up on my shoulder.

Staggering under the weight of Mickey, I followed Butchie as fast as I could through a narrow walkway on the right side of the place to a set of large iron-clad double doors leading to a cellar. Butchie gave the window a couple of bangs to get the doc's attention, and just a moment later, the doors were opened. The doc was ready, I gathered, on a tip from Butchie himself prior to the job.

"Jesus," the scrawny, thick-bearded fella said when he saw Mickey and the trail of blood leading from the sidewalk. "Come on down; hurry," he whispered hard.

Butchie and I each had an arm and leg of Mickey's and carried him down the stone staircase, through the dingy basement, and to his work station: a green padded bed raised to waist high, scratched and torn, and stained with blood from his previous appointments. The bed was surrounded by the oldest of fixtures, including a pair of filthy glass cabinets with an array of medical instruments hardly sanitary enough for this type of work in a hospital or a licensed physician's office. But on this night, they would do.

Butchie and I stood and watched the good doctor—who was up to his elbows in blood—attempt a miracle: to stop the bleeding, remove the bullet, stitch him up, and hope for the best. But Mickey had already lost a lot of blood, and he began convulsing and spitting up more of it. Finally, his eyes rolled to the back of his head. His grunts were haunting, and in a flash, I saw the time we'd spent together pass by—seventeen years' worth. Butchie turned to me with a look, an expression, indicating the end was near. He should know; he'd sent plenty to the "hole" himself and had stood over many who took their last breath after he was done with them.

Mickey's shrieks started to dull; his physical body became much less animated. A calm came over him when he tilted his head to his left side and called to me. The doctor backed off, knowing the inevitable was just a moment away. I went to him and grabbed his left hand tight.

"Tony," he said.

"Hang in there, Mick," I said.

But he shook his head. "It's over."

"No!" I said.

"Tony, find my Betty…tell her I love her."

"I will," I told him.

And just like that, the air escaped from his body, and his head returned to a resting position, face up, eyes open. He was still and cold to the touch. And ever so slightly, his grip loosened until he couldn't squeeze any more.

He was gone.

I brought my head forward. I felt Butchie's hand on my left shoulder, and then he gently pulled me away. I stood up, with tears running down my face, as the doctor pulled a sheet over him.

"I'm sorry," the doctor said. "I did everything I could do."

"Can you give us a minute, Doc?" Butchie asked politely.

"Certainly."

So the doctor left the basement and went upstairs, leaving Butchie and me alone with Mickey's body. I was catatonic for a moment until Butchie raised his voice. "Hey!" he said.

I turned to him, lucid and aware.

"I need you right now."

"No," I said.

"What do you mean, no?"

"I mean, no. I'm done. I did my part. What else do you want from me?"

"We still have to go to the shop. They're expecting us."

I just shook my head. "They're expecting you, and Sammy and the others are there. So you go; do what you have to do. I'm going to stay here."

"And do what?"

"I'll figure it out."

I think at that point, Butchie finally understood I'd had enough, and so there was no more resistance from him, and his expression shifted to that of a more compassionate human being.

"OK," he said. "I'll go and handle it from here."

"OK."

He said, "I'm going to head upstairs, get cleaned up, and tell the doc you're down here."

"Thanks."

Then he turned, headed for the stairs, and walked up to the next floor.

In the meantime, I found a chair, pulled it next to Mickey's body, and just sat and reflected for a few minutes. Then the doc came back down, and he also pulled up a chair and sat on the other side of Mickey.

"Would you like a cigarette?" he asked, offering a Lucky Strike out of a pack.

"Yeah," I said. "I'd love one."

So we lit up together.

"A good friend of yours, this guy?" he asked me.

"He was," I said. "He really was."

"I'm very sorry for your loss," said the doc.

"Thank you."

"It looks like you fellas had a hell of a night."

"It was…it was hell."

"I suppose if you ended up here, what other kind of night could it be, right?" he asked.

"Yeah, Doc, I suppose you're right," I said.

"You live around here?" he asked.

"I'm over in East Boston. Born and raised," I said. "Yourself?"

He said, "I grew up on the South Shore."

"I'm sorry to hear that," I said jokingly, and in fact, we both got a chuckle out of it.

"Yeah, I was married, had a practice down in Hingham for a good while, but then I got divorced. The bitch took everything, even the practice, so here I am."

"I'm sorry to hear that."

"It's OK," he said. "I rarely complain because I feel like wherever we are in life, at the end of the day, we chose to be there."

"I couldn't agree with you more, Doc," I said.

"Well, you're more than welcome to stay here for the night, get cleaned up…I have some clothes if you need them."

"Doc, that's a hell of a gesture, and I really appreciate it, but I think what I really need to do is to go home—be with my family."

"It's what every man should do," he said.

"So could I bother you for a big favor?"

"I suppose that's what I'm here for. What do you need?" he asked.

"I'd really appreciate a lift, you know, if you weren't too tired or nothing."

"You've had a difficult evening, and considering what happened here, I think it's the least I could do."

"Thanks again, Doc."

"No problem," he said. "And call me Ray."

"You got it, Ray."

"And you are?" he asked.

"I'm Tony."

We shook hands, and he said, "Let me get my coat."

He got up and left. I reached out and gripped Mickey's forearm, said a quick prayer, and made the sign of the cross.

When Ray came back, I asked, "What will happen now…to Mickey?"

He took a deep breath and said, "I only try to fix them; I never dispose of them. Your friend will be back to take him tonight; what he does with him is anyone's guess."

"I was afraid of that. Can you tell him…just tell him to be good?"

"Of course," he said. "Ready? I don't want to miss him."

"I'm ready."

So we left. I got in his light blue Chrysler, which was parked right in front, and I directed him carefully—even insisted we not go near the waterfront—and took him a roundabout way, essentially from the opposite direction, until we came up on my car. I couldn't see or hear any commotion from our position, which was comforting in a strange sense.

Nonetheless, I said, "Listen, Ray, you'll want to go back exactly the way we came, all right?"

"You bet."

So we shook hands. I thanked him for the ride and got out. That's when I headed back to the club.

It was after two o'clock at that point, and the streets were devoid of any people as far as I could see. I walked to the front, looked both ways, and then unlocked the door and went in.

It was dark; no one was there. I flicked the lights on and walked in. The first thing I did was head upstairs, where I always kept some clothes in case I ever needed to crash there. Such times were few and far between, and it only really happened when I stayed late to close the joint up. I then went back downstairs and into the bathroom, stripped down, grabbed a washcloth, and scrubbed myself as best I could. I put the new clothes on and placed the bloody threads, jacket and all, in a paper grocery bag and rolled it tight.

And that was it.

I shut the lights off, locked up, and went to the car with the bag.

I made it home finally. I went inside with the bag and headed straight for the shower. When I finished, I took my boots and tossed them in the tub and then used the hose to the shower to give them a good cleaning as well. When I got out, I changed, took the bag with me to the bedroom, and ever so quietly, went to the closet, opened the safe, stuffed the bag in, and closed it.

I felt a slight sense of relief.

Though the bedsheets, along with Marie next to me, provided a certain level of comfort I really needed, I didn't sleep a wink. After a couple of hours of lying there, I got up and paced around until I realized how hungry I was. I went to the kitchen, found some leftover pasta in the fridge from the previous night, fixed myself a plate, and then inhaled it. When I finished, I cleaned up and went right back to bed. I finally dozed off for a few hours, until I heard the phone ringing at about six o'clock. I leaped out of bed and answered it. It was Butchie.

"I took care of Mickey," he said. "I put him on the beach in Winthrop, against the wall and facing the water. I figured you'd like that."

"OK."

"You all right?" he asked me.

"Not really, but I'll get through it. Everything go as planned?"

"Yeah. I'll fill you in later."

"OK," I said. "I'll see you in a few."

Then we hung up.

I knew that day was going to be a circus. We'd taken the gold right from under Global's nose—not all of it, but any amount was enough to shake the waterfront to its core that morning. The pier would be flooded with law enforcement within minutes, if not sooner, once either one of those security guards was discovered. So I braced myself, as I knew each and every longshoreman on that day was a suspect in the eyes of the authorities and would undoubtedly face intense questioning.

I needed to be on my game.

CHAPTER 28

THE MORNING AFTER

Marie got up when she heard the phone ring from Butchie's call. I grabbed a pair of jeans hanging off the bed and slid them on and then walked into the kitchen to see Marie scrambling some eggs. She saw me but hardly seemed excited.

I sat down when she said, "How was your night?"

"It was...uneventful," I said. "How was yours? Were the kids good?"

"Well, Isabella was already asleep, and Tony Jr. was quiet, so, yes, they were OK," she said, continuing to scramble the eggs. Then she stopped abruptly, turned around, and asked me point blank if I was having an affair. This I did not need.

"No, Marie, I'm not."

"Are we OK?"

"Yeah, of course we are. We're better than OK. In fact, I will never leave you and the kids alone again—never again."

"You mean that?"

"With all my heart, baby" I told her.

"You never returned my call last night; I was worried sick."

"I fell asleep for a couple of hours upstairs by accident; by the time I woke up, it was too late to call."

"It's never too late," she said.

"Well, luckily, there won't be a next time…I'll be right here, OK? You were right. I gotta stop saying yes all the time."

She breathed a deep sigh and said, "You must be exhausted. Do you really have to go to work?"

"I really do, yeah."

"Is everything going to be OK there? You know, after what you told me about not getting as much work?"

"It is, and everything is going to be fine, except—"

"Except what?" she asked.

"The eggs are burning!"

"Shit!" she said. She spun back around, grabbed the pan, shut the gas off, and took a good look at them. "They're OK, right?"

"They're perfect."

After thirty minutes of sitting, talking pleasantly, and eating, I went back into the bedroom, got fully dressed, and said good-bye to Marie and the kids, who by that time, which was around seven thirty, had gotten out of bed and gotten dressed themselves.

So the morning at the Costa household was like any other. But on the waterfront, it was something else.

As I approached the terminal, I was forced to veer off to the right to let a couple of speeding cop cars pass me, and that's when I knew it was going to be one hell of a day. My attention was grabbed once again, this time by the drone of helicopters flying overhead toward the pier. I continued on, and just a mile ahead was the gate. I proceeded slowly until I arrived in the parking lot. Then I walked to the gate, where Charlie Goodman, a part-timer who worked just a couple of days a month, stood outside shaking and shivering. I knew him pretty well. He'd worked on the waterfront for a couple of years—nice enough guy.

"What's up, Charlie?" I asked him. "What are you doing over here?"

"Good morning, Tony," said Charlie in somber fashion.

"What's all the commotion about?"

"It's quite a mess in there. Someone busted into the warehouse and made off with one of those giant black boxes of gold, I think. The feds, staties, locals—they're everywhere talking to anyone they can get their hands on!"

"Jesus," I said. "You OK, Charlie? What are you doing standing out here?"

"I'm OK, just freezing my balls off," he said. He pointed in the direction of an investigator and continued, "I'm waiting for the knucklehead over there to let me go in. The prick stopped me and started asking me questions."

So I looked over, and as I did, the guy waved us both in.

"Finally!" said Charlie, and we both walked in the yard together.

Most of the commotion was to the left, naturally, by the warehouse where the guard was shot—but there was no guard as far as I could see. The yard was still a zoo, though.

"Must have been some take for all this to happen, huh, Charlie?"

"And how."

From there I said good-bye to him and then merged into the mess of people scrambling around. I looked around in awe, in disbelief. What a spectacle this was, from one end of the pier to the other. There were news trucks and reporters wielding microphones in front of anyone who was willing to talk. This was a big deal. The biggest since the Brink's heist over in the North End over two decades prior. I was anxious, but I knew I needed to keep my composure, to steady myself, to morph into a complete dunce who was walking into mass confusion brought on by God knows what.

I felt terrible. As it had all unfolded the previous night, it had been like a dream, but daylight said otherwise and brought the events to life in a very real way.

Then I saw Freddy Scofield. He was in my gang. I approached him when I saw him finish up a conversation with a state trooper.

"Freddy!" I called to him. "What's the deal over here?"

"The warehouse got robbed last night, and the sons of bitches tried to take out one of the guards while he was patrolling the yard," he said. "They must have been some cowboys to do a night watchman in, I'll tell ya that."

"Try?"

"Yeah, the lucky bastard is still alive over at Mass General," he said.

What a relief, I thought to myself.

"Well, that's good at least," I said. "They got any suspects?"

"No, but one of the trucks over there on that construction site went missing, and they found some of their equipment inside," he said, "and they have a bird's-eye view of the warehouse, ya know?"

"But how the hell would they know if there was gold in there?"

"I have no idea," Freddy said, "but ain't that something? I'll tell ya, whatever they came away with must have been pretty doggone worth it to come in guns blazing."

From where I was standing, I could hardly find a longshoreman who wasn't tied down by an investigator, until I saw Wally loping gingerly with his head down.

"I'll catch you later, Freddy."

"All right," he said.

I caught up with Wally before he disappeared into the mob scene.

"Hey," I called to him. He turned with a big grin. "You good?" I asked.

"I've been better, Ton'," he said. "Mick?"

I shook my head as if to say *he was gone*. Wally's expression turned, and it was telling; his heart was broken.

"What do we do now?" he asked.

"I gotta talk to Butchie. Seen him?"

"He's here, in the hall, probably getting grilled by one of these cops since he knows the most about the shipments."

"OK, I'm going to go see him," I said.

I turned to walk away, but Wally called to me and said, "Hey, Ton'!"

I turned back. "Yeah?"

"Was it worth it?"

But I didn't have an answer, only a blank stare. I halfheartedly shrugged my shoulders, and then I turned back around and kept going, but I supposed my silence spoke volumes and probably clued Wally in to how I felt: I regretted the day I chose to go along with this thing. I always have, in fact.

I was steps from the hall entrance when a guy in a suit extended his arm across my chest like a bar and stopped me. "I don't believe anyone has spoken to you yet," he said. Then he lowered his arm and exposed his badge. "Walter Stamkos, FBI."

"How can I help ya?" I asked him. Then he proceeded to ask me what my name was, occupation, years on the job, where I lived, my telephone number, and so on. He scribbled my answers on his notepad. He was exasperated and tired—that was obvious. Between everyone at the waterfront and the construction site, it was a wonder how they could keep up with all the information given. But he perked up when he asked where I was last night.

"I was at a social club with a few fellas playing cards."

"Can anyone verify you were there?"

I gave him names—Stevie, Patrick, Henry—and the club's phone number. These were all guys who were playing in that card game I'd watched for one hand. Then I gave Wally's and Butchie's names because we had our own game upstairs. There was no need to bring attention to Sammy or Connor by adding their names to an alibi, and Mickey was no longer with us. But it didn't matter, the guys had seen me at the club, and if anyone questioned it, I was going to say I fell asleep upstairs.

He finished writing and said, "Thanks a lot, Anthony," with a deliberate emphasis on my name and a smug look and then walked away.

So I continued to the hall through a cluster of law enforcement agents and longshoremen. I made it, walked in, and there was Butchie, all smiles, with a foot up on a chair while he was speaking to a couple of state troopers—always working his charm no matter who was sitting across from him. Then he saw me.

"Tony, get over here," he said.

I took a walk over, and when the two guys sitting turned to me, I nodded, and they nodded back.

Butchie continued, "Gentlemen, this is Tony."

They remained seated but shook my hand.

"I was just telling the boys here about the card game last night," Butchie said.

It must be nice, I thought, *to not give a flying fuck about Mickey dying just a few hours ago. Just sitting there pretending it was a big party.* I was pissed.

"It was a long one," I replied to him.

Just then the two cops stood up, and the shorter one sighed. "Well, this has been one hell of a morning. It's best we get going," he went on. "We don't want to hold you fellas up any more than we already have."

"Good day, gentlemen," Butchie said.

"Gentlemen," I said, extending my good-bye.

They left, leaving only Butchie and me in the hall.

"It's cool, I know those guys," he said.

"Let's go," I said.

"Where?"

"We need to talk," I said.

CHAPTER 29
THE FULL AFTERMATH

When the smoke cleared and the waterfront was finally operating without law enforcement getting in the way of the flow of business, Butchie and I took a lap together and discussed much of what we needed to regarding what had transpired the night before, what we dealt with in the morning, and what was to likely come.

"You know," he said, "this is a federal matter now. That shit came in from overseas, so it's them guys who we need to worry about."

"I figured as much."

Butchie said, "Anyway, since we grabbed only one chest, our cut was significantly less."

"Naturally."

"So we're lookin' at about 250K each, factoring in Kevin's cut, which I did. After all the bullshit, the drop went down pretty good. Phil even had his guys chopping up the truck while we were there. I'll grab the cash in a couple of days."

"What about Mickey's?" I asked him.

"What about it?"

"I'm sure there's someone out there who he'd like to see have that money, don't you?" I said.

"That's not how this works, Ton'."

"I don't give a shit," I said. "He made a mistake, and it cost him his life, but he did it with the best intention. He did it for us."

"I'll speak to the guys," he said.

"Good."

Conversation over.

It was never a trust issue when it came to Butchie, because if he said someone close to Mickey was going to get his cut, it would happen. He never would have screwed me; I just wish he'd wanted to do the right thing from the get-go.

At 1:00 p.m. that same day, we got word that Mickey's body had been found. Once that happened, the feds could now focus their investigation on the longshoremen.

But, first, a good number of us wanted to grieve, and so we got together and pitched in to pay for all of the funeral expenses. But we didn't know who to give the cash to, not until that night when, after the cops were done collecting evidence from his body, his mother was able to drive down from Maine, view her deceased son, and claim him. And that's who I was going to give Mickey's money to, but not yet. Not until the heat cooled down from the robbery.

Mickey's burial was scheduled for Wednesday, February 5, which was in a couple of days, but it was in Portland, Maine. Nonetheless, about fifty guys from the waterfront made the two-hour trip. Even Butchie came, but he didn't stay long. Marie accompanied me because she knew Mickey very well, and she was heartbroken. So we got the kids ready for school and took the drive up to the cemetery in Portland.

It was sad, but I kept it together. Marie had her moments when she teared up, but all in all, she was OK.

While there, I sought out Mickey's mystery girl, Betty. It was tough trying to match her name to a face when I didn't know a single soul, but to the best of my ability, I tried to visualize the snapshot I'd seen for just a few seconds. I then zeroed in on a woman sitting alone in the back who fit that image in my head, and approached her.

"Your name wouldn't happen to be Betty, would it?"

Surprised, she said, "Why, yes. Do I know you?"

"No," I said, "you don't. But my name is Tony."

"How can I help you, Tony?"

"I knew Mickey well, like a brother," I said. "He spoke very highly of you. In fact, he told me once that he loved you and that one day he was going to marry you."

And that was it. She broke down and cried a river of tears, got up, and hugged me as tightly as anyone could. Her tears triggered mine. It was terrible.

By noontime we were already headed home, and when we got home, I saw a message on the machine and listened to it; it was Butchie asking me to give him a call. So I immediately picked up the phone and dialed; when he answered, I said, "Hey."

"Hey, we're meeting at the club early, about four, can you make it?"

"I can make it," I said, and then he hung up.

I arrived promptly and went right upstairs. Butchie, Wally, Sammy, and Connor were already there, and it appeared the topic of Mickey's cut had come up and the group had overwhelmingly decided to forfeit Mickey's cut to me so that I could deliver it to his mother when the time was right.

"I took a ride to Kevin's bar and gave him his twenty-five, so he's all set," Butchie said. "So, each guy here is walking away with just over $200,000, boys!"

Sammy and Connor reacted cheerfully, but Wally and I could not.

Then he reached down, grabbed a black duffle bag, and emptied nearly 1.25 million dollars on the table. "Let's divide it up," he said.

We each took our share, plus I added Mickey's to mine, but there was another matter Butchie needed to let us know about.

He said, "There's a guy, Billy, down in Southie; he belongs to an Irish gang down there, a real tough crew. I knew him as a kid, not well, but enough to know he's for real."

"So what's this got to do with anything?" I asked.

"Billy heard about the robbery and sent for me…wants to know who took the gold. He also probably wants to know if it's someone he can shake down or not."

"What are you going to say?" Wally asked.

"Not a goddamn thing. No one knows who took it, and it's going to stay that way. And if somehow he ever catches wise that we took it, I'll put him and his whole fuckin' crew in the ground, and no one will ever find them. This cash is ours, and the gold belongs to the guys in the North End, and that's that." He went on, "I kinda got a feeling we'll just shoot the shit about the old days anyway, have a few drinks, and that'll be it."

"When's this meeting taking place?" I asked.

"Tomorrow night."

"You be careful," I said.

"I'll be fine," he said.

Sammy asked, "You want me to come?"

"No, guys, it's fine," he said. "Don't get carried away—it's just a meeting between old acquaintances. But it just goes to show you how big this thing really was, ya know? It's been on the news every night since; we're like fuckin' celebrities, for Christ's sake."

I said, "That's not what we're going for, Butchie."

"I know that," he said. "I was just pointing it out." Then, very agitatedly, he asked everyone, "We good?"

And we were. So we all shook hands, said good-bye, and left, but separately.

When I walked out of the club, I remember thinking I was going to get thrown to the ground and cuffed on the spot, but in hindsight, it was sheer paranoia on my part.

I got home and stashed all the dough in my safe. Then I remembered the bag of bloody clothes was still in there. Luckily, though, Marie was out and the kids were in school, so I took the bag to the parlor and tossed them in the fireplace with a couple of logs. Five minutes in the flames, and they were well done.

Problem solved.

Now I had over $400,000 in a safe, and perhaps I'd have to explain how I got it to someone in the event the house got raided. Plus, I knew half that money was going to Mickey's mother up in Portland eventually, and the rest I could say I'd been saving over the course of twenty years or so—not likely—but only I would know the truth.

The real dummies were at Global because they were simply too lax and should have had more security on the warehouse. I can only assume they thought that once the gates were closed and the warehouse was locked up, there would be no problem. But they underestimated our ability to go around our own security.

Stupid.

However, it was in my moment of solitude that afternoon when it finally hit me. Had I never asked Mickey to join the crew, he'd still be alive. The feeling of guilt that washed over me was overwhelming, not to mention well deserved. And so I broke down as I sat on the edge of my bed. No one was home; it was just me, alone with my thoughts, and they were tearing through me, and I couldn't stop them. I only composed myself when I heard the front door open. It was Marie, so I got myself together and appeared natural, but on the inside, I was imploding.

It was Friday morning, February 7, 1975. The waterfront was quiet; in fact, there were no ships. Still, there was an eerie silence spreading across the docks that morning. Something was up.

So I took a walk to the hiring hall to check out the mood, and the mood was a downer. I saw only a few guys, four to be exact, sitting at a round table with their heads in their hands. One of them, this guy Dennis, lifted his head when he heard me approach, and right away he said he was sorry, as if someone had died.

"Denny, what's wrong?" I asked him.

He stood up straight and said, "You don't know?"

"Know what?"

"They found Butchie."

"Who found him? Found him where?"

My mind was all over the place, but I was set straight when Dennis said, "He's dead. Butchie. They found him wrapped up in a Dumpster in Southie."

I sat down. I was completely mystified and had no words to say. Dennis sat down with me, but after a few moments, I had to ask him, "What happened?"

"I don't know, Ton', but whoever did it...they worked him over pretty good."

I was stunned—completely dumbfounded and speechless. I didn't know what to do or say. Everyone on the waterfront knew how close we'd been. I mean, we'd had our ups and downs, but I'd loved the guy. He was my closest friend, and he was now gone, too.

There's no way to really prepare for something like that. Two friends, in less than a week, dead, murdered—and in brutal fashion.

So I went home, told Marie and sobbed on her shoulder. She was shocked, of course, but then she began asking questions and wanted to know if I was in trouble. As far as I knew, I wasn't. So that's what I told her. But, boy, it was tough. Coping with Mickey's and Butchie's deaths concurrently was just miserable.

To make matters worse, we got a knock at the door. Lo and behold, it was a couple of federal agents reminding me of what had happened to Butchie and extending their false condolences at the same time.

The fact was, the deaths of both Mickey and Butchie made it easier for investigators to connect some dots, so it made sense that some suspicion was headed my way. They accused me of being involved, but I denied it, of course. Still, though, they had nothing. Unless the other guys did something stupid like buy a Rolls Royce or a twenty-karat diamond ring, I felt I was pretty safe.

The investigators never asked to come in, but when they left, it was with a parting message: "I would watch your back if I were you."

CHAPTER 30

THE SHADOW

Life went on.

I kept in close contact with Connor, Wally, and Sammy to see if they experienced anything alarming or out of the ordinary, but there was nothing. Perhaps a good sign, but I could never be too sure.

In the meantime I felt it was safe enough to take the drive to Portland, Maine, and pay Mickey's mother a visit.

She was a sweet old woman who was deeply saddened by the death of her son. We spoke for a couple of hours, and most of the time we were trading stories of what a good guy he was. When we finished speaking, I went out to my car and grabbed the money that I'd placed in a black duffle bag.

I handed it to her and said, "This belongs to you."

"What is it?" she asked. "Something from Mickey?"

"Yes," I said, and then I unzipped it and showed her the contents. "He was saving it for quite a while, and I think he would have wanted you to have it."

She teared up, got a closer look in the bag, and then looked at me and said, "Thank you." She embraced me tightly, and when she let go, we said our good-byes.

I never saw her again.

On April 23, 1975, it was time to deliver my son's birthday wish.

I was coming home from work, and as my car came to a full stop in front of my house, I saw my son's face in the window, with a smile from ear to ear. His Red Sox cap was pulled down over his eyes, and his MacGregor 2000 baseball glove was dangling from his fingers. My son's big hazel eyes gleamed with excitement; he gave me a huge gap-toothed smile, as that night we would visit Fenway Park for the first time together to watch the Sox take on the dreaded New York Yankees.

I turned the key and shut the car off, and no sooner did my left foot hit the pavement than my son was past the front door and jetting down the stairs. I removed myself from the car just in time to catch my leaping son in my arms and squeeze him tight.

"Dad!" he shouted.

"Are you ready for tonight's game?" I said.

"Yup," he said with a pronounced nod and a smile that hadn't quit.

I set him down on the sidewalk.

"Come on. Let's go say good-bye to your mother before we go."

"OK!" he thundered excitedly.

He scurried back up the stairs and into the house. I followed gingerly, and when I made it past the front door, I heard Marie giving last-minute instructions to Tony Jr. "Don't leave your father's sight," she said. "Be good, not too much candy, OK?"

"I promise, only three trips to the food stand," I said, grinning.

"Very funny," Marie responded.

On the way to the park, I frequently glanced over to Tony Jr. in the passenger seat, only to see the same grin I'd seen when I pulled up to the house just a few moments earlier. I remember feeling so much joy witnessing my son so happy to see his favorite player, Fred Lynn, in action, in person. But I couldn't share his excitement, not on the inside, because my mind was elsewhere—on the bullshit I had been dealing with the last couple of months or so. I thought to myself, though, *This is the greatest day of his life. To be able to deliver this much happiness to my own little boy—nothing beats this, nothing. And the night has only just begun.*

It was roughly ten minutes to game time. Tony Jr. was getting antsy in his seat to my right, watching the centerfield clock tick down to the first pitch. So I asked him, "Want a hot dog?"

"Yeah!" he shouted.

We sat in the middle of the row in section thirty-three. The seats were great, and rather than getting up and making people move, I decided to flag down a vendor who was walking up. Furthermore, waving down a vendor at Fenway, which can be a fun spectacle at times, was a part of the experience I wanted my son to enjoy.

"Hot dogs!" the young man wildly shouted to the crowd. I raised my hand and caught his attention.

"How many?" the kid asked. I put up the two-finger sign, so he grabbed a pair of dogs and chucked them at us one at a time. I caught them both, much to my son's delight.

"Two dollars!" he shouted.

I reached in my pocket, grabbed a couple of bucks, and handed them to the guy flanked to my left; he continued the money train until the last person in the row closest to the vendor handed him the dough.

The Sox were up big when we hit the seventh-inning stretch. That's when I decided to give Marie a call to check in, so me and the little guy got up, I took him by the hand, and we sidestepped past eight or so fans who were already standing. We took a left down the stairs and then a right hook down the tunnel. Straight ahead was a pay phone.

I picked up the receiver, dropped a dime in the slot, and dialed with the same hand, while I held on to Tony Jr. with my other. The place was teeming with fans, so I didn't want to chance having him disappear into the crowd; plus, I wanted him to speak to his mother.

A couple of rings and Marie answered, "Hello?"

"Hey," I said. "It's me."

"Hey!" she said. "Are you guys having a good time?"

"We're having a blast," I told her, "and he's still wide awake, so I think we're going to stick it out till the end."

"Wow, OK," she responded. "I thought he'd be fading by this time. Is he next to you?"

"Yeah, I'll put him on."

"OK," she said.

I handed Tony Jr. the phone, and I heard him saying things like, "Yeah!" and "He got a hit!" I began to zone out and just watched the crowd maneuver about the tunnel as the game was about to resume. I was brought back by the phone tapping my thigh. I took it back from my son.

"OK," I said to Marie, "the inning is about to start up again, so we're going to head back to our seats. I'll call you before we leave."

"OK," she said. "I'll be up."

We hung up the phone.

Though a mere twenty minutes had gone by since we called Marie, Tony Jr. was beginning to fade. The little guy was exhausted and slumped over, with his right cheek resting on my left arm. I reached across and nudged him back to consciousness and asked, "Want to get going?"

He nodded with his eyes half shut.

"OK," I said. "Let's go and beat the crowd."

Once we made it past the row, this time I needed to carry him, so I hoisted him up and again walked to the pay phone. Keeping him snug, I dialed home again, but this time it rang and rang...no answer. I hung up, put the dime in again, and dialed. It was the same result. Perplexed, I thought, *She must have dozed off.*

So I headed for the gate.

Tony Jr. was drooping over against the passenger door and passed out, while I wasn't far behind. It had been a long day between work and the game, and now we were nearly home at the late hour of 10:30 p.m.

I felt relief when I turned left onto my street and headed up the hill. When we approached my house, I noticed there were no lights on inside, and it reinforced the notion for me that Marie had fallen asleep.

I turned left into my driveway and saw that the garage door was closed. I was too tired to open it, so I slowly rolled the car up to within a foot of it. I turned the car off, and that's when I saw the shadowy figure move quickly from the back and toward the car. It took about a second for my tired eyes to focus, and when they did, I knew this was all wrong. Before I could react, this person was standing just outside my door and pointing a gun at me, and then *Pop! Pop! Pop!* More shots were fired, and I threw myself over Tony Jr. I was hit, that much I knew from the pain I felt and the blood that rushed out of my body, but what about my boy?

My senses were shocked back into action, kicking my adrenaline on high gear. In the background I heard a car screech away, so I had to assume the worst was over. I uncovered Tony Jr. and began shaking him, but he was unresponsive. I was frantically calling out his name. "Tony! Tony! Stay with me!"

It seemed like forever, but finally I managed to open his door and take him beneath my arms. I slipped him out his side and placed him gently on the front lawn. I ripped his shirt open to find a wound in his abdomen, so I turned him over and noticed an exit wound as well in his lower back.

I started to feel light-headed, but I was fighting it. Marie stormed out of the house in hysterics, and after what seemed like several minutes, an ambulance came to a halt in front of my house. I saw the paramedics approach, but the memory of what they looked like has been lost. I looked at the first responder and said, "Please, help my boy." And then it all went black.

I awoke to a bright haze and blurred figures moving about. I was incapacitated both physically and emotionally and had no idea why I was where I was.

This is a nightmare, I thought. *I will wake up.*

And then I knew where I was. I was draped by more than one layer of white linen, with multiple IVs lodged in my veins and an oxygen mask securely fastened to the front of my face. I could hear the mutters of physicians and nurses in close proximity. I was in a hospital, in a bed, but I was awake, which was a good thing.

A doctor appeared, hovering over me and waving a pencil-like flashlight across my eyes. I responded to the rays, and he said, "Mr. Costa."

I nodded.

"Do you know why you're here?" he asked.

I nodded again.

I was propped up and in pain, but I was awake enough to know my wife was sitting by my bedside to my right, but she was stiff and tearful when she locked eyes with me.

Weakly and hoarsely I croaked, "Marie…Tony Jr.?"

"We still don't know," she said, wiping tears away.

My eyes filled up enough to drop a few tears down my cheeks. Just then the doctor walked in and closed the curtain, leaving the three of us alone.

"Mr. Costa, Mrs. Costa," he said. "My name is Dr. Erickson—"

I cut in. "How is my son?"

"He's in ICU at the moment," he replied. "His wounds are extensive, but the bullets, where they entered and exited, missed his vital organs; however, he did lose a lot of blood. The surgery went well, but at this time, we just don't know."

Marie and I exchanged a look, and by expression, I could tell she already knew how serious our son's condition was.

"As for you," he said, "I expect a full recovery. You were hit three times, but lucky for you, the bullets were from a .22-caliber handgun and traveled through a window and into your back. One did come close to your spinal cord, but we were able to extract it without any permanent damage left behind. The other two bullets were extracted also, leaving, well, almost superficial wounds, but with some swelling. Once that goes down and the pain subsides, you can go when I check you out one last time."

"How long?" I asked.

"I'd say four, maybe five days," he said.

"OK."

I healed quickly, and on that fourth day, the doctor discharged me on paper, but as far as me leaving the hospital, I couldn't. I needed to be there for my son.

He was unconscious and hooked up to a mass of technological devices monitoring his vitals. I was at his bedside and holding his hand and praying. I was also apologizing incessantly, but telling him everything was going to be all right.

I thought to myself that whatever happened, I couldn't escape the fact that something I'd done in the past had come back to haunt me, and now my son was paying for it. This wasn't a robbery, as nothing was taken from my person or the car. This was a hit, and I was going to assume the shooter had no idea when I pulled in that my son was with me, as he was beneath the line of sight and sleeping.

Marie joined me. She put a hand on my shoulder and said with a shaky voice, "Let's go and talk."

I kissed Tony Jr.'s hand before I stood and walked out with Marie. I followed her into what looked like a private conference room for doctor-patient discussions.

As soon as we got into the room and shut the door, she said, "I'm taking Isabella, and we're going to stay with my parents for a couple of days. Then I want you to pack up your stuff and go. I'm leaving you."

CHAPTER 31

DEAD BY MONDAY

Friday, May 30, Tony Jr. was still in a coma fighting for his life. I'd been living apart from Marie and Isabella for about a month at that point, in a little hole-in-the-wall on the top floor of a three-story building in the North End. It was the middle of the afternoon, and I was stretched out on my sofa, daydreaming about the pain I would soon inflict on the person or persons responsible for my son's condition when I heard a knock at the front door. I got up from my relaxed position and went to the door. Before I opened it, I carefully looked through the peephole to catch a look at my visitor; I learned it was a familiar face and a friend—Joey Federico, all dressed up in a suit and tie.

I didn't hesitate in letting him in.

"Joey," I said.

"Tony."

"Please, come on in."

Still cautious, I took one last peek outside to see if anyone suspicious was lurking. No one was, so I closed the door and bolted it.

"Make yourself at home," I told him.

And he did. He sat on the sofa, leaning forward with his hands folded, elbows on his knees.

Joey said, "I went to see you in Eastie, but your wife told me you were here. I'm sorry; I had no idea."

"Forget about it, Joey," I said. "These things happen, ya know?"

"I do," he said.

"So it's great to see you. Can I get you anything?" I asked. "Some coffee, juice?"

"No," he said. "No, thank you. I can't stay long; I'm working."

"Working, huh? What are you, undercover or something?"

"Detective, actually," said Joey.

"I see. Well, congratulations."

"Thanks, Tony," he said. "You know, it never would have happened if it weren't for you—"

Abruptly I said, "Joey. What brings you here? Because I know it wasn't to thank me for that. Is it about my son? Do you know something I don't?"

"No, Tony, it's nothing like that," he said. "Not per se. How is the little guy holding up?"

"We're praying, Joey, so it's in God's hands now."

"I have been praying for him as well," he said.

"Thank you," I responded. "So?"

"I'm here as your friend, Tony. I need to explain a few things to you and ask you a couple of questions as I go."

"Go ahead."

"First of all, the guys who we think murdered your friend Butchie...only one of them is responsible for the attempt on you and your boy."

I said, "So it was that Billy and his gang, huh?"

"In a sense, but that's not the whole story."

"I'm all ears, then," I said.

"How well do you know a guy named James O'Donnell? He's from Dorchester."

I thought for a few seconds and then shook my head. "Doesn't ring a bell."

"What about John Reed...I believe he went by JR?"

"JR?" I said. "There was a JR that Butchie was tight with, but that was a lot of years ago. I couldn't tell ya if the guy was alive or dead to be honest."

"He was found dead yesterday, brutally murdered, much like the way your friend was. We felt there was a connection and believe the person responsible is James O'Donnell, or Jimmy, as his friends call him." Joey took a second to continue, and so I became more eager to hear what he had to say next. "It was an act of revenge."

"Revenge?" I said bewildered. "Over what?"

"This guy claims that many years ago, JR put a hit out on his brother over a bad debt, and that you and your friend Butchie carried it out right on the pier."

"Jesus Christ." This time I shook my head, but in disbelief.

"So you know him?" Joey asked, observing my reaction.

"He's the brother, huh? The one Butchie said was on the chopping block, but he was put away."

"Then you do know him?"

"Joey, you gotta believe me; I never killed anybody. I was in the wrong fuckin' place at the wrong fuckin' time. This guy got it all wrong."

"Tony, listen," he said. "I believe you, but it's not me you need to convince; it's him. Because over a wiretap we heard him say, basically, 'Two are down, but there's one more to go'—and that's you."

"How did he even know?"

"Because they tortured that poor JR until he spilled his guts, and whatever he said, it doesn't matter, because he threw your name into the mix. Your friend must have told him how it went down the day his brother was murdered."

"So now what?" I asked. "You got a wiretap on him, so you're investigating him, right? That means you're bringing him in?"

"Not yet, not for anything serious. These things take time, years even," he said. "Which makes me nervous that he may, at some point, come back and try and finish the job."

"Not if I get to him first."

"Tony, this guy is no joke. He waited nearly twenty years to catch up with you guys, and in his sick mind, he feels he did you a favor by blasting up your car and not putting you through hours of torture like he did the other two."

"But I *am* being tortured, Joey. My son is lying in a hospital bed being kept alive by machines. He can't talk. He can't hear. He can't feel. He can't eat or sleep without all the wires connected to him. That's my torture. But I'm not gonna lie, 'cause you know what? To some degree I am relieved."

"What are you talking about?"

"Because I'm no longer looking over my shoulder. I'm the one who's going on the fuckin' hunt, and when I find him, I'm going to kill him."

"I would advise against it."

"Joey," I said. "Are you for real? What did you think I would do with this information? I have nothing right now, you know that? My wife ain't talking to me, and she took my daughter. My son is fighting for every breath. So you better believe it, I'm going to do this fuckin' guy in! I mean, why else would you tell me this shit?"

"In case the guy made another move on you, you'd be prepared."

"I'm sorry, Joey," I said. "I appreciate that—I really do. But I'm just done. I can't do this anymore. It's like one thing after another, so I gotta end it."

And that was not the waterfront talking, it was me and the way I was raised. You gotta protect your family, and at all costs.

"You can try to stop me," I said. "But it won't matter."

"I'm not going to do that, Tony, you know that. But I will try to reason with you, and I will pray for you."

"Don't pray for me; pray for him…and I would start now, because right now I want to know where to find this cocksucker."

"Think of the consequences, Tony," he said. "What if you get caught? Or, what if you succeed in killing this guy and his crew comes after you?"

I said, "Then I'll hunt them down, too, one by one, until there's no one left. Now tell me where to find this guy."

"You're talking like a crazy person," Tony.

"I'm just a father ready to take revenge on the one who hurt my son," I said. "Where is he, Joey?"

Just then he stood up, took a long pause with his hands in his pockets then said, "I suppose even if I don't tell you here, today, you're going to find out anyway."

"That's right; I will."

"He's at eighty-four Mead over in Charlestown. He lives alone, but you won't find him there."

"Why not?"

"He's been detained on assault and battery charges… from slapping his girlfriend around, but he'll be out by the end of the week, but on house arrest until…well, I guess it doesn't matter now."

"House arrest, huh?" I asked.

"That's right."

That was all I needed to know. I then got up and walked Joey to the door. I opened it, and before he went through, he said, "Listen, Tony, whatever you do—"

"Yeah?"

"Don't miss. You only get one shot at things like this."
"I don't plan to."
"I figured as much," he said. "Be seeing ya."
"Take care, Joey."

I had one piece: a Smith & Wesson model 19 .357 Magnum. I darted to the bedroom closet where I kept her in a shoe box. I separated a rack of clothes, knelt down, and there it was. I opened the box and held it in my hand, grabbed a clip, popped it in, and aimed it. This was all I needed. I then put the gun in my belt, closed the box up, put it back on the floor of the closet, and went back and sat on the couch. I began to think about how I was going to attack him.

I was going to do this alone. No one else. I was mentally and physically exhausted from dealing with others in trying to plan anything. I wanted no more of it. I never wanted to be in that predicament. I was done. But this had to happen. There was no stopping me. No person, no cop or priest, not even a bullet was going to stop me.

I sat and thought up the plan right then and there. For hours I barely moved until dusk became night, and I settled into bed. I came up with little except the vision seeing the guy dead.

I was too revved up. That was the problem that night after seeing Joey, but I calmed down eventually, as I knew I had a few days of peace and planning.

In the meantime, I was there for my son. I was at his bedside day and night holding his hand while Marie read him stories. The more I was there, the more Marie began to relax her animosity—to the point where we spoke a lot about me moving back in and repairing our marriage.

It was nice. Over the course of a couple of weeks, I got a taste of what life was like before the incident: I slept over a few times and helped get my daughter ready for camp, because school, at that point had just ended for the year. But it was all overshadowed by my son's condition, which had not worsened but had not changed for the better either. The doctors explained that every day he remained in a coma, it was less likely he'd make it out alive.

It was wearing thin on Marie. She lost weight, and when she wasn't at the hospital, she was home lying down and clutching a photo of our son from his third birthday party.

I stayed strong for Marie and Isabella when I saw them, but I had my moments in private when I broke down.

Still, I knew that killing Jimmy wasn't going to improve my son's health, and it wouldn't repair my marriage or cause me any fewer tears…or would it?

I'd find out soon enough.

CHAPTER 32

REVENGE

Thursday, July 3, 1975.

I cased Jimmy's place in Charlestown for a couple of hours; I drove around the block a few times and carefully watched the neighborhood to determine where I was going to park and where I'd enter the apartment. I devised a plan in my head while there, and so I went home.

My eyes were dead that day, Friday, on the Fourth of July. So much anger had filled my heart, but so did the guilt, because I knew wholeheartedly that the decisions I had made in my life had led to my son's suffering.

Now, contrary to those in most occupations, longshoremen worked on Independence Day like it was any other day. The only holidays we got a break from were Labor Day and

Christmas Day. On Christmas Eve we were allowed to go home at 2:00 p.m.

Unfortunately for partygoers, the weather was to start out a perfect day—sunny and dry—with heavy rain to follow late in the afternoon. So the streets were packed with people heading to some sort of celebration or just enjoying the outside air and waiting for the fireworks to go off at the Esplanade in Boston, on the Charles River—a longstanding tradition that I hope will never die.

I was scheduled to work, and that was a good thing, because that was going to put me on the time sheet from 8:00 a.m. to 5:00 p.m. on a ship as an upman.

I no longer got the cushy jobs like counting shipments and pallets and whatnot. Those days were long gone, but truth be told, I didn't give a shit, because I loved the guys I worked with, and if I was on the ship all day sweating my nuts off, at least that time of year, then that was quite OK by me.

That day began like any other since the attempt on my life, except for one thing: I was home in Eastie, not at the North End apartment.

I awoke at around six o'clock, and alone, as Marie had spent the night by my son's bedside at the hospital, while Isabella was staying at Marie's parents' place for a few days.

I gave the hospital a call before anything to receive an update on Tony Jr.'s condition—no change. I made some coffee but took just a few sips and tossed the rest out. I showered and got dressed. I left the house and went straight to the hospital.

No surprises. I saw Marie sitting asleep in a chair, leaning to her left and propped up by her left hand balled in a fist. I approached quietly and sat next to her, held her hand, and watched her eyes flutter to an open position.

"Hey," I said, "do you need anything?"

"No, I'm fine."

"Doctors say anything?"

"The usual."

"He's a fighter, Marie," I said. "Don't ever give up."

"I will never give up on our son."

"Good."

I paused, and in a matter of a few seconds, Marie dozed off. Then I sat for the better part of an hour, interrupted only by the routine checks by the nurses.

At 7:45 a.m., I shook Marie gently to let her know I was heading to the pier and that I'd be back later. I stood up, bent over my son, and kissed him on his forehead.

As soon as I left, my thoughts shifted gears in an instant from sorrow to rage.

I arrived down at the docks about twenty minutes later, ready to begin the first step in my plan.

Work. Be seen. Be natural.

And so it went. Four hours of unlashing. During this time, many of the guys were asking me how my son was; they gave support and offered to kill whoever was responsible, naturally. It was nice to hear, and thoughtful, but not needed.

At around one thirty, I hit the hiring hall to grab a coffee.

"You staying here all day, Tony?" a guy named Georgie Banks asked me.

"Yeah, sure am," I said to him.

After thirty minutes or so, I cut the break short and headed back to the ship. Then, at five o'clock, I made my move.

Jimmy's apartment sat on the corner of Main and Mead in Charlestown, which both wrapped around Edwards Playground. This meant I could enter Jimmy's back door via the field by hopping a fence and making myself at home.

Simple.

I parked on Mead. I had resident stickers that were given to me by Uncle Dom a while ago that could be used in neighborhoods all over the city. So I placed one on the windshield for the purpose of blending in and deflecting any unwanted attention. As well, I screwed in a fake plate my friend had made for me while he spent time in the can.

There were a lot of eyes on me that day, because the neighborhood was packed with people, but they were preoccupied with having a good time in the streets, boozing, lighting off firecrackers, and tossing them in the streets.

Between a pair of apartments lay a path to a fence, which served as a barrier between the residences and the playground. I got out of the car, walked through a sea of drunken idiots, and took it. Then I walked through a three-foot slit in the iron and hung a right. Jimmy's place was roughly twenty feet away. With my gun drawn, I hugged the fence while the rain began to pick up. With each step my heart rate quickened. Then I came upon it. I placed the gun in my belt and hoisted myself up and over the fence.

The yard was small and unkempt, with a shitty-looking picnic table, some matching chairs, and weeds protruding from every crack in his cement walkway, which led directly to Mead Street.

I approached the back door cautiously, wading through the puddles. I gripped the gun with two hands and placed my ear to the door; it was quiet as a grave inside at first, and then I heard something. There were voices, but judging by the distinctive speech patterns, I believed they were coming from a television. I followed the chatter to the left of the door alongside the back to a window. I peeked in. I was right. A TV was on, and sitting across from it was a person, but I wasn't sure who, as the back was turned to me. I didn't give a shit; I was going in.

I moved back less cautiously and checked the door handle; it was locked. So I readied myself with an eye to busting in, with one boot to the cheap, cruddy wooden door. I positioned myself and then brought the force of my right leg and steel-toe boot through the door, cracking its hinges and swinging it open. I pushed forward to the person watching. When I got a look at him, I could not believe my goddamn eyes.

"What the fuck are you doing here?" I said to Jake O'Sullivan, my union leader, as I pointed the pistol directly at his forehead. His eyes were wide as craters, staring down the barrel of my gun.

"You shouldn't be here, kid."

"Well, there's not much we can do about that now, is there? Where is he?" I asked.

He said, "He's not here."

"You put him up to all of this? Did you set up Butchie?"

"Butchie was a foolish thug who thought he could do whatever he wanted and get away with it. He wasn't so lucky after all, huh?"

"You know what, Jake?" I asked him. "It looks like I'm the lucky one today, because I can take care of both of youse at once."

Then he started to cower.

"You know I had nothing to do with your son; that was all him."

"That may be," I said, "but someone gave him my address, and seeing as how you're sitting here in his place like you own the joint, I'm going to guess that person was you. Now…where is he?"

"You'll never get away with this," he went on. "People will talk. You'll get made before the sun comes up tomorrow."

"At least I'll have a tomorrow."

Till that point Jake hadn't moved a muscle aside from the ones controlling his big mouth. But that changed. I saw his right arm twitch He had a gun nearby; I could sense it. So I cocked mine.

"Don't do it," I said. "I'll put two in your forehead before you get it past your side."

So he changed his mind and retreated, and he changed his demeanor as well. Suddenly, he grew a set of balls.

"That's what I thought," Jake said. "No guts."

"Quiet."

"You need a reason to kill me? Well, I'll give you one. You're right, I'm the one who told him how to find you, and I'm glad, the way everything turned out. I always knew you were soft."

"Watch it, Jake," I told him.

"You know something?" he said. "Fuck you and your son."

And that was it. He went for his gun, and I squeezed the trigger. Two pops! One in his chest by his heart and one between his eyes. He was dead.

I heard a toilet flush and a door open from upstairs. The other scumbag had been taking a shit that whole time. I hid in a spot behind an extended wall that essentially separated two rooms: a small dining room with a table, but no chairs, and a floor covered in papers and all kinds of crap. The other room was where Jake lay dead.

Jimmy came down the stairs and said, "Hey, what the fuck was..." and then he caught sight of Jake and his lifeless body. Jimmy ran over to Jake and then took out a gun that was tucked between his jeans and white T-shirt.

He got up closer to Jake, and when he came into my view, I crept up behind him and fired off a round, but because there was so much shit on the floor, I must have stepped on something that alerted him to my presence. He turned just enough so that the bullet hit the left side of his chest, close to his shoulder. His momentum, though, took him a few feet and out of my line of sight.

We played a cat-and-mouse game for about a minute or so, until I followed the blood trail into the kitchen, where I saw him sitting upright on the floor in the corner, bleeding badly from his open wound.

I'd hit him better than I'd thought, because the blood was running out of his body like a river overflowing. His breath was hard, but his gun was still resting in his right palm, so I kept mine on him.

But his face—it was like I was seeing a ghost. I could see his brother's reflection, the one Butchie had murdered all those years ago. The one I'd helped hide between two pallets in the hole of the ship. It was haunting.

"Let go of the gun," I said.

And he did. So I walked to him, knelt down, placed my boot on the gun, and then grabbed it and backed up, all while keeping my barrel aimed at his good eye.

"Do you know who I am?" I asked him.

He nodded.

"I didn't kill your brother," I said.

He just looked at me. No response. No change in expression.

"But you forced my hand when you shot my son."

Then the crazy prick started laughing.

"This is all funny to you, huh?"

He continued to hoot and then shook his head and said, "I don't even care," and laughed some more. As he repeatedly coughed up blood, he said, "He was a fuckin' asshole anyway," and he coughed some more.

"So all this was for nothing?"

"Nothing?" he said. "It's never for nothing. Your buddy, that fuckin' piece of shit..."

"Butchie?"

He nodded and said, "I had the money for my brother, I told him, but he killed him anyway."

"He had no choice," I said.

He took a deep breath and said, "We always have a choice."

"It still had nothing to do with me."

"Tell that to the judge." He laughed again. And after a few hard breaths, he asked me, "Aren't you going to kill me now?"

"Yes."

"What are you waiting for then?"

We were all part of the same great game at that point. I was just like him, a killer, at least on that day. I wasn't proud of it, but that was the stone-cold truth. Jimmy had said we all have a choice, and he was right. I chose to be who I was. I chose to do the things I did. It wasn't the waterfront that made the choices for me; it was me. I chose it all and chose wrong many times. At that moment I chose to not finish him, but it didn't matter, because his eyes began to flutter, so I lowered my gun. He choked and choked until he lay motionless in the same position I'd found him in. He was dead. It was over.

I took a moment to look around at the mess I had created. No regrets.

I made for the back door but looked through its window first to see if anyone was out there. It was clear. I hopped the fence and went back the way I'd come, sweat-stained cap tilted, head down, and walked to my car under buckets of rain and through a sea of disorderly people paying no mind to the weather or my existence. Everyone in the crowd was messed up on booze, drugs, you name it. I could have been Jesus Christ, and they wouldn't have noticed.

I drove back to my home in Eastie, where I showered, changed, and replaced the license plate. I got in the car and headed back into town to see my kid.

On the way I stopped on the Chelsea Street Bridge and tossed the gun over the side. The gun was untraceable, but it could still be linked to the shell casings, so I heaved it in the drink.

It was just after seven o'clock when I arrived at the hospital, and the scene in front of me appeared as if I had never left. My wife was at the bedside, watching my son, and so I took my normal seat in the room.

"Any news from the doctor?" I asked.

She shook her head in frustration, while maintaining her gaze on my son.

"How was your day?" she asked.

"It wasn't too bad."

"You should get some rest; you look exhausted," she said.

"Yeah."

So I lay back a bit, as much as I could, and dozed off soon after.

I awoke to mayhem. When I focused my eyes, I saw nurses buzzing in and out, but it was my wife who caught my attention. She was smiling for the first time in weeks. When I caught sight of my son, I knew why. His eyes were open, and he was nodding and shaking his head as the doctor asked him questions.

My boy was back. Marie offered a look of pure joy as the tears rolled down her cheeks. I couldn't have been happier and teared up myself. The moment was surreal. After all he'd gone through, he was going to make it.

After several minutes the room cleared out, leaving just the three of us to a private moment.

I asked Marie, "What now?"

"We go home," she said, "and become a family again."

I went home a couple of hours afterward and took up a spot in my bed. Despite the overwhelming joy I felt after seeing my kid's eyes open for the first time in months, I was still making peace with what I'd done just hours prior. Naively I had predicted a good night's sleep after I carried out my revenge, but I was wrong. It was anything but on that first night and every night thereafter, with a few exceptions along the way.

Though I had no regrets about my revenge or the manner in which I exacted it, I only wished I had never put myself or my family in that position in the first place. So I vowed never to do it again if I could help it.

CHAPTER 33
TIME TO PLAY BALL

I went to work on Monday, and once again, the cops in suits paid the waterfront a visit. They first spoke to the business agent, then the new stevedore, and then checked the time logs, I was told. I was on a ship when a friend of mine, Pauly, came on board and told me, "A couple of fellas with the badges are on the pier waiting to speak to ya, but I told them you weren't here, and I think they believed me. Just giving you the heads-up."

"It's OK, Pauly," I told him. "I'll take care of it, and thank you."

I came off the ship a couple of minutes later, and it seemed they were still waiting for me.

Right on the dock I approached them with a smile and said, "Good afternoon, gentlemen. Sorry about that; my friend didn't know I was still on the ship."

"Good afternoon," a short, bald, stuffy-toned guy said. "Tony Costa?"

"That's me. How can I help you?"

"I'm Detective O'Malley, and this is Detective Brady." He went on, "Mind if we ask you a couple of questions?"

"Not at all; shoot."

O'Malley began by asking me direct questions regarding the nature of my relationship with Jake O'Sullivan.

"He's my union president, but I don't see him too much." I said.

O'Malley continued, "And where were you on the evening of the Fourth between the hours of five thirty and eight thirty?"

"I was working down here until five o'clock or so and then headed straight for the hospital to see my son. You can ask my wife if you want."

"We may. Did you happen to make any stops along the way? "O'Malley asked.

"No."

"The reason we're here," O'Malley stated, "is that we found two bodies early this morning belonging to Jake O'Sullivan and a fella named Jimmy O'Donnell. They were murdered—did you know that?"

"Jesus, that's terrible," I said. "No, of course not, I'm just hearing this now."

"Really?"

"That's right, Detective."

The two cops exchanged a look, and then O'Malley went on, "The thing is, Tony, that we have a problem with your story, because we checked the hospital records, and they say you didn't arrive until at least seven in the evening."

"No, uh, that's not possible."

"And we did some digging—well, you know, that's what we do—and we found a witness that said they saw a vehicle driving around the block over and over the night before, and on the very same street where these fellas were murdered. Ain't that something?" O'Malley said sarcastically.

"It's quite a coincidence," I told him.

O'Malley went on, "The witness's description, well, it sounded like they were describing something you drive...a tan Oldsmobile, right?"

"That's true, but it couldn't have been mine, officers."

"We're detectives. But, are you sure you weren't there? On Friday either?" O'Malley asked. "Because that's ninety minutes, plenty of time for you to leave the waterfront, commit the murders, and make it to Mass General by seven, don't you think?"

"Am I under arrest here, fellas?"

"No, but you could make it a lot easier on yourself right now if you'd just tell us the truth. Tell us where you were during those ninety minutes!"

"I told you already."

"What do you think, Teddy?" he asked his partner. "Should we believe him, or should we cuff him and book him on first-degree murder charges?"

"He don't want to play ball, Detective, so I don't see no other choice," his partner said.

"I tend to agree," O'Malley said, and the prick took a couple of steps toward me, and right to my face said, "Look around you. Look at all your so-called friends here. We're going to talk to every last one of them until someone cracks. And believe me, there's always one who does. And when we root out the first canary, the rest will start singing. I own you, Costa—you better believe that. You think you're the only guinea that's committed a murder in this town? I've dealt with scumbags like you my whole life."

I stood stone-faced and completely unaffected by his words, because I knew two indisputable facts: (1) He had nothing on me, only suspicion as a result of a few circumstantial pieces of evidence that pointed in my direction. (2) Ain't no fuckin' way a longshoreman was going to give me up; it just wasn't the way down there. We were all rock solid. Not to mention the fact no one knew anything anyway. The hit was carried out by me, and me alone.

So he asked me again, "Where were you that night?"

"I told you, Detective, I was at the hospital."

"Turn around, Costa, hands behind your back" O'Malley said. "It looks like we're going to do this the hard way."

He took the cuffs out and I did what he said. And then a voice boomed, "He was with me, Detective."

We all turned and looked, and walking toward us with his arm extended holding his badge was my friend, my guardian angel, Joey Federico.

Boy, this angered O'Malley.

"What the hell are you talking about?" O'Malley snapped at him. "Put that badge away; it means nothing. This is my investigation!"

"I'm not disputing that, but I am assisting as a witness. You see, I was with Mr. Costa; in fact, I gave him an escort to the hospital, and it was right at five thirty, on the Fourth. Had a cup of coffee with him before he finally went upstairs to see his kid. So he couldn't have been at the crime scene; he was with me."

"I don't believe this horseshit!" O'Malley then looked at his partner, and they exchanged a dumbfounded look.

"And you're willing to testify to that?" he said to Joey.

"It's my duty to, sir, so, yes, of course. So please put me on record as having escorted Mr. Costa at 5:30 p.m. on the night of July 4, 1975, before having a cup of coffee with him in the cafeteria."

"Why the hell would you be escorting this man to the hospital without any emergency going on?"

"Truth be told, I pulled him over for running a stop sign, and when he explained to me where he was going and why, I saw fit to lend him an escort."

"You have proof of this?"

"Yes."

"You better not be playing me false, buster," O'Malley said right in Joey's face.

At that point it was a standoff between the two, until O'Malley was just fed up, turned to me, and said, "You're not out of this yet, Costa!"

I said nothing. With that, the two dejected cops stormed off.

"Since when did the nut take over the nuthouse?" I asked Joey.

"What are you talking about?"

"You can get into a lot of trouble by doing what you're doing, you know that?" I said.

"You let me worry about that; you just take care of everything you need to on your end."

"Let me get this straight. You did all that just for me?" I asked Joey. "I'm touched."

"Yeah. Yeah," he said. "I felt bad about the way I reacted the other day, and I knew you were going to off that son of a bitch…didn't think it would be two, but I started planning your alibi right from the get-go. I followed the investigation from a safe distance, and when I heard those two were coming to see you today, that's when I decided to make my move. You should be all set now."

"I gotta tell ya, Joey. I didn't think you had it in ya."

"Hey, easy, wise guy," he said.

"Thank you, Joey, really. I owe you."

"I have a son, too, Ton'," he said. "So I get it. Anyhow, if it weren't for you, I wouldn't have this job anyway. Who the hell knows where I'd be? And if, God forbid, your uncle found out I did nothing to protect his favorite nephew, I'd have to change my name and leave the friggin' country."

We laughed together at that one.

"How is he, by the way?"

"He's pretty good, thanks. Hanging in there. I'll tell him you were asking about him."

"Please do," Joey said.

"I will."

"Well, I've had enough of this place already for one day," said Joey. "How the hell do you do it? Working out here with your hands, lugging that shit, breathing in the stench of that dirty water in Boston Harbor, and working with these animals…"

"You know what, Joey? I can't think of anything else I'd rather do," I said to him.

"I just don't see it. But you always were a little crazy yourself."

"So they say," I said.

CHAPTER 34
OPERATING WITH A LICENSE

Eight long years had passed since anyone made a mention of the gold that went missing out of the warehouse on that fateful January night in 1975—eight years of peace. The media dubbed it "The Waterfront Heist," and it was one of the biggest unsolved mysteries the country had ever seen.

After all, Mickey and Butchie were no longer with us. Sammy took off to Ireland; Connor sold his bar and gave up the dogfighting business and then bought a three-bedroom condo down in Naples, Florida, and no one ever heard from him again. And since neither were longshoremen when the robbery took place, no one even mentioned their names as being possible coconspirators. Wally remained close and put his mother in the best nursing home in Boston, until she passed away in 1981. As for me, well, I walked away with all that money, a nice chunk of change, especially for that day and age, and it was enough to relieve the stress of our financial issues for good.

The investigation into who killed Jimmy O'Donnell and Jake O'Sullivan fizzled rather quickly after Joey alibied me out. Forever grateful, I kept in touch with Joey; our families became close, and as it turned out, he became one of my best friends.

A funny thing happened on the waterfront, though, after I sent a cold-blooded killer and our union leader to the ground. Guys started looking at me funny, and when I walked along, people moved out of the way. But it wasn't out of fear; it was out of respect. They suspected what I had done, and though they never spoke to me directly about it, from time to time, I got a nod from a guy as if he was saying *I know what you did, and your secret is safe on the waterfront.*

At the start of the eighties, I longed for a change from laboring on the ships, driving trucks and forklifts, or working in the garage, so I set out to earn my crane operator's license.

In 1983 I applied, got accepted, and spent a week in Baltimore training. I came back, and after a couple of times operating under supervision, I was on my own, and I was flying.

I became one of the best operators the docks had ever seen, lifting more containers off the ships in a safe and timely manner than anyone else. And I was happy doing it. The pay was great, and as a result, I was able to sell the house in

East Boston and relocate my family to the Boston suburb of Stoneham, Massachusetts.

The year 1988 marked my fifth as a crane operator, and in that year, another dicey opportunity came up.

I was approached one afternoon by a drug trafficker, a local guy from Dartmouth, Massachusetts, and a pretty big deal, if you asked the feds or his friends in Colombia. I had actually become acquainted with him on a visit to see my uncle Dom in Walpole, so he needed no introduction. His name was Will Youngstown.

He was escorted over to me by a longshoreman named Danny Walsh, who happened to know the guy from his days growing up in the same town.

Danny said, "Will, Tony; Tony, Will."

We shook hands. "It's good to see ya again," I said.

"Likewise," said Will. "Listen, I don't want to take up too much of your time, so I'll come right out with it. I need a guy, a guy on a forklift who can lift a shipment from a box truck and place the stuff in a particular area of the warehouse, and I will need it done in a very timely fashion. I need someone good. Someone solid. We have a tight window, and I can't have any problems. The job pays $25,000 for twenty minutes of your time. You interested?"

I looked at Danny, and he said, "I told him you were the best."

By that point in my career on the waterfront I was pretty good on a forklift, and I could have handled the job with ease. However, I said, "Will, although I really appreciate the offer, I honestly truly do, because it's a very generous offer for sure, but at this time, I'm afraid I'm going to have to refuse."

He looked at me like I was nuts and said, "That's your right, of course, and I respect your decision. Then, would you happen to know of another who might be interested?"

"I might. I'll talk to someone, and if he agrees, I'll send him to Danny, and you guys can work it out."

"Is he good?" asked Will.

"He's very good and always looking to make a few extra bucks doing things such as this."

"OK, great," Will said. "I'll wait for Danny's word, then."

With that, we shook hands and went on our way.

I felt comfortable turning him down. It wasn't worth the risk, considering the truck was probably filled with dope, and if something ever went down, I'd be looking at some real jail time. Not to mention the fact I knew how those Colombians handled their loose ends, and it wasn't pretty.

The following day I met up in the hiring hall with the guy I had in mind; his name was John Tully. I explained the opportunity to him in full, and he never hesitated when agreeing to do it. The only thing I stressed to him was that he'd better do the job and do it well, because it was my reputation that was on the line, considering I was vouching for him. John was a stand-up guy and a great forklift operator, but it needed to be said.

I told him to see Danny, and two days later, he made the lift without incident. He got paid, and that was that.

I was out of the game forever and wanted nothing to do with anything even remotely close to breaking the law. I stood by that decision and never looked back.

In 1995 I turned fifty-five years old, had thirty-seven years of service in the union on the waterfront, and was still going strong on the cranes. However, all those years of wear and tear on the docks had led to frequent back and shoulder pains, and so I wasn't quite as mobile as I used to be. I was a shell of my old self—gray haired, slightly hunched, and a good thirty pounds heavier than I was when I started working way back in 1958.

The added aches and pains and extra weight made things tough on me at times, but I didn't let it slow me down until one day in August 1997 when I was having a cup of coffee on the pier, just shootin' the shit with a guy. Suddenly someone driving a forklift carrying two pallets of heavy boxes stacked high hit a very steep pothole, causing the merchandise to tip over and tumble off the truck. I pushed my friend out of the way, but I had no time to avoid the avalanche myself, and several of the boxes—which were filled with computers—knocked the hell out of me, sending me to the ground.

I separated my shoulder and tore tendons in my knee, and after a month of surgeries and rehab, I was deemed unfit to work on the waterfront in any capacity, thus prematurely ending my career as a longshoreman.

I took an early retirement package but a very good one, with all the benefits a person could ask for, including a great pension and free health care for Marie and me for the rest of our lives.

And believe me, we would need it.

A mere two weeks into my retirement, Marie was diagnosed with a rare form of cancer, and the doctors gave her just a few months to live. She battled if for a year before she finally succumbed to it. But, boy, was she a fighter—she fought harder than I ever could have.

It was tragic for me, and especially the kids, who were both grown up by that time and out of the house. But we stuck by one another for support like any normal family would.

The death of my wife marked the lowest point of my life, and without her, I was lost. I lived alone, took care of myself, and tried to do all the things I had seen Marie do to keep the house running, but I just couldn't. I wasn't Marie. And though Tony Jr. and Isabella, along with Isabella's two little boys, my grandsons, all visited me many times to keep me company, it just wasn't the same anymore.

My brother stuck around. He became a sergeant at the station, finally got married, had two girls and a boy, and settled in Tewksbury, Massachusetts. Just two weeks after his wedding, my mother had passed away in her bed at the nursing home. I know she would have been proud him. My dad lived long enough to see my brother finally tie the knot, but then one day after several of my calls went unanswered, I went to the house to check on him, and unfortunately when I did, I saw that he had passed away. I found him sitting in his favorite chair with a glass of wine by his side; by all accounts he went peacefully at the ripe old age of eighty-seven.

Even Uncle Dom, that son of a bitch, was still alive and pushing ninety and living well in a fifty-five-plus community. He ran the joint. It was nonsmoking, but every morning at eight o'clock, you'd see him outside with a cigar and coffee, reading the newspaper on a lawn chair outside in the common area. He didn't give a shit.

I loved that guy.

CHAPTER 35
WHEN IT'S ALL SAID AND DONE

Eighteen months after I called it quits, my local decided to honor me by throwing a party and thought it best to use the club as the venue. They waited that long out of respect while Marie was battling the cancer.

As if that wasn't touching enough, they sprang for a limo to come and pick me up at my house and deliver me right to the front door, there and back.

I had seen a lot of guys come and go on the waterfront, and for all kinds of reasons: death, injury, retirement, incarceration, and so on. But no one else had the pleasure of such a send-off as I got on February 21, 1999. To say it was bittersweet…well, that would be an understatement.

My closest friends, guys who'd essentially grown up on the pier with me, were all gone. Butchie, Mickey, and Wally—all deceased. Wally had had a bad stroke, leaving him confined to his bed, until his heart simply stopped one evening. He died a year before I retired. Perhaps I would have joined my friends had the bullets meant for me found the right arteries to pierce.

Did I have regrets? Sure. But who doesn't?

I have my memories, too. Some good, some bad.

I held a great one in my hand early on the day of the party. It was a picture taken back in 1962 by a photographer working for the *Boston Herald*. It was black and white and creased in several spots, with white edges around the border. It showed five of us longshoremen posing for the shot right on the dock, with a cargo ship anchored just behind us. From left to right, it was Mickey, Butchie, myself, Wally, and then Franky B. Looking at that photo brought me to tears. *Oh, what I'd give to see those guys tonight*, I thought—if not for the entire evening, just for a few minutes.

I wore a suit—nothing flashy—just a navy-blue, three-button jacket with a tie. And that tie was a bitch. I must have knotted it a handful of times before I felt I got it right.

The party was to begin at six o'clock. At around five o'clock, I became anxious, so I got up repeatedly from my couch and pulled back the corner of the drapes in my living room with my right hand to see. But there was nothing. Not until five thirty did I see my ride—a silky black stretch limousine idling at the curb in front of my house.

It was time to go.

I let the drapes go and banged around to my left, past the open French doors, turned right to the front door, and exited, locking it behind me. The driver then got out of the car, scooted around the front end to the passenger-side back door, and opened it. I began the stroll down the brick stairs, one painful step at a time. The accident had left me with a slight limp in my right leg and a couple of pins holding my knee in place. I told the driver, "I'll just be a minute."

"Of course, Mr. Costa," was his reply. "Can I offer you some assistance, Mr. Costa?"

"No, but thank you very much."

"Of course, Mr. Costa," he said.

This kid was great; I needed to make sure I took care of him with a few bucks.

I hit the walkway with both feet and approached the backseat. The driver said, "You have a beautiful home, Mr. Costa."

"Thank you. Thank you," I said. "I nearly killed someone to get it."

He chuckled, probably thinking I was kidding, but I wasn't.

I slid into the leather backseat just enough so the door wouldn't close on me. I thanked him, and he closed the door.

It was comfortable and roomy, with all the luxury fixings, including a stainless-steel glass holder and a bottle of champagne surrounded by cubed ice in a bucket nestled in the center of the console.

"Help yourself to some champagne," he said. "The glasses are in the door-handle area."

There they were, a pair of them, held by a circular cup lined with bristles to keep them from clanking at every bump and turn.

"I think I'll wait for the party, but thank you," I replied.

This kid was polite. I really liked him.

He checked his mirrors, then the road on his left, and we began to pull out. We were a far cry from the club, and it was obvious. The side streets of Stoneham were lined with towering trees over the power lines. The roads were wide enough for two cars to pass each other with ease, even with vehicles parked on either side. I had been there for about ten years and still found the neighborhood pleasing to my eye.

"Is there anything you need before we hit the highway, Mr. Costa?" he called back to me.

"I'm good, thank you," I let him know. "Just head straight to the club."

"You got it, Mr. Costa."

We hit the on-ramp to Route 93 South, and my worries began to intensify once again. But there was little traffic, and we cruised through Medford before we slowed to prepare to exit off the highway. We left the burbs—that was obvious—and entered the outskirts of urban living in Boston. We took an exit and passed through Everett, Revere, then Chelsea, and then came up on East Boston, where the club was.

We stopped, and the kid got out, ran around the limo, and opened my door. I handed him a twenty. While he protested, I made him take it.

There were a lot of people there, so many I couldn't keep track. Most I recognized, and the ones I did not were of the younger generation on the waterfront and were gracious enough to make an appearance. It was nice, another sign of respect.

After a few minutes of hugs and handshakes, I sat at a table with a couple of guys and got caught up on what had been happening on and off the pier the last few months. Then, out of the corner of my eye, I noticed someone, a young man, looking over. He had an agenda, I thought, to come over to me, and I was right.

He was a big kid, young, maybe twenty-one years old, six feet tall or more, and he probably weighed three hundred pounds at least.

He reached out with his right hand. We shook hands as he said, "Mr. Costa."

"Hi," was all I came back with.

He replied, "My name is Christopher…Christopher Kelly."

My eyes widened with surprise. "You're Wally's kid?"

"I am," he said. "My mom called him Patrick, but, yes, he was my dad. I just wanted to come by and say congratulations. My father had so many kind things to say about you, so I figured I could say it for the both of us since he's not with us anymore."

"I know. It was a shame what happened to your father," I told him.

"My family misses him very much."

"As do I," I said "very much. You know, your father was the strongest guy on the pier and one of the toughest around town. Nobody wanted a piece of him—I can tell you that. Nobody. I owe my life to him. He did a lot for me. Please, sit."

"I really can't, Mr. Costa; I have to get going, I had a prior engagement, but thank you very much."

"Sure. Sure, I understand, kid" I said. "Thank you for coming by, and listen, if we ever run into each other again, call me Tony, understand?"

"Yes, sir, of course," he said. "Take care, Tony."

"You, too," I said, and then he left.

It was exhausting. I had a few drinks and many laughs. And when the time reached eleven or so and the crowd thinned out, I looked around and saw a bunch of guys huddled at the bar, where Gus used to work. He'd been gone a long time, fifteen years or so at that time. Now I saw a young kid back there, and I had no rapport with him or the group remaining. They were young longshoremen, nice fellas from what I could see. But nothing like the guys I knew, and nothing like me. They had no idea. They would never know what it was like to extort a shipping company and have it pay us for more men than were needed for a job. They'd never know what it was like to work under another guy's social security number just to keep his seniority ongoing while he spent time in the joint. The waterfront now is more streamlined, with fewer cracks in the surface that guys can use to get away with things.

I'll say this, though: Whether a kid worked on the waterfront back in the sixties or today, it's one hell of a job, and it still has the greatest union in the country. And anyone working down there now, man or woman, is strong. Because no matter how dirty longshoremen get fixing a crane or how cold they feel unlocking pins on the containers when the winds are whipping off the harbor at subzero temps, the job gets done. And at the end of the day, it comes with good pay and great benefits and—you better believe it—a great deal of pride and prestige.

You could say I was the last longshoreman, the last of an era. The last of a special breed the world will never see the likes of again. Let's hope not, anyway.

The End

About the Author

Marc Zappulla hails from the Boston suburb of Medford, Massachusetts. He received a bachelor's degree in psychology from Endicott College. He has worked as a ghostwriter for sports figures such as Hockey Hall of Fame goaltender Gerry Cheevers and strength and conditioning coach Brian McNamee. Zappulla was inspired to write his first novel by his father's thirty-year career as a longshoreman. Zappulla lives in Boston and is busy working on his next book.